COMING HOME

Other books by Elisabeth Rose:

The Right Chord

COMING HOME

•

Elisabeth Rose

AVALON BOOKS
NEW YORK

Published by Thomas Bouregy & Co., Inc.
160 Madison Avenue, New York, NY 10016

Library of Congress Cataloging-in-Publication Data

Rose, Elisabeth, 1951–
Coming home / Elisabeth Rose.
p. cm.
ISBN 978-0-8034-9914-0 (acid-free paper)
1. Violoncellists—Fiction. 2. Sydney
(N.S.W.)—Fiction. I. Title.
PR9619.4.R64C66 2008
823'.92—dc22 2008017329

PRINTED IN THE UNITED STATES OF AMERICA
ON ACID-FREE PAPER
BY HADDON CRAFTSMEN, BLOOMSBURG, PENNSYLVANIA

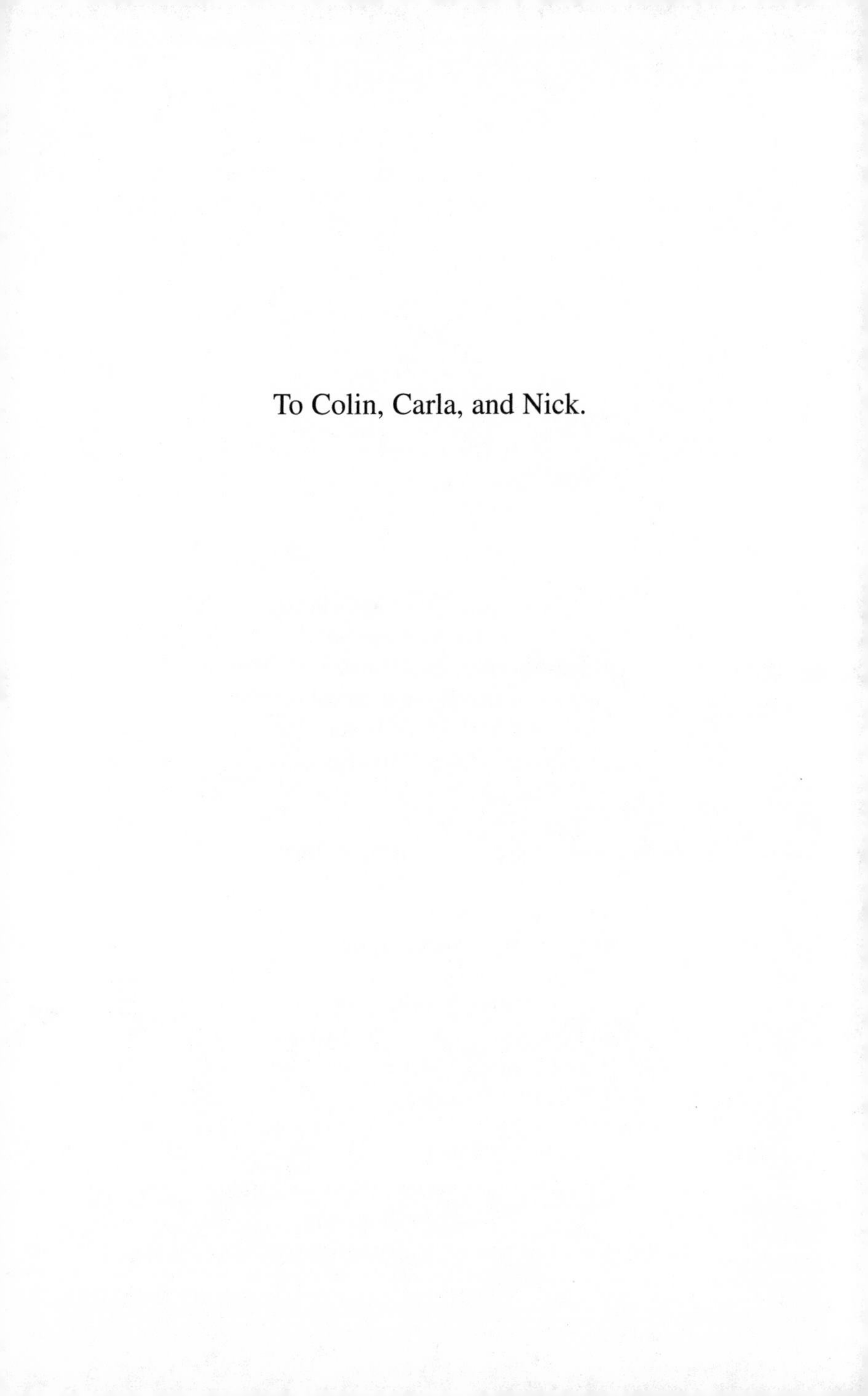

To Colin, Carla, and Nick.

Thank you to the Rusiti family whose lovely
home is the model for Charles' house.
Thank you to my father and Pam
for reading the manuscript.

Chapter One

It occurred to Libby, as she sat in the taxi on the way to dinner, that she may have been mistaken by Cressie's mother for a Lame Duck. A Lame Duck, as classified by Betty Swift, was a sad, lonely, single person with nowhere to go on important feast days and those national holidays normally celebrated by families.

Lame Duck. With capital letters.

This wasn't Christmas or someone's birthday. This was an ordinary Sunday night in September. Libby was thirty years old. Single. No immediate family. Alone in the world. Going to a dinner party at the Swift's, those magnets for the lost and lonely . . .

"Mom had a couple of her Lame Ducks to dinner again. I don't know where she finds them," Cressie would say, returning to their shared student house after a family anniversary, a birthday, or even just a normal meal with her parents. They'd both laugh with the smugness of youth.

"I am not a Lame Duck," Libby said out loud, startling the taxi driver into saying, "I never said you were, ma'am," and giving her wary glances in the rearview mirror for the rest of the trip.

But she kept that thought firmly in her head when, clutching a bunch of cheery, bright-yellow daffodils, she rang the bell of the house she hadn't seen for nearly eight years. This was a dinner with dear old friends, catching up after years out of the country. Years in which she'd been productively employed in many different orchestras, surrounded by colleagues, meeting new people at each change of position. She could hold her own in Icelandic, Dutch, German, and French. So there!

Bob Swift flung the door wide and yelled, "Queen Elizabeth. Gorgeous as ever! Why are you standing out there? Come in, come in. Betty said you hadn't changed and she was right."

He hadn't changed either, apart from his girth, which had expanded in all directions at once. His hair, never a strong achiever, had given up the struggle and retreated to a thin gray line of resistance around the perimeter of his shiny bald head. Libby was grabbed in a familiar, stifling embrace and soundly kissed on the cheek.

"Bob, you're looking well," she said when she was able.

He slapped his hand on his stomach, setting up a jellylike wobble and laughed. "It's all the exercise. Those marathons really keep you fit."

"It's wonderful to see you again." She followed him

into the living room, which also hadn't changed. Still the same squashy, old brown leather couch and Bob's favorite dark-blue velvet armchair by the fireplace. Still the same homey smell of dinner cooking and air freshener, the same blue carpet and the same cream-colored walls, the same overflowing bookshelf in the corner and fiddly little ornaments on the mantelpiece with evidence of past sporting prowess in the form of cricket and netball trophies. The dust collectors, Betty called them, but she hadn't thrown any of them away or packed them into boxes to languish in the shed.

"Libby, how lovely," cried Betty's voice from the depths of the house. Not waiting for a reply or visual contact, she continued emitting welcoming squawks until she bustled into view wearing a floral apron and wielding a corkscrew in one hand and a can of cat food in the other.

"I'm so glad you could come. I said to Bob when I got home, 'Guess who I ran into today?' And he couldn't, of course. Well, how would he? I hardly believed it myself. We thought you were in Europe being famous and there you were in Pitt Street." She chortled with glee. "But I recognized you instantly."

"Hello, Betty. I was amazed to see you, too. Although, you've sold raffle tickets for some charity or another as long as I've known you, so I shouldn't have been in the least surprised."

"She's a chronic volunteer," said Bob. "She's addicted."

Libby leaned forward and kissed the warm cheek that her hostess proffered, fragrant with a mix of perfume and cooking. An image sharp and piercing flashed across her mind of her own mother—she was the same age as Betty, or would have been. Libby smiled, quickly blinked away a rising tear, and said softly, “Really lovely to see you. Thank you for inviting me.”

“This is your second home,” said Betty. “You know you’re always welcome. Now, I’ve a few things to finish off in the kitchen.”

Libby sniffed. “Something smells good.”

An enticing aroma wafted through the house. A baked dinner, Betty’s mainstay. Libby’s mouth literally watered in anticipation. How she and Cressie and sundry other friends had devoured Betty’s roasts. Starving students, Betty decided. Not eating properly. Compared to the food at the Swift household, they weren’t. Cressie joked she had to leave home before she was too large to get out the door.

“What are you going to do with that, love?” asked Bob, eyeing Betty’s can and opener. He winked at Libby. “You’ve come on a good night. Chicken and turkey mince is my favorite, but I don’t think she’ll get it open with a corkscrew.”

“Have you still got the same cat—Abraham?” asked Libby.

“Yes. Fancy you remembering him,” shrieked Betty. “I was about to give him his dinner. This is for you.” She handed the corkscrew to Bob. “Make yourself useful. Come and see Abraham, Libby. He’s fifteen now. Still has all his faculties though.”

“Sounds like a university.” Bob laughed uproariously

at his own joke although no-one else did, which had never bothered him before and apparently didn't now.

Libby handed the daffodils to Betty, who oohed with pleasure. "Aren't they lovely. It's yonks since I was given flowers. Come through to the kitchen."

"She's got a memory like a sieve. I gave her flowers on her birthday," cried Bob.

"Yes. My thirtieth birthday." Betty laughed and patted Bob on the cheek. "Only twenty years ago."

"Make that thirty, love."

Bob winked at Libby again, who smiled and stifled a sudden yawn. Tiredness hit her like a sandbag. She'd forgotten how exhausting an evening with these two could be even without a jet-lagged brain and a body that thought it was four in the morning. Dinner at the Swift's was casual, friendly, and overwhelmingly welcoming but never calm and relaxing. Guests needed all their wits and energy to keep up with the hosts.

Libby followed Betty. With any luck the other guests would be good talkers and take the pressure off, and she could sneak away early to crash into bed. Maybe she shouldn't have come on this, her second night back home. She wasn't really fit company. But Betty was difficult to refuse, and Libby had accepted because she loved Cressie's parents, plus a solitary meal wasn't inviting, and she was jet-lagged, having been back in Australia for exactly five hours. Her judgment had been severely clouded.

Black-and-white Abraham gave her a yellow-eyed stare from his corner of the kitchen, then deigned to sniff at the food Betty had dumped in his bowl. He obviously knew what he'd been offered didn't equate with the smell issuing forth from the oven.

The doorbell rang, and voices shouted jovial greetings in the other room.

"That'll be Joe and Selina from next door. You won't remember them. They're Greek."

Libby wasn't sure whether that was why Joe and Selina should have fallen through a crack in her memory, or if there was another reason for their forgetability. It wasn't lack of conversational ability. Judging by the racket from the living room it would be a rowdy night, and she wouldn't have to contribute much.

"Who else is coming?"

"Bob invited the new neighbor. He's just moved in and his wife hasn't arrived yet from Perth. That's why we're having this little get together really, to welcome him. And then there's Cressie's ex." Her voice dropped. "He was shattered when she married Nick." Betty gave Libby a meaningful look.

A Lame Duck! Maybe she wasn't it, after all. Cressie and Nick had been married nearly eighteen months. This guy should be over it by now.

"And have you got anyone special, Libby?" Betty asked. "You must have had plenty to choose from over there in Europe. All those lovely dark and passionate Mediterranean types, lonely millionaires and so forth waiting for the perfect girl on their yachts and their islands."

Apparently Betty still read far too many romances.

"No one at the moment. I didn't have much time to go

on dates and I was mainly in the Northern countries—Germany and Holland."

Where the men were blond, industrious, meticulous, and humorless in her experience, especially German Klaus. Or there was that morose but extremely good-looking Russian viola player who insisted on taking her to depressing, arty, black-and-white movies on their precious nights off—Russian dialogue with Dutch subtitles.

"Yes, working at night makes it hard and those countries are so cold, aren't they? But still, Libby . . ." Here it came—the old "why aren't you married yet, you're thirty" routine—but Betty amazed her by saying, "You don't want to rush into anything and get stuck with some man just because he's got a good body."

Is that what Cressie had done? Or had Betty? Libby stifled a snort of laughter as she pictured Bob . . . but he hadn't always been rotund. The wedding photo in the living room showed a dashing young man with Betty, slim and pretty on his arm.

Betty sniffed suspiciously, opened the oven to peer inside and a cloud of smoke billowed out, making them both cough.

"Bob will insist on heating up pizzas without a drip tray. The cheese melts everywhere and he never wipes up," she confided cheerfully, flapping a tea towel about. "Don't worry, dinner's looking marvelous. A lovely hunk of beef. I do so love a roast and I thought you'd like one now you're home again. And you living on your own. Singles don't tend to cook proper dinners, do they? Slap some mushy frozen thing in the microwave. Tasteless muck, that's all I can say."

A piercing beep-beeping made Libby wince and slap her hands to her ears, and also saved her from replying to the question, which had Lame Duck crawling all over it. A crowd of people rushed in, filling the kitchen with shouts and exclamations and bodies. The two portly, gray-haired figures had to be Selina and Joe—same age, same shape, same volume level.

"She's set the place on fire again," roared Bob. "All hands to the buckets."

He grabbed a chair, stood on it, and fiddled with the smoke alarm on the ceiling while Betty waved her tea towel about vigorously. Someone turned the exhaust fan on over the stove top, and suddenly the brain-penetrating cacophony ceased.

"Here's Charles," cried Betty. Libby caught a glimpse of a head of dark-brown hair in the kitchen doorway before the new arrival was mobbed.

He said, in a cultivated English accent, "The door was on the latch so I came in. No-one seemed to hear the bell."

"We've just averted a near disaster. Betty tried to torch the place," yelled Bob. "But dinner is safe. Have a drink, Charles. Let me introduce you. Here are Selina and Joe from next door—that's over that side." He pointed while Selina and Joe shook hands with Charles. "And Libby. Friend of Cressie's from way back. Libby's a world-famous cellist just flitting in for a breather in Sydney before she takes the world by storm again."

Libby stepped forward ready to set the record straight, but the man smiling at her over the heads of the two neighbors snatched the very words from her mouth by saying, "We've met. Hello, Libby, what a surprise! Marvelous to see you again."

Marvelous? What a surprise? *He* was surprised?

He leaned forward and kissed both her cheeks in a very familiar manner just before both his arms wrapped around her and held her firmly against a very broad and totally unfamiliar chest.

Libby gasped. His right hand squeezed her arm tightly as he released her. It was the sort of squeeze that implied prior meetings, and things left unsaid, actions still to be taken, words still to be exchanged. Private and personal. His fingers slid down her arm, stopped at her hand, and held on.

This wasn't a Lame Duck. This was way too fast a mover. This was a swooping hawk. He must be the new neighbor. The one whose wife hadn't arrived yet. Libby was positive she'd never seen him before in her life. But there was something vaguely and disturbingly familiar about that round-toned voice.

"You've met? We had no idea, did we, Bob?" said Betty in transparent delight. "When was it?"

"Yes, indeed, when was it exactly?" asked Libby, eyeing him as he stood there with his fingers holding hers in a proprietorial way. Not bad-looking, in fact alarmingly good-looking. Nice straight nose and full lips. Firm body, no flab. His hazel eyes bored into hers for a second, then he looked at Betty with a grin.

A little squirm of protective anger that he should possibly be making fun of these two kindly people, her friends, made her pull her hand free and add, "I don't really remember, but then I've met so many people in the last few years, you know . . . all over the world." She gestured helplessly and smiled her most innocent smile at him. "Sorry."

"It was in Vienna," he told her calmly.

Libby stared. Eight years ago she'd been in Vienna. She'd gone straight there after graduating, to study with Heinz Wanhal, who had since died. Two years in Vienna. She frowned. Could she have met Charles? An Englishman. She would definitely have remembered that smile and the dangerous glint in those eyes. But the voice . . .

"Vienna, how I love Vienna," piped up Selina who had laughed like crazy at the smoke and so far had said nothing apart from hello to Libby and Charles.

"You've never been to Vienna," declared Joe. He had bushy eyebrows that leapt about above his eyes like big hairy caterpillars: the ones that appear on gum trees at certain times of the year and have a frightfully venomous sting—spitfires. The name leapt into Libby's mind. She watched them, fascinated, her bewildered brain momentarily distracted from the extraordinary claim Charles had made.

"I have!" Selina bristled with righteous indignation. Her dark eyes flashed and crackled.

"Venice, you went to Venice." Joe emphasized the point with a vehement hand gesture and the caterpillars nosedived.

"And Vienna! I know the difference between Vienna and Venice. I'm not stupid." Selina raised both hands in despair at his stupidity. Heavy silver bangles jangled on her wrists.

"No, not with me, you didn't." Joe glared at her. Now the eyebrows joined in a straight line. One big, long caterpillar.

"No, I went before I met you. When I was a girl." Selina smiled triumphantly at him.

"I can't remember that far back. My memory capacity isn't large enough." Joe laughed loudly and grinned at Bob, who chuckled. The caterpillars samba-ed.

"Hah!" Selina gave him a playful punch on the arm and laughed, displaying big white teeth.

"Shoo everyone, out of my kitchen," interrupted Betty. "Bob, give people drinks."

Libby blinked and refocused on Betty, dragging her befuddled attention from the eyebrows.

"Don't mention Vienna," murmured Charles in Libby's ear, as they shuffled behind the neighbors—who had moved on to argue about what Joe should or should not be drinking—on the way back to the living room.

"I had no intention of mentioning Vienna," said Libby. What on earth was this Charles doing here? He didn't fit at all. But then she should know better—this was Bob and Betty's house. No one and everyone fit in here. Bob handed them a glass of wine each. Useless to protest but if she drank alcohol she'd probably fall over. The doorbell rang. Would this be the Lame Duck?

"Aah, Gregory." Had to be. This one fit the description perfectly—glasses, unkempt hair, worn jacket, corduroy pants, distracted air, socially uncomfortable. Perhaps the despair of losing Cressie to Nick had reduced him to this sorry state.

"This is Gregory, our new neighbor," announced Bob.

"He's here holding the fort and establishing a toehold until his wife Alison arrives in a few weeks with the tribe: two little girls. Greg's at the university. He's a geologist. Studies earthquakes."

He beamed around at the assembled company while Greg squirmed beside him and stared at the floor, as though he hoped an interesting fissure might appear to swallow him up.

"Earthquakes?" cried Joe stepping forward with his hand outstretched. "Where do you go to study those? Do you climb volcanoes?" Now the eyebrows were ready to climb mountains, shooting up at an alarming angle.

With an earnest expression on his face, Gregory began explaining the difference between vulcanology and his field of expertise. Charles stood beside Libby observing the exchange with a smile dangerously close to a smirk on his face.

"What do you do?" asked Libby more loudly than she'd meant. Gregory may not be as attractive a man as Charles, but he was certainly highly intelligent and in a fascinating area of work. Supercilious Charles was still shaping up to be a stinker even if he wasn't married. He had a distinct aura of British upper class superiority about him—roughing it out in the colonies.

"I'm an architect."

"Really?"

"Yes, why does that surprise you?" He looked down his refined nose at her.

"Have we truly met before?" Libby asked instead of answering.

"Yes," he said.

"In Vienna?'

"Yes." He obviously wasn't going to give her any more clues. He was enjoying himself too much at her expense. Charles, the observer of human weakness and foibles.

"Are you the . . . Do you know Cressie?"

"Yes." The Lame Duck! The heartbroken, deserted boyfriend. He should get over it, Cressie wasn't coming back to him.

"Nick, her husband, is a lovely man," she said sweetly. She'd only met him once, at the wedding when she was Cressie's bridesmaid. A flying visit home from Germany and back in eight days. But Nick was gorgeous.

"Yes. Although I wouldn't use the word lovely myself. Not in connection with a man." Charles studied the wine in his glass, held it up to the light.

"I shouldn't drink anything or I'll pass out," said Libby suddenly. Her head was already fuzzy. Tiredness dragged at her limbs and eyelids with lead weights. She looked around vaguely for somewhere to sit down.

"Are you all right?" Charles peered at her in concern and placed a warm hand supportively on her upper arm. He took her glass and put it on the mantelpiece between a tiny porcelain shepherdess and Troy's Under Twelve Best Bowler award.

"My brain thinks my body is somewhere like Singapore, still in transit." Libby tried to smile, but her lips failed and she yawned instead, covering her mouth quickly with her hands. "I probably shouldn't have come tonight."

"I'm glad you did." His hand was still on her arm. He'd moved closer. Glancing up, Libby found herself gazing into eyes fixed intently on her own. Deep-brown flecks covered almost all the jade-green background, dark lashes provided the frame. His gaze was intimate, searching, and deeply unsettling. "Would you like to go home? I'll drive you."

Libby blinked, dragged her eyes and her crazed mind away from the hypnotic depths of those dark pupils. Something she saw there made her think he . . . No, get a grip. Jet lag. Messes with your head. "No, thanks. I'm fine. I probably need to eat."

"Just give a yell if you feel faint and I'll try to catch you before you hit the floor."

"It won't come to that." That remark sounded more like the man she'd just met. In her befuddled state she'd upgraded polite concern to something . . . else.

"I'll be ready just in case. I'll stay right by your side."

"Thank you," she murmured, not sure if she wanted his undivided attention. The intimacy, imagined or otherwise had gone, now he was laughing at her. She made a supreme effort to get her brain in gear. "Tell me exactly how we met?"

"Oh, you trod on my foot."

"What?"

"You trod on my foot," he repeated.

Libby began to laugh. He smiled calmly as the laughter took hold, and she had to pull out a tissue and wipe her streaming eyes carefully. She must appear hysterical now; she probably was. This whole evening was assuming certain Alice-in-Wonderlandlike aspects.

"I'm sorry, my brain's not working properly. And neither's yours. That's the most ridiculous thing . . ." Laughter bubbled up again, and she had to wheeze and gasp for a few more minutes until she could continue. ". . . the most ridiculous thing I've ever heard."

"It's true."

"Where?" she asked. "Where precisely did I stand on your foot?"

"On my right big toe. You were carrying your cello downstairs, and I was coming up. I politely turned aside to allow you to pass, and that's how you repaid me."

"Which stairs?"

"The stairs in our apartment building."

"In Vienna?'

He nodded and glanced around in a ridiculously furtive manner. "Ssh, remember, don't mention Vienna."

Dim memories began stirring. She frowned. Memories began stirring all right, of an obnoxious man in the apartment below who thumped on the ceiling, which was her floor, when she practiced, and yelled things in an English accent about "wretched cat's yowling" and "dim-witted, selfish, classical musicians."

"What floor were you on?" she asked with narrowed eyes.

"Third."

"I was on the fourth."

"I know. Right above me."

"You were that person who complained all the time and nearly got me evicted! I had to do some serious pleading to be allowed to stay. I don't know what I'd have done if I'd been thrown me out. I was terrified.

The student accommodation was full. Hardly any landlords allowed practice and I could barely afford that place."

Charles bowed his head penitently. "Mea culpa."

Libby's mouth dropped open in astonishment. "And here you are claiming to be my long lost friend?" No wonder she'd been instinctively wary despite the attractive packaging. Her female intuition was right.

"That was a long time ago. I don't hold grudges."

"You were vindictive enough in Vienna, complaining to Frau Gunther."

"I was studying for a very important exam and you did practice a lot. All the time really. Got on the nerves."

"You could've gone to the library."

"You could've gone to the music school or the park. You moved in just at the wrong time. A week later and I would've been finished," said Charles.

"I couldn't practice in the park! How ridiculous. It was snowing. Why didn't you just come up and explain?"

"Would you have stopped practicing?"

"No, but I did cut down. I had important work to do, too. I was Heinz Wanhal's last student, and he only gave me an audition because I pleaded and begged and came from half way round the world. He wouldn't have seen me again if I wasn't good enough. I only had that one chance. I had to do hours of practice and I was his private student so I couldn't practice anywhere else."

"I did come up and knock once, but you didn't open the door."

"I probably didn't hear you."

"I certainly heard you," said Charles. "All day. I was

prepared to be polite, but you had a way of ignoring people. Frau Gunther said you were dedicated and shy. I just thought you were selfish."

He stared into her eyes and a flush crawled up her neck, prickly and hot.

"You know, you're just as obnoxious now as you were then," she blurted, flustered by the intensity of his gaze and the way he wouldn't let her free or the way she couldn't release herself. He smiled and broke the spell by sipping his drink.

"I'm sorry, that was a bit . . ." Libby searched in vain for something true but still polite. She was about to plead jet lag but he beat her to it.

"Rude?" he suggested. An infuriating smile lurked just under the surface of his bland expression. "Uncalled for?"

"Yes, I'm sorry. Did you pass your important exam?" she asked stiffly.

"Yes, with honors."

"Well, you've nothing to complain about. Excuse me."

Libby gave him a frigid little smile and stalked off to talk to Selina and Bob who were discussing rose growing, which Libby knew nothing about, but it seemed like a safe topic.

"We're delighted to have you back, Libby," cried Bob. "We'll all come and hear you play. Selina, this girl is a virtuoso."

"Are you performing with an orchestra?" asked Selina. "The violin is a wonderful instrument."

"Cello," interrupted that voice behind Libby. He'd followed her. "Libby is a cellist. A very good one."

That was rich coming from him. How would he know? Libby clamped her mouth firmly shut. He said pleasantly, "I'm looking forward to hearing her play again."

"But you don't like classical music, do you? And dislike the cello in particular?" That just leapt out despite the clenched teeth.

"It's growing on me as I age." He smiled blandly. "Some of it."

"You make it sound like fungus, Charles." Bob roared with laughter. Charles gave a little chuckle and stared at her complacently.

Libby opened her mouth to explain to them, explain why she had returned so abruptly to Sydney and why even though she didn't want to do anything but play cello, she couldn't. But the doorbell rang again, and Bob rushed to open up. A youngish couple were revealed standing hand in hand with expectant smiles on their faces. He was tall and gangly, she petite and red-haired.

"Wayne, we'd nearly given you up. And who's this you've brought along?"

"I hope you don't mind, Bob, but this is Danielle."

"Not at all, the more the merrier we say. Come in and grab yourselves a drink. I'll tell mother to lay an extra place." He turned and yelled the instructions in the general direction of the kitchen.

Betty rushed through with extra cutlery and a plate and disappeared into the dining room. She greeted the new arrivals on the way back and paused by Libby to murmur, "Finally. We'd almost given up hope that he'd find someone else. Cressie will be so relieved. Danielle's a pretty little thing, isn't she?"

So Wayne was the Lame Duck. Or had been until the appearance of Danielle. If that was the case then what on earth was disturbing Charles doing here if he wasn't Cressie's discarded, shattered husk of a boyfriend? Which he plainly wasn't.

"When did you get back?" asked Charles.

Libby decided, for Betty and Bob's sake, to be polite to this man who'd freely, even proudly, admitted harassing her eight years ago—he'd abused her through the floorboards, detested the type of music she played and gone so far as to complain to their landlady. Given a choice, she'd have chosen a conversation with Abraham.

"The plane landed yesterday morning at six-thirty. I ran into Betty selling raffle tickets after I'd checked into my hotel and went looking for food."

"You're in a hotel? No family in Sydney?"

"No, I'd stay with relatives if I could, I've been away so long."

Charles said, "I'd rather sleep in the park than stay with my family."

"That's sad." But the feeling was probably mutual.

Charles shrugged. "So where are your family?"

"My parents died in a car accident five years ago and I'm an only child." Libby still couldn't prevent the slight tremble of the lip at their memory, and the shock of the news, which came via a phone call to her in Munich from Don, her father's closest friend and the family solicitor.

"Sorry. That's tough." There was a flash of real sympathy in his tone, he almost looked sorry he'd pried, but it was more likely embarrassment at her display of emotion.

Libby deliberately hardened her voice. "Yes, but it's okay now. The world's full of orphans and many of them are children far worse off than I am."

"You're all alone." The hazel eyes regarded her intently. They looked greener all of a sudden behind the dark lashes. His eyebrows were neat and elegantly arched. Aristocratic. They contributed to the haughtiness of the face.

"I don't mind."

"Very independent."

"Yes, I like it that way." Did that sound too defiant? Libby smiled grudgingly to take the edge off and he grinned back.

"Me too."

She looked away. There was something unsettling about him. She couldn't quite put her finger on it. He seemed to be on the point of bursting out laughing. As if he knew something she didn't. He acted as if their one time, very slight, and abrasive encounter made them old friends. She didn't know him at all then. She wanted to know him even less now.

"What brings you back? Are you playing here in Sydney?"

"I," she began, but Betty cried, "Dinner's ready, folks. Take your places."

She pointed and suggested and organized until everyone was seated to her satisfaction. Libby sat between Joe and Bob. For some inexplicable reason Betty had insisted Charles sit at one end while she sat at the other, the end nearest the kitchen.

He, with impeccable manners, seemed very comfortable assuming the role of head of the table. Had he been raised in a manor house with a nanny and servants? Was he surveying everyone from his place like the lord of the manor overseeing his minions?

Why did he hate his family? That was very sad. A stab of sympathy made Libby look at Charles with softer eyes. Was his haughtiness and rudeness simply a façade? Did she want to find out? A small, central part of her, did.

Food was served, and the serious eating business commenced. Just as Libby remembered, Betty was a marvelous cook and, just as Betty had suspected, her single person meals were mainly prepackaged and microwaved, tasteless by comparison, mush.

After they'd stuffed themselves with roast beef followed by hot apple crumble and ice cream and drunk hair-raisingly strong coffee, Libby decided she really would have to make a move whether it was polite or not. Everyone had adjourned to the living room and sat or sprawled about discussing the merits of a TV show she hadn't heard of, let alone seen. She helped clear plates, and in the kitchen Betty and Bob, predictably, assured her she wasn't eating and running.

"Absolute nonsense," cried Betty. "You look exhausted. It was lovely of you to come and put up with us old fogies at all."

"She's the old fogey." Bob flung his arm around Betty, winked at Libby.

Betty ignored him. "Make sure you give Cressie a call. Now that she's in Adelaide we don't see her nearly enough, but I rang and told her you were coming here tonight, and she'll be expecting you to ring. I told her you didn't have an address yet. Where are you going to live?"

"How long are you here for? Will you play with the orchestra?" asked Bob. "What are your plans?"

The questions were overwhelmingly unanswerable. Libby looked from one kindly face to the other and burst into tears. The reaction was immediate. Hugs from two generous sets of arms, and Bob's hanky shoved into her hand. She sniveled and sniffed and tried to draw away, but Betty clasped her strongly against her bosom and said soothingly, "Don't worry, it's the jet lag. It scrambles your brains. You're too tired to think straight."

"I think you should stay here tonight with us," said Bob firmly. "You can sleep in Cressie's room."

"No, no, I'm sorry. I don't know why I did that. It must be tiredness."

"I think you should move in with us," continued Bob, "permanently. We'd love to have you."

"Yes," cried Betty. "Definitely, yes."

"No, thanks. I think I need a good sleep, that's all." Libby pulled herself away and managed to produce an embarrassed, watery smile. They'd kill her with kindness. She'd been too long alone to become a surrogate daughter. "Can I call a taxi, please?"

"No," said Charles's voice behind her. "I'll take you."

She whirled around in dismay. He was standing with that irritating smile on his face again.

"Marvelous idea. Thank you, Charles," cried Bob.

"You have a hot shower and pop straight into bed when you get to that hotel," ordered Betty.

"I can take a taxi," protested Libby weakly, as she was virtually frogmarched to the front door and propelled down the steps. She managed a wave to the other guests as she passed, and they chorused goodnight and went on with their intense discussion of the movie *Dante's Peak.* Greg was explaining once again to Joe that he didn't study volcanoes.

Betty and Bob accompanied Libby to Charles's vehicle parked across the street. They hovered anxiously as he unlocked the doors, and Bob helped her in as though she were either fragile or ninety.

"Thanks for dinner," Libby said, trying to regain some degree of control over the situation. But the Betty and Bob juggernaut rolled on and she knew she'd just been definitively cast in the role of Lame Duck recently vacated by Wayne.

"You come and visit any time you want, love, the door's always open. Come and take potluck," called Betty through the open driver's door.

"Thank you."

Charles started the engine. He didn't say anything, just pulled out into the street and drove in the general direction of the city center.

Libby surreptitiously wiped her eyes. She must look terrible. They'd bundled her out pretty smartly not wanting to startle the other guests. No, that was unkind. Bob and Betty were concerned only for her well-being. They were wonderful people, she loved them. Libby leaned her head back against the seat and closed her eyes. Not even that lethal coffee would keep her awake. Lead weights settled on her lids. It was unnaturally nice of Charles to drive her . . .

"Libby," said a voice. A gentle voice. A voice like smooth velvet, deep—crooning her name like a lover. She sighed. And stirred. "Libby, wake up."

They must be landing soon. Stopover in Singapore. Her eyes flicked open, and her brain tried vainly to assimilate the information it was receiving. Not on the plane. No engine noise. City noises. Dark. A car? A man talking to her. A man? She stared. He looked vaguely familiar in the dim light.

"Charles, remember? I'm taking you to your hotel. I just need to know which one."

Libby exhaled loudly. "I'm sorry. I didn't know where I was for a minute."

"Can you remember which hotel you're in?"

"The Park Regis on Park Street," she said crisply. He'd spoken as if she were an amnesia victim or a panic-stricken child.

"Fine." He eased back into the traffic.

"Why are you taking me home?" she asked but rephrased it quickly. "I mean, thanks for taking me home but isn't it out of your way?"

"No," he said.

"I thought you lived near Bob and Betty."

"No."

"Where *do* you live?"

"Willoughby."

The city was on his way, sort of.

"How do you know them?" she asked after a few moments of silence. Orientation silence while her brain sifted and filed information.

"I did some renovations last year at the offices where Bob works and he was my contact."

"And they took it from there," finished Libby. Typical of them. They were indiscriminate in their invitations. One day they would discover they had a serial killer sitting at their dinner table. Charles was saying something about Bob, she realized. Her mind must be wandering.

"I need sleep," she said, suddenly embarrassed. He'd seen her cry and hadn't asked why. But a man wouldn't, especially this one. He didn't want to get involved in anyone's life, that was obvious. He was probably actively scared she might tell him why she cried. Except she couldn't because she didn't actually know why herself.

He didn't comment. She recognized the old brown sandstone walls of Central Station before they plunged across the intersection and entered Elizabeth Street. He took a left at the lights, slowed.

"Here you are." The blue-and-white Park Regis Hotel sign shone on her left.

"Thanks. Thanks very much. I'm sorry I . . ."

He cut her off. "Have a good sleep."

She opened the door. "I intend to, don't worry." She got out and leaned down to wave goodbye. "Good night. Thanks."

He waved back and said, as she closed the door,

"Sleep tight." Then came a few more words lost in the roar of a passing bus.

He looked at her expectantly, but a waiting taxi blasted its horn for him to move. Libby nodded and smiled and quickly shut the door. She stood staring after his car as it disappeared down Park Street, took a right at George, and disappeared. Had she heard correctly? It sounded as though he'd said, "something, something, something—pick you up—something dinner."

Chapter Two

Charles drove home across the Harbour Bridge humming under his breath. He couldn't believe what had just happened. Libby McNeill, the most beautiful girl he'd ever seen in his life, had arrived for dinner at Bob and Betty's. Amazing. Staggeringly and wondrously amazing. He slapped the steering wheel in delight. At Bob and Betty's of all places. Who'd have thought they knew a girl like Libby? The connection with Cressida never entered his head. They would be the same age, but Cressie hadn't studied music. None of the Swifts were musicians.

Talk about luck! He'd had to decline many of their invitations because they never gave him much notice—spontaneity was the keyword with the Swifts—and since he'd met Tiffany many of his evenings were spoken for. "Bring her along," they insisted, but he knew Tiffany wouldn't appreciate the Swift brand of hospitality. Far too rowdy and unsophisticated for her refined tastes—that, coupled with an eclectic guest list that he found entertaining and very relaxing after some of the high powered and/or boring work-related functions Tiffany asked him to escort her to but which she would regard as supremely uninteresting.

Plus there was something else about walking into that friendly, warm, and welcoming atmosphere. Something he wanted to keep to himself, for himself. Something absent from his own miserable childhood in the large and chilly mansion in London he was supposed to call home. Bob and Betty's house simply oozed love and acceptance. He'd never realized how much a physical structure could absorb from its inhabitants.

If only he could plan that into his building designs. If only he'd had parents like Bob and Betty. If it hadn't been for Glory and Henry . . .

Glory had been with him several months now, and she'd enjoyed the two Bob and Betty dinner parties she'd attended, but found the evenings noisily tiring. At eighty-one she was usually snug in bed by 9:30.

"You go," she told him when the next invitation arrived. "I'm happy staying home with a book." But he couldn't go out to dinner and leave her alone too often.

This time, however, the gods were smiling when Bob rang. Glory had some old-folks do on so Charles accepted.

And Libby was there.

The first time he'd seen her in Vienna he'd been speechless. There she was striding across the street, coming towards him with that bulky cello in one red-gloved hand and a slim leather case in the other, breath steaming, cheeks pink from the frosty night air. Thick dark curls escaped from under a red-knitted cap pulled down over her ears. Confident, young, bursting with vitality and beauty. And she lived in his building.

She'd swung up the steps before him and charged through the heavy green-painted wooden door before he could reach it to hold for her. By the time he sprinted up the steps and politely, frustratedly, chatted with elderly Herr and Frau Willing who were also returning and insisted on telling him about the play they'd recently seen, she'd disappeared.

But Frau Willing knew as much as could be learned about Libby, and living up to her name, was very willing to share. She had a kind heart and a romantic soul and seemed to recognize instantly Charles's lovestruck state. Libby was Australian, she said, studying with Heinz Wanhal, the best cello player in the world but now in his eighties. Libby didn't chat much with the neighbors but wasn't unfriendly, just busy. She would be practicing constantly. Her apartment was on the fourth floor, and she'd just moved in. Her German was quite good.

Charles had nearly completed his postgrad studies. One more week and he'd be leaving Vienna for London.

She practiced constantly. The rich, full sound swirled around the building. At first it was a novelty and he quite enjoyed it, but by the third day he'd had enough of the Elgar *Cello Concerto* to last a lifetime. He discovered himself humming her warm-up exercises and scales under his breath as he studied his notes. He stopped typing to strain his ears as she attempted the same difficult passage, which involved high notes that slipped and slid from under her fingers. Over and over again.

He ground his teeth and tried to block it out. Impossible. He went upstairs armed with a polite smile, and knocked on her door. She didn't answer. The cello sang on heedlessly. Herr Willing came down from the apartment above as he stood on her landing debating whether to thump with his fist on her door.

"She is very talented, that one," he said and smiled. "We are fortunate to have such a musician to play for us. For free."

Charles swallowed the bile and agreed. Both Willings were elderly and almost certainly partially deaf. He accompanied Herr Willing downstairs, went into his rooms, and stuffed cotton wool in his ears.

He spoke to Libby just the once. On the stairs, exactly as he had related to her. Except that she'd also spoken. He had his little speech all ready, a polite request to refrain from practice for just a couple of hours each day so that he could study. But his tongue had tied itself in knots at the proximity of his idol, and he'd only stuttered, "Good evening."

She'd replied, "Good evening. Excuse me, please," and gone on down the stairs without a second glance, barely pausing to acknowledge his existence, apparently not even registering they'd spoken English.

He'd never forgotten. Eight years and he'd never forgotten the loveliness of that face at close quarters, the delicacy of the skin, the glorious violet blue of the eyes and that little polite smile, in passing, she'd thrown him from luscious, full lips. All this was etched forever in his mind. She'd rendered him—self-confident, articulate, highly intelligent Charles Hogarth—speechless.

And he'd never forgotten how she ignored him, how she loved her music and her cello more than anything. It made him sick to his soul. He'd grown up observing that obsessive brand of love. He instantly recognized and abhorred the singleminded pursuit of perfection that shut out the uninitiated, and more tragically and personally for Charles, shut out the child. It was a sixth sense, honed to perfection in the uncompromising mind of a sad, lonely, and embittered little boy.

He'd left Vienna and left Libby with a sigh of relief at not being exposed to such conflicting emotions for any longer. She was too beautiful to resist and too dedicated a musician to consider pursuing. He was glad he had to leave. A bittersweet departure.

But seeing her tonight, all that doubt and muddled emotion was swept away in the overwhelming rush of pleasure. She was gorgeous, even more beautiful in her maturity, and she had a vulnerability she'd not had before. He was that gauche, torn student again. He literally couldn't keep away from her, could barely keep his eyes off her all night. Betty must have noticed. Everyone must have noticed.

As he drove and thought and his hormones gradually resumed their normal circulation, the mature, present-day Charles recognized in himself the signs of an infatuation that could lead to trouble. The humming ceased and a worried frown creased his brow by the time he'd crossed the Harbour Bridge and reached north Sydney.

Beautiful women were his weakness; he knew that

after various close shaves and hysterical tirades. He'd learned over the years to insulate himself, control himself, and clinically choose those who were of the same mind. He wasn't looking for permanency and messy emotional entanglement. Tiffany understood. Tiffany was of his world and had the same calculated approach to relationships. She wanted a reliable escort and companion, which suited him just fine.

Spontaneously inviting Libby to dinner had all the hallmarks of a terrible mistake. She was uncharted waters, she was a mapless jungle, she was a vast emotional minefield waiting to blow him to pieces. She was a Siren. He was drawn to her like a helpless, captivated sailor in thrall of her beauty, heedless of the jagged, death-dealing rocks . . . She made him think like one of his demented mother's appalling opera librettos.

Charles thumped the steering wheel with the heel of his hand. Blast! Why had he opened his stupid mouth to invite her out? Maybe he could simply not turn up?

Never. He'd never stand a woman up. Such crass, ungentlemanly behavior was cruel and far too callous. He would call her in the morning and cancel with apologies and sincere regret. Yes, that was better. Plead an emergency involving Glory, the only relative he had here in Australia, and the only relative he could, in any way, abide.

Sleep on it. See how he felt in the morning. But seeing her again . . . just once. Wouldn't hurt.

Libby slept for sixteen hours straight. She woke and lay gathering her cotton-wool thoughts into coherent order. They were all depressing, but there were many things to do. First she needed to find somewhere to live. Cheap. Then she needed a job. Urgent. Then she would have to send for her goods and chattels, and try to establish a new life for herself. Without playing.

She flexed her arms and winced as the pain bit into her left shoulder and ran down to her forearm. Her fingers curled and the tendons complained violently. Repetitive strain injury. Chronic and almost irreparable. No playing of any kind, no hand or arm movements that would exacerbate the injuries and cause pain. Complete rest was the only cure. For months and months, maybe years. Then slow therapy to regain the strength. Thus spake the Dutch specialist she'd seen before fleeing the country in despair.

What could she possibly do? What work? She could do nothing but play the cello, but she couldn't even teach in the state she was in. Unemployable.

Libby lay flat on her back and stared at the ceiling. She had capital—money invested thanks to the inheritance from her parents—but she needed a permanent place to live as soon as possible. The family home was rented out, paying its remaining mortgage off. Don Fraser, her father's lawyer friend had organized all that for her years ago after the accident and anyway, she didn't want to live in the Turramurra house again. Not with so many memories floating about. It was too big for one person, needed a family. She may even sell it. Don recommended against that at the time saying not to make a hasty decision. She had assets but no cash. She needed a job.

Libby showered and dressed then picked up the phone. Betty answered.

"I wanted to say thanks for dinner last night and apologize for being such a mess."

"There's no need to apologize, Libby. We understand perfectly. Are you feeling better today? It was so nice of Charles to drive you home, wasn't it? He's such a kind man. Very busy, we don't see him often. He makes the social pages, though, usually with a very attractive girl." Betty gave a little trill of delighted laughter.

Libby said, "It was nice of Charles to leave early for my sake. I'm almost back to normal, I think. I have to go flat hunting so I'll let you know when I have an address and phone number."

"You do that. Keep in touch."

"I will, I promise."

Libby sat in a nearby coffee shop eating a late lunch while studying the To Let ads. She had a vague idea of the area she wanted, but everything was ridiculously expensive, especially as she didn't have an income. Her savings would only stretch so far and for so long. She'd either have to share or rent a bedsit where she slept and ate and practiced all in the same room. No. Cut the practice bit. She was so used to having that as a consideration, she hadn't even registered she was doing it.

She circled a few ads then went back to her room to telephone the agents and set up appointments to view. Next she needed a job. Her options were severely limited—even more so than she'd thought. She couldn't do anything requiring finger dexterity or lifting of any kind. That cut out secretarial, receptionist, any sort of computing—even if she could type or work a computer which she couldn't beyond basics—and also waitressing. She was too old for most of the shop assistant positions and had no experience for most of the others.

By page three of the vacancies section she was seriously considering the suburban letterbox leaflet drop rounds, and dressing up as a rabbit for a "Jump into Spring" shopping center promotion. There were also the "earn a thousand dollars a week from home" positions, which involved telephoning people and irritating them at dinner time by doing surveys, or selling lottery tickets for worthy charities. But she'd need a home first to do that from.

She circled two talent agencies, which offered modeling, TV, and film extra positions to virtually all comers no experience required; a music school requiring a part time teacher of music theory; a small private ad from someone who wanted German translations done; and another requiring "person with musical knowledge to do research."

Maybe she could cobble together an income for a few months until the situation with her arm was clearer. Impossible to imagine never playing her cello again.

No answer from the research and the German numbers, an answering machine at the music school, and two very enthusiastic receptionists at the talent agencies. "Come in," they both said, "for an interview and a photo." She made appointments for later in the week.

Then she lay down on the bed and went to sleep until the bedside phone rang stridently in her ear.

"You have a visitor, Miss McNeill."

Libby sat up.

"Visitor?" Her fuzzy sleep-drenched brain attempted to calculate the country she was in and what time it might be. The desk clerk had an American accent, which didn't help, and neon lights flickered red-and-blue patterns on her wall from across the darkened street.

"A Mr. Hogarth."

"I don't know Mr. Hogarth," she said, bewildered.

Subdued background muttering, then, "Charles Hogarth. He's come to take you out to dinner."

"Oh! Yes. Tell him . . . No. I'll be down in a few minutes." She must have heard what she thought she'd heard. And promptly deleted it from her mind as too unlikely.

Libby leapt off the bed and headed for the bathroom. Charles Hogarth. Downstairs waiting for her? Handsome Charles Hogarth. That subversive thought stopped her in her tracks. She frowned as she filled the basin with water and washed her face. He was more than handsome, he was downright attractive. But he hadn't asked her to dinner, he'd thrown the invitation at her at the last minute and she hadn't even heard it properly. He apparently thought she had or he wouldn't be here.

Libby massaged moisturizer into her cheeks and stared at herself in the mirror. He hadn't given her much chance either to accept or decline. What sort of person was he?

A kind one according to Betty. One who didn't like cello playing.

One with a temper if her memories were correct. But to be fair, people can change in eight years. Had Charles?

Was he always as supercilious? And another thing—why wasn't a good-looking man of his age already spoken for? Should've asked Betty. He may well have some deep personal problem preventing his forming a lasting attachment with a woman. Newly broken heart? Perhaps the love of his life had died a tragic early death and he'd vowed never to love again. That'd make for a fun evening.

But he was too keen to take her out for a man who'd sworn off women. Ditto for the broken heart theory. She applied mascara and picked up her lipstick. Plus he'd driven her home last night. He hadn't needed to. Not at all. But that last minute invitation with no chance to respond? Smacked of "lord of the manor."

What on earth was she doing? Libby glared at herself.

"You're not going out with a man who *tells* you he'll pick you up," she exclaimed. He assumed she'd be ready and waiting, and even though she'd actually been asleep, she was falling over herself to get ready for him now.

Libby snatched up her bag, her key, and marched out to the elevator. She would go downstairs, apologize for wasting his time and politely decline his offhand invitation. She remembered now—he'd been looking down his handsome nose at the company last night as if they were all beneath his social level.

But she took one good look at him waiting in the foyer and knew this man was most definitely not the monster she'd built in her mind, and he was most definitely extremely sexy. Her determination to send him packing faltered under the spell of buzzing hormones and an intense rush of desire that weakened her alarmingly at the knees.

Last night's impressions were hazy to say the least. Now, unclouded by jet lag, tears and tiredness Libby saw Charles as she had never seen or noticed him before. He was studying a historic photograph of Sydney Harbour on the wall, and in profile his nose was straight and his chin firm. He had longish dark-brown hair, streaked gold in parts from the sun. Maybe he surfed. His body was certainly the right shape. Broad shoulders, lean and fit. His jacket and slacks hung neatly and crisply from his frame. Early to mid thirties?

He turned as her heels sounded loud on the parquetry floor. He stared for the briefest of moments as if stunned, then he smiled. Libby gasped as if she'd been hit by a sandbag—right in the chest. This was followed by nonfunctioning knee-joints. Her mouth opened and heat rushed to her cheeks. She swallowed. Her smooth, leather-soled, elegant, Italian shoe slipped on the shiny floor and she skated inelegantly for a few floundering paces before crashing into his hastily outstretched arms.

"Hello," he said.

Libby managed a sort of gurgling noise in response and straightened herself up still clutching his forearm, which resembled an iron railing under the linen jacket sleeve. She drew a deep gasping breath as much at the sudden stabbing pain in her arm as anything else and glanced down. Her foot had landed on something more pliable than parquetry.

"Oh! I'm so sorry. I've trodden on you again." She leapt back and removed the offending foot from his toe.

Charles nodded. "Perhaps I have big feet."

"No, no, you don't," Libby cried. "It's me. I must be clumsy. I'm not usually, I don't think. You probably do, though." He grinned and she added quickly, "Think I'm clumsy."

"No, not particularly. As an architect I frown upon slippery surfaces in public thoroughfares. Just inviting lawsuits." He extended his hand. "Shall we?"

Libby paused. He was making that assumption again. She said, "I wasn't expecting you." To her surprise a look of embarrassment flitted across his face.

"Why not?" he asked with a certain degree of caution.

"I didn't hear what you said properly when you dropped me off and you drove away before I could answer."

Now he seemed relieved and a tiny smile reappeared. "What would you have said if you'd heard properly?"

"What did you ask?

"If you'd have dinner with me tonight."

"Funny. The bit I heard sounded more like 'I'll pick you up tomorrow.' " Libby watched him deciding how to reply and added mildly, "I prefer to be asked than ordered."

"But you're here now." Charles was looking at her with that expression of private amusement she remembered so clearly from last night. "So you must have decided to accept."

"No, I came to tell you what I thought of your manners."

"Go on."

"What?"

"Tell me." The smile widened, and she frowned in a desperate effort to maintain her annoyance, dignity, and most of all independence in the face of this most obnoxiously confident of men. With a very infectious smile.

"I have already. I said I prefer to be asked than ordered."

"Libby, will you have dinner with me tonight, please?"

He stood there gazing at her with his brown-flecked green eyes and his penitent face, and she recognized that vulnerable, almost secretly hoping expression again, and heard herself saying, "Yes, thank you."

Charles ushered her through the heavy glass door, keeping one hand firmly on her arm. Libby proceeded with as much dignity as was possible under the circumstances. He swung her to the left when they reached the street.

"I thought we'd walk. Do you mind?"

"No," she said. Then after a few steps, in case he thought a ten-block hike was an evening stroll, "How far?" she asked. Italian elegance wasn't designed for long marches. If only she'd thought to change her jeans for a skirt when she rushed out to berate him.

"Just down Chinatown way." Four blocks.

They crossed George Street at Town Hall. Foreign backpackers and sundry homeless people lounged on the steps of the building watching the passing crowds.

"I played Elgar's *Cello Concerto* in there," said Libby, gazing up at the imposing dark stone frontage. "With the City Symphony Orchestra."

"I thought you were still learning it in Vienna," Charles said. "All that practice you did."

He watched her face as she decided whether he was trying to insult her or not. He wasn't; he'd just wanted her to know he knew the piece, but she didn't even register that he'd remembered what she'd been playing way back then. His stomach, which had been a churning mass of nervous tension all day, hardened into a solid, dull ache.

He didn't want to upset her. He just wanted to be with her.

If she wasn't a musician, she'd be his perfect woman. He could put up with any other profession—or even no profession—but that one. This evening was going to be a torture of repressed attraction combined with the bitterness of memories that had nothing to do with Libby, but had everything to do with how he related to her. He should've acted on his survival instinct from last night and called it off. But today the thought of seeing her again was irresistible: just once wouldn't hurt if he was careful and reserved. If she kept talking about music, it would be easy not to follow up.

"Learning never stops," she said seriously. "I performed it as part of a concerto competition when I was a student."

"Did you win?"

"Yes. If I hadn't I don't think Herr Wanhal would've bothered with me. It gave me a certain credibility."

"Why are you back in Australia?" asked Charles. "Performing?"

She was probably going to tell him she was on a concert tour of Australasia and would be leaving in a week. Much better if she did. It was obvious all she thought about was music. Charles inhaled deeply, hoping to ease the ache in his stomach. Maybe he was growing an ulcer. Glory kept telling him he should relax more.

He glanced at Libby walking so casually beside him. She wore her clothes with an incredibly stylish elegance. Blue jeans, those crazy, dangerous shoes, and a simple tan jacket over a white T-shirt—she was stunning. Irresistible. He must be mad.

The longer he spent with her the less he'd be able to stay away from her. The thought of life with a self-obsessed, highflying professional musician was unbearable. Constant practicing, ridiculous rehearsal schedules, constant travel, dramas, hysteria, nerves, the works. He'd escaped from that years ago as soon as he was old enough. He didn't want drama and uncontrolled passions in his life. He wanted order and normality. He'd achieved it until last night.

Libby said, "You say performing as though I were about to embark on a career as an axe murderer."

"Are you?" Even her voice was musical. Siren sound.

"Of course not! What is it with you and musicians? Why do you dislike us so much?" Now she was cross.

Charles pressed his lips together firmly. If he told her who his parents were she'd gush all over the place about how lucky he was to have grown up with such incredibly talented people. Then she'd ask why he didn't follow them into music and it would all get messy and horrible, and he'd sound surly and bitter. Glory was the only one who understood how he felt, how deep the resentment was, how he hated his heritage.

He shrugged, laughed lightly. "Bad experience. The ones I've met were totally obsessed with themselves and ponced around as though they were God's gift to the world."

"Thanks very much. I can't imagine the sort of people you've come across, but we're not all like that," said Libby in a tight voice.

Charles stopped himself from saying she had been in Vienna, but Libby said it for him. She'd stopped walking, and her angry words hit him in the back like stones. "You think I *am* like that, don't you, based on your experience in Vienna? Why on earth did you ask me out tonight, Charles?"

Charles had continued several paces, but he spun about now and faced her. He looked down into her angry, bewildered face and told the truth instead of kissing her, which he really wanted to do and had wanted to do since Vienna.

"I wanted to see you again. I thought dinner together would be nice . . . catching up . . . you know . . ." His eyes left hers, accusing and hard. He glanced over her shoulder briefly, then back. "I'm sorry I offended you, Libby . . . I didn't mean to." He licked his lips and firmed them, frowning slightly as he mangled the next truth ever so slightly. "I feel awfully guilty."

"Why? For offending me or for something else?" Her expression changed. "Are you married?" She stepped closer.

"No! But I do . . . I am seeing someone."

"A girlfriend." Libby stared at him, searching his eyes for signs of a lie. There was nothing except remorse and guilt. He thought he was two-timing his girlfriend and had second thoughts. Ridiculous. What did he expect from this evening? She almost laughed. "What do you think? I'm expecting an engagement ring?"

"No," cried Charles, sounding terribly English. "Of course not."

"Glad we've got that straight," she said. The blank shock on his face almost made the laughter explode. She relented. "Look, Charles. This isn't anything more than a dinner between old acquaintances. Catching up, as you said. Tell her that if she asks, and I certainly won't disagree. There's absolutely nothing to feel guilty about."

Charles met her gaze. The beautiful eyes glinted with a steely sheen of annoyance. This passion was all on his side. The bitter disappointment at her dismissal of him as potential suitor was all his. Libby didn't care one way or the other. She expected nothing. He was an idiot. A crass, rude, and stupid idiot. He nodded abruptly, drew on all his childhood training. The stiff upper lip.

"Yes," he said. "Yes, you're right. I'm terribly sorry. I don't know what I was thinking . . . saying."

Libby stalked ahead a few paces. He stood mesmerized, watching the way the breeze lifted her dark hair, the way the street lighting gleaned off its ebony waves. She was perfection. He'd dreamed of this woman for years. He didn't know her at all. She remained a dream, unattainable. He wanted her as he'd never wanted anything or anyone in his life.

She turned with a tiny beckoning gesture of her hand. "Come on. Are we having dinner or not?"

"Yes," he said without hesitation.

Charles took her to a Spanish restaurant tucked down a side street just before they reached Chinatown. Libby kept her anger under tight control. This man amazed her; she was even more amazed at herself. Why hadn't she simply turned on her heel and left him standing after insulting her that way? Why?

Perhaps it was that instant when he looked completely vulnerable and lost. The moment before he told her he felt guilty—as if that would matter to her, as if she thought something might be brewing between them. Then when she'd completely dismissed his reasoning, he'd stared into her eyes and she'd imagined . . . must have imagined because it couldn't possibly be the truth . . . she'd imagined he was disappointed.

Perhaps that was why she'd spun away from the expression in his eyes, and why after several paces she'd relented.

Lying restless in bed later that night, Libby couldn't remember much of what they'd discussed over dinner. Vienna. The weather in Sydney as compared with Europe. That had lasted them through the main course. Bob and Betty and what wonderful characters they were. They hadn't had dessert, just coffee. The whole affair was a miserable, stilted, uncomfortable failure. And she couldn't get to sleep.

Charles had walked Libby back to the hotel. The whole night had been a disaster. He wished they could start again. He wished he could flick his fingers and Libby would walk toward him and trip; then he'd catch her in his arms and they'd laugh. And this second time around he wouldn't tell her what he thought about musicians. This second time he'd smile and admire and listen and secretly love her. But there was only one chance and it had gone.

"I'm sorry, Libby," he said in the slippery parquet foyer of her hotel.

"Nothing to be sorry for, Charles," she said. She held out her hand, and he shook it out of habit. "Thank you for dinner. Good night."

"Thank you. Good night."

Libby turned on her dangerous heel and headed for the elevators.

Charles watched her go. He sighed and shoved his hands in his pockets. It was better this way. Now even if he was tempted to pick up the phone and suggest they try again, she'd politely decline. Much better. But horribly and unexpectedly painful, to the point that his stomach cramped violently and his chest felt as though someone had shoved a knife into it. He suddenly wanted to cry.

But of course, he wouldn't. He'd trained himself as a child not to.

Chapter Three

Charles let himself into his house in Willoughby. Glory was still out. Two social functions in two nights. Those senior citizens certainly knew how to entertain themselves. He made himself coffee and sat in the living room mournfully. He was considering a second cup when the front door clicked open and shut, and light steps sounded in the hall.

He plastered a smile on his face as Glory appeared.

"Did you have a nice evening, dear? You're home early. I thought you were having dinner with a Viennese friend." Glory dropped her handbag on the table. She removed her jacket and folded it over the back of a chair.

"I did," he said. "How was your trivia night? Did you win?"

Glory threw up her hands in dismay. "You try answering trivia questions with a table full of people who are losing their memories and their marbles and are argumentative know-it-alls with it."

Charles smiled. "I'm glad you're settling in."

"You're a dear boy, Charles. I know I'm a pain-in-the-neck landing on you like this. The last thing a young man needs is a decrepit relative cramping his style." She gazed at him fondly and Charles smiled, dutifully this time.

"You're not decrepit," he said. "Any signs of decrepitude and you're out."

"I feel it right now," she replied with a laugh. "Two nights socializing in a row. Too much for me, I'm afraid. I'll sleep like a log."

"Off to bed?"

"Yes, good night dear." She leaned down and kissed his cheek softly.

"Good night, Glory."

Charles sank back into the cushions with his coffee cup resting on his stomach. He heard Glory pour herself a glass of water in the kitchen, her feet scuffing gently on the hall carpet as she headed for her room. The door closed with a click.

What could he do? She was his only relative in Australia and vice versa. Great Uncle died years ago, Glory couldn't live alone any more. At eighty-one she was becoming forgetful and evermore fragile despite his denials just now. Two months ago he'd moved her into his house.

She steadfastly refused to consider aged housing and there was a chronic shortage anyway. Unbeknownst to her, he'd investigated all the options and put her name on several waiting lists. He'd never tell her, but she *was* a worry. He couldn't be with her during the day and felt guilty leaving her at night. He dreaded to think of the day she might require nursing care.

Glory also politely detested Tiffany. Charles loved his great aunt dearly, but the sooner she moved somewhere more suitable, the better.

The first apartment Libby viewed was hideous. Advertised as a studio, it was basically a motel-sized room in a building that seemed to house men on the various lower rungs of life's ladder. Two were sitting on the front steps in the sun when she arrived, and they greeted her cheerfully with raised beer cans. The interior smelled of stale cooking, cigarette smoke, and alcohol. Kitchen facilities were shared.

The next was a two-roomed mansion by comparison, but it was on a very busy road, next to a pub, and opposite a fire station.

"You'll have to go farther out to find anything decent at that price. These and similar are your options in the inner city area," the agent told her sternly with an I-told-you-so look in her eye.

Libby thought longingly of her cozy flat in Rotterdam, but she shoved that image brutally aside. This was now. Her life would be completely different from this point on. Get used to it.

Libby went back to her room and made herself a cup of instant coffee. She stared out the window at the traffic and pedestrians on the street below. Occasionally a screaming siren rent the air, horns tooted, bus brakes hissed and squealed—all sounds of people going about their lives. They all had things to do: jobs, some of them extremely important involving saving lives and helping people in trouble.

What could she do? Nothing.

On Wednesday afternoon Libby went to the first of the talent agency appointments. The woman, Desiree, who greeted her, appraised her as though she were on show at a slave auction. Libby thought Desiree might even go so far as to examine her teeth and pick up her foot the way people buying horses do. She filled out an endless questionnaire and was shunted through to a studio to have her photo taken by a jovial young man who exclaimed over her eyes.

"Elizabeth Taylor eyes. Forget Bette Davis!" he cried.

"We'll call you," said Desiree when he'd finished. "But don't hang by your thumbs waiting."

The second agency appointment was much the same although the man who photographed her was surly, and the woman who questioned her, preoccupied.

"We can't promise anything," she said.

Libby rode the bus home to the hotel, despondent. She would have to move soon. The hotel was too expensive to live in after this first week. It was a luxury she couldn't justify. The whole job situation was hopeless. She was of use to neither man nor beast.

She rang Cressie in Adelaide and had a long, sometimes teary chat reminiscing and catching up and explaining why she'd returned so abruptly to Sydney. She omitted any reference to the strange individual who'd taken her to dinner. It was too embarrassing and humiliating, especially as the man was a friend of Bob and Betty.

Later that evening Betty phoned. The Swift grapevine was swift indeed.

"You must come to stay with us," announced Betty firmly after a flurry of "oh dear" and "what a shame." "Why didn't you say you couldn't play any more? You can move in straight away."

"I may have to take you up on that soon but not right away," said Libby when she could force a word in. "I really need a job."

"Have you considered a live-in position? A nanny or some such?"

"I have absolutely no experience with children," cried Libby. "I'd be a disaster."

"How about house sitting? That'd be perfect. You leave it to me," said Betty with determination. "I have many contacts. I'll spread the word at the seniors' club where I help out. They're always going off on holidays, or their children are. Someone may want help in the house."

After Betty had rung off, Libby sat by the window and stared down at the busy street. Charles popped into her head as he had done frequently since this same time yesterday. She could not believe someone could be so insensitive by saying such things—all because she was a classical musician. Or was it any musician? Did he have it in for country singers and rockers as well? Such a bizarre reaction. He'd known all along that's what she did. He'd even told Selina she was a beautiful cello player and sounded as though he meant it. And he'd recognized the Elgar.

Tears sprang to her eyes and a prickle of heat went down her spine as she relived the humiliating conversation. What did he think he was doing?

She'd made the mistake of thinking he was an attractive man and worse still, thinking he may have improved since Vienna when, in actual fact, he had deteriorated to a puddle of slime. But he'd been so nice up till then and, as they'd set out to walk to Chinatown, she'd tentatively started to relax and look forward to the evening ahead. Why couldn't they have just had a meal like old acquaintances? Why did it have to become so tense and dramatic?

Forget him. Put him out of her head. Treat him like something nasty she'd trodden in and had to wipe off her shoe. Or like a bad smell that had wafted in through the window and caused the room to be aired out. The chance of meeting him again was exceedingly slim. The only place their paths would conceivably cross was at Bob and Betty's, and she, and most likely Charles, would make quite sure that didn't happen.

"Hello, is that Libby McNeill?"

The voice on the phone was elderly and female. Please let it be one of those people she'd left messages for—music theory lessons, German translations. The silence from those areas had been deafening. "My name is Gloria Bennett and I heard through Betty Swift you may be interested in a live-in position. I'm in need of a companion."

"Oh!" Libby's mind lurched into gear. Betty and her contacts. Live-in position? "What exactly did you have in mind?"

"I'm eighty-one, you see, and I live with my nephew in Willoughby, but he's too busy to have to bother with me and he's at work all day. I'd like some company and I need someone to help about the house, help me get about the place to my appointments." She sounded mentally competent: very alert and well-spoken.

"I'm not trained as a nurse," said Libby doubtfully.

"That's all right, dear, I'm not sick," said Gloria and laughed. "There's a lovely bedroom with its own bathroom. We have a large house and there's plenty of room for another person. I hear you're a musician so that would be wonderful."

"I'm not able to play at the moment. I have an injury to my arm," said Libby.

"How tragic! You poor thing. Would you like to visit? We could have afternoon tea and see if we like each other. Size each other up." Gloria laughed again, softly.

Libby smiled. She glanced at the bedside clock, at the newspaper lying open with crossed-out jobs and a depressing array of circled accommodations in increasingly far-flung suburbs. Willoughby was close to the city and upmarket.

"Thank you. I think I would. I've never done this sort of thing before."

"Neither have I," said Gloria. "But there's a first time for everything. You know what whoever it was—some chap whose name I could never remember even before I started losing my memory—said? 'Try everything once except incest and Morris dancing.' "

Libby burst out laughing while Gloria chuckled at her end of the line. She dictated the address and telephone number and invited Libby for three-thirty that afternoon. Libby could catch a train then walk three blocks. Too easy.

She sat cross-legged on her bed. Was this as good an offer as it sounded, or were there hidden catches and lethal booby traps? She couldn't judge anything until she'd seen the house and more importantly, met Gloria Bennett.

Her life so far had been totally devoid of elderly relatives, her own or anyone else's. In fact she didn't mix with the elderly at all. The last octagenerian she'd had dealings with was Maestro Heinz Wanhal in Vienna and he'd been a tetchy old devil prone to discussing her playing with scornful utterances in fractured English laced with ripe Italian and German invectives. Not a good advertisement for the ageing.

Gloria sounded friendly on the phone and there was also a hint of pleading that Libby agree to visit before making a decision. The old lady was lonely and didn't want to be a problem for her nephew. She knew that much about the elderly, they hated becoming dependent and a burden. On reflection, she was in a similar position herself. Maybe she and Gloria would be well-suited. And Gloria liked musicians.

All the houses in the street were elegant old Sydney redbrick with small tiled porches, white gables, and neat front gardens. They probably all had enormous backyards and were worth a small fortune. Number fourteen had a beautiful garden. Libby paused at the gate and sniffed the perfume rising from the soldierly rows of pink-and-purple flowers lining the path to the front steps.

The front door had a rich blue, yellow, and red floral stained glass inset and was flung open almost the instant she'd rung the bell. A small gray-haired woman in burgundy-silk Chinese pajamas and black-cotton kung fu slippers stood beaming at her from behind round-framed spectacles.

"Libby, do come in," she cried. "Excuse my clothes, I've just come home from my tai chi class."

Libby stepped inside. At first sight Gloria appeared perfectly fit and capable of looking after herself.

'This is the old part of the house. The fronts are heritage-listed, but the backs can be altered as long as it's not visible from the street," said Gloria. Libby gazed around at the high ceiling rooms and the beautiful dark, stained wood floor hallway covered in bright, predominantly red-patterned Persian rugs, that led through to the rear of the house.

She followed her would-be employer into a large, open family area that incorporated a kitchen enclosed by a workbench. A polished wood staircase led up to a second level and the entire back wall was French doors and glass windows looking out on to a spacious and beautifully maintained garden. The whole space was painted off-white and the furnishings were black leather and wood with cream vertical blinds to screen the windows.

Everything appeared functional, elegant, and comfortable. How she would love to live here.

She smiled at Gloria who was appearing friendlier and more appealing by the second. Did she want to be a companion to the elderly? A glorified Jane Eyre, except she would have a senior citizen charge instead of a child. How hard would it be to live in this house with this charming old lady?

"What a beautiful home." It was, and already she could imagine herself calling number fourteen home.

"My nephew is an architect," said Gloria proudly. "He designed all this himself. Sit down while I make the tea."

Libby sat in a comfortable squashy leather chair as alarm bells began sounding faintly in her head. Another architect in Willoughby? How many were there?

"What's your nephew's name?" she asked casually.

"Charles Hogarth," said Gloria, pottering about in the kitchen area. "He's a dear, dear boy. He took me in when . . ." A crash of shattering china made Libby jump. "Oh goodness!"

Libby sprang to her feet and rushed around the bench to the kitchen. Gloria stood amidst broken crockery holding a teapot handle in one hand.

"Oh," she said again in a tremulous voice. "That was my favorite pot. I do so prefer a properly made pot of tea instead of those horrible tea bags." She looked at Libby in despair and became an upset, frail, elderly woman in an instant.

Libby took the broken handle from the knobbly arthritic fingers and placed it on the bench.

"Don't worry," she said gently. "We can go shopping for a new one. Show me where the broom is and I'll clean this up. We'll start again."

"Thank you, dear. I'm turning into a silly, clumsy old woman. I don't know why Charles puts up with me."

Libby pondered the same question as she swept and tidied and made the tea in the plunger coffee pot instead. Gloria rallied, put homemade shortbread on a plate, and they sat at the dining table together drinking tea from delicate rose-patterned cups with saucers.

The fact that Charles cared for his elderly great aunt flew in the face of all recent experience. Gloria loved him, that much was evident. He must love her despite his protestations about keeping well clear of his family. There was more to Charles than met the eye. Was he really the selfish, cold observer he appeared? Or was the real Charles the one who smiled at her in the hotel foyer and made her heart, and the rest of her body, do somersaults? Why then, the crass behavior?

It was all irrelevant. He had a girlfriend he admirably refused to cheat upon, even thought he was doing so by dining with a female acquaintance.

"Come upstairs and I'll show you your room."

"Can you manage the stairs?" asked Libby as she saw the relatively steep ascent with no handrail. Gloria didn't move quickly or confidently despite her apparent good health. "You stay here and I'll nip up and have a quick look."

There were two bedrooms and a bathroom in the upstairs extension. One room was set up as an office with a computer and desk. There was plenty of space for a music stand and cello. Ultra modern fittings, beautifully designed, a view from the windows over the leafy back garden. In a word—perfect.

Gloria waited anxiously at the foot of the stairs. "I don't go up there at all. Charles' and my rooms are at the front of the house. His has an ensuite and I have the other bathroom to myself so we'd all be quite away from each other. He'd hardly know anyone else was here. You'd be very private."

"Doesn't Charles know about a companion for you?" asked Libby in sudden, chill realization.

"No, not yet. I thought it would save him worrying about me when he's at work. He does, you know. He phones me to check up. I have my own money. My Henry left me very comfortable so that's not a problem—your wages, I mean."

"Won't he mind?" He would when he found out who the companion was. "He'll have to live with me, too."

"He's not here much. He has his own life and this will give him far more freedom. He can stay out all hours with his girlfriend." Her lip curled slightly. "Though what he sees in her I don't know. What sort of a name is Tiffany, I ask you? Sounds like a fluffy cat or that jewelry shop in New York. What a wonderful actress." Gloria sighed. "Audrey Hepburn in *Breakfast at Tiffany's,*" she explained when Libby looked blank.

"I think maybe you should discuss it with him first," said Libby, tactfully resisting comment upon Tiffany. She'd immediately thought of a dinner service design. "I really don't think it will work out, Gloria."

Gloria clutched Libby's arm. "You won't need to do

any cleaning, Charles has a cleaner. I wish you would think about it, Libby. We'd get on very well and I know Charles will approve. How could he not like a lovely girl like you?"

Libby saw the desperation on Gloria's face and in her voice, heard the cry for help, and her heart softened. She really did like Gloria.

"Well," she said doubtfully.

"At least wait and meet Charles. We always have take away Chinese together on Fridays. You can stay and eat with us. He'll phone me soon to let me know he's on his way."

Libby gazed around the beautiful room and imagined herself settling in upstairs in the comfortable, private bedroom overlooking the garden. Gloria was alert, intelligent, and extremely mobile, if slow. She wouldn't have to clean house, her duties would be preparing meals and accompanying Gloria to her appointments. She could even take on some part-time work without it interfering with the job of companion.

If Gloria was correct, Charles would hardly be an issue. They could ignore and avoid each other. By caring for Gloria she would actually be doing him a favor, and he should be grateful to her for freeing him to fraternize with his amour, which would keep him even farther away from the house. Surely she should give him the benefit of the doubt. He might think it a wonderful idea. Or not.

"All right, I'll stay for dinner."

"We'll break it to him gently. I'll just say I have a friend eating with us tonight." Gloria giggled and her eyes gleamed. "We'll have such fun together you and I. We'll rent *Breakfast at Tiffany's* one evening. You'll love it. So romantic."

Libby smiled as Gloria began warbling "Moon River" in a high quivery soprano.

At five-thirty Charles rang home.

"Gloria Bennett," his great aunt said firmly.

"Hello, how are you?"

"I had tai chi today, so I'm serene and centered." She sounded very chipper, suspiciously so.

"Good. I'll be home about seven."

"All right, dear. I have a friend here so choose an extra dish." So that was it. He heard a brief, muffled conversation before she said, "Anything will do, she's very easy going."

Charles hung up with a sinking heart. An evening with two elderly ladies. What a way to spend Friday night. But Glory loved their regular meal together, and he'd made a point of keeping Fridays free. He could always go out afterward because she went to bed early and was safe enough tucked up asleep. Heaven knows who the friend would be. Still, if Glory was happy and wanted to entertain that was fine. He owed her that much; she'd rescued him from depression and despair as a child and he'd clung to her like a lifeline as a teenager. She was more of a mother than his real one had ever been.

Gloria went off to her room to change her clothes. Left on her own Libby investigated the books and CDs lined up neatly in their respective cabinets. Hardly any classical music. Not surprising. Plenty of jazz, some rock, some New Age—must be Gloria's, they didn't suit her image of Charles, he was definitely not a touchy-feely type—the Elgar *Cello Concerto*! Libby snatched the CD from the shelf. Played by Jacqueline Du Pré. Her interpretation of the work was Libby's own favorite.

Why on earth did Charles have this?

Was it to remind him of the nuisance woman in Vienna? Maybe it gave him a yardstick by which to judge dreadful moments in his life. Listen to that and realize nothing could ever be as bad again? Until now.

Libby replaced the CD carefully and went to sit on the couch amidst big burgundy-and-cream cushions, with the lemon, lime, and bitters Gloria had insisted she have while waiting for Charles.

The front door clicked open. Charles's voice called, "I'm home."

Libby drew a deep breath, steeled herself. At least she had the advantage, forewarned is forearmed. Charles would be stunned.

Pole-axed was more like it. The expression on his face was almost laughable, and Libby nearly did laugh except for the blankness that followed rapidly after the first confused shock.

"Libby? What are you doing here? Where's Glory? Glory?" he called, spinning around wildly. The two plastic carry bags of Chinese food dangling from his fingers swung in an arc and narrowly missed crashing into the doorframe.

"Don't hurl our food about, Charles. This is Libby

McNeill. I told you I had a friend for dinner." Gloria appeared, smiling, behind him. She had on a grey wool skirt and lightweight pastel-pink sweater now.

"A friend? Libby?"

"Hello, Charles." Libby rose from her chair. She clutched her glass to keep her hand from trembling. He was staring as if she were a mirage. The blankness had gone, replaced by something else. Shock, possibly.

"Do you know each other?" asked Gloria in a bewildered voice. "Libby?'

"We met in Vienna." Charles sounded half strangled.

"And again the other night." Libby attempted a smile and failed.

"Is Libby your friend from Vienna? The one you had dinner with? You told me that was a man."

"No, I didn't. You assumed."

"You should get your story straight, Charles. Put that food down and explain what's going on," said Gloria sternly. "Both of you!"

Maybe Gloria had been a schoolteacher in her day.

Charles charged into the kitchen and dumped the plastic bags on the bench. He flung open the fridge. Gloria motioned Libby to sit down again, and Libby sat meekly. What would Charles do next? His great aunt Gloria seemed to hold some sway in the house. She was remarkably formidable when she chose.

"Sit, Charles," she said. "And speak."

"I think Libby should go first. She should explain herself," he said, and plopped down on the couch opposite clutching a small green bottle of cider.

Libby met his eyes briefly and her breath caught in

her throat. She had a wild and preposterous urge to jump up and kiss him right on his full lower lip. There was something about that desperately controlled aloofness that made her want to hug him. He'd probably throttle her.

Gloria stood between them looking from one to the other. She fixed on Libby. "How did you meet Charles?"

"We lived in the same building in Vienna. I was a cello student and I drove Charles insane practicing all day. He used to thump on my floor from his room underneath. Made me furious. He nearly got me evicted." Gloria startled her by giving a shout of laughter. "Then I trod on his foot on the stairs. I didn't even notice, but he told me I had the other night. I'd bought this fantastic pair of heavy winter boots, you see, for the snow . . ." She trailed off.

"Why didn't you tell me?"

"I didn't know you were related until this afternoon then I . . ." Libby flicked a look at Charles. She didn't know how to continue. She turned back to Gloria. "I'd really like the position."

"What position?" yelled Charles, leaning forward. "You still haven't explained how you came to be sitting here in my house?" He thumped his bottle down on the coffee table. White foam fizzed out and ran down the side.

"Don't you speak to Libby like that," snapped Gloria. "Libby has kindly agreed to be my live-in companion. I got her name from Betty Swift as someone needing a position and a place to live. Betty mentioned it yesterday when she came to the Seniors' Club to help out with the

Scrabble afternoon. I've been thinking about this problem for a week or two, Charles, so when Betty put Libby's contact details on the notice board I copied them down." She drew a deep breath, exhaled. "She said Libby was wonderful and she was right. We suit each other perfectly, and I shall pay her wages from my own money." Her voice began to waver. "She'll save you from having to worry about me."

Gloria sat down abruptly with trembling hands and lips. To Libby's amazement Charles didn't explode. Instead he got up from the couch to squat beside Gloria. He took her hands and folded them in his. He kissed her cheek. When he spoke his voice was more loving and gentle than Libby could believe possible, coming from that source.

"Glory, don't be upset. It's an excellent idea and you're right. I do worry about you, but you should have discussed it with me first, not just hired someone out of the blue."

"He's right," interrupted Libby. She stood up quickly. Never had she felt so much an outsider. "I said the same thing, Charles. I didn't know this was your house until I got here. I'm sorry. I'll go. It wouldn't work, Gloria, I told you, remember? I'm sorry. It would've been . . . I would've . . ."

Libby didn't trust herself to say more. She grabbed her handbag and made a dash for the front door. It was dark outside, and she slipped and nearly fell as she negotiated the front steps, but then she ran down the path between those strongly scented flowers and hurried to the right along the footpath in the direction of the station.

She didn't even notice the tears on her cheeks until she tasted salt on her tongue. It would have been such a perfect position. Gloria had gone about it all wrong. Everything had gone wrong from the start. She herself had messed up the date with Charles by attacking his opinion instead of laughing it off. He'd been underhand asking her out and belatedly wishing he hadn't. She thought he liked her. He had until she'd ruined it. Now she was just "someone." Someone he didn't want in his house, let alone his life.

Libby slowed to cross a larger road. Cars streamed by, blinding her with their lights. She walked to the left and waited at a set of traffic lights with a pedestrian crossing. She wiped her eyes and blew her nose. The station was only two blocks farther. The house was in such a perfect spot, a beautiful place. Charles was very talented, designing those extensions, and he adored Gloria. Betty was right, Charles was a kind man.

Why wasn't he kind to her? Because he basically didn't like her?

Libby stuck her hands in her jacket pockets against the evening chill. Was that it? Charles really didn't like her? Could she have misread the occasional interested gleam in his eye? But that was the usual reaction of the male to her appearance. She was used to stunned, ogling men. Like that photographer raving over her eyes.

Libby was not so inexperienced with the opposite sex as to be blind to her attractiveness. She knew she was pretty; people kept telling her she ought to try modeling and men always had a slightly stunned look at first sight. She'd learned to ignore it because men interfered with her music and she didn't want that sort of distraction. Men became a hindrance. They wanted her complete attention and she couldn't give it.

Looked at objectively, none of them had ever physically attracted her as much as Charles, though. But none of them had ever insulted her so blatantly as Charles had the other night. Many had been guilty of asking her out while otherwise spoken for. He was one of those. Except he was slightly different. A man with a conscience, even if belated. Lucky Tiffany.

The lights stubbornly refused to change. Traffic roared by. Libby jammed her finger on the pedestrian button. Why did it have to be so difficult? Why, of all the elderly women needing a companion, did Gloria have to be Charles's aunt? Charley's aunt. Libby snorted and giggled. Tears welled up again.

She rubbed her eyes furiously, bit down hard on her lip. She didn't even know why she was so upset. It wasn't as if she knew either of them. They weren't friends. Charles was barely an acquaintance. But he'd sandbagged her in the chest again this evening, and it was lucky she'd been sitting down . . .

And she truly thought she may have found a solution, even if temporary, to her immediate homelessness. Gloria was such a sweetie, they would have . . .

"Libby?"

The voice made her jump and emit a small shriek of surprise. She spun around. He was there behind her, panting slightly, face flushed from hurrying, unruly hair across his brow. His expression wasn't angry or blank or haughty. It was anxious.

"Gloria told me everything."

"What do you mean?" Could the remains of tears be visible in the patchy street lighting and the passing headlights?

"Your situation. Your injury. How you can't play any more. I'm sorry, I had no idea."

"So?" The lights finally changed. Libby stepped on to the road. Charles followed.

"Libby, please wait."

"Why? I'm still the same person, Charles, whether I can play or not. I'm still a musician. Nothing will ever change that." He grabbed her arm so she had to stop, glaring up into his face. "What do you want?"

"I want you to come home and have dinner with us. I owe you dinner and an apology."

"Gloria sent you?"

He nodded. "I was to bring you back or else." He didn't smile, but his eyes were gazing intently into hers and they weren't angry now. "But *I* want you to come home, too. Not just because of Glory."

Libby glanced down at the hand holding her arm. She couldn't pull away. The grip was firm but not aggressive. It was comforting, offering aid and security. He'd said "come home."

"I'm sorry, Libby," he said softly.

"I'm sorry, too." He seemed to be nearer. His other hand touched her cheek. She couldn't move under the spell of those green, hypnotic eyes. He'd run to catch her, to find her. His expression had changed to one of wonder, vulnerable and tender. His mouth was coming closer with that deliciously inviting full lower lip. Libby swallowed, and her eyes began to close in anticipation of those lips touching hers. Her heart pounded in her chest. She could barely breathe. His thumb caressed her mouth gently, warm breath fluttered on her cheek.

Chapter Four

A car horn blasted. "Get off the road," yelled a voice.

Someone laughed, an engine roared. A van shot past. Charles grabbed Libby's hand and sprinted to the safety of the footpath. Two red patches burned on his cheeks, his mouth was now a grim line. Her own face was probably flushed. Suddenly the chill had left the air.

"Hungry?" he asked overly loudly as he began walking.

"Yes."

Libby stifled a giggle at his flushed embarrassment. She hadn't been caught kissing in public since she was sixteen. Correction—nearly kissing in public. She'd stake her life on it. He was about to kiss her. Charles wasn't such a stuffed shirt after all, and he was still holding her hand. Squeezing her fingers, in fact. She grinned at him as he glanced down at her.

But Charles didn't return the smile. His face had

resumed the reserve and haughtiness of before. He let her hand go and walked silently with his own hands shoved in his pockets, all the way back to the house.

Libby strolled beside him, her breathing returned to normal, her heart thumping along as usual. Deep inside a little ray of hope lightened the darkness which had become her future. Charles didn't hate her, far from it. He wasn't a cold, hard man at all, he was remorseful for the way he'd spoken to her, and he was seriously considering allowing her to move in. The little shining ray of hope broadened and strengthened. She must be very, very careful. Unless Charles wanted another try for a kiss, in which case . . .

A spurt of laughter made Charles throw her a frowning glance, but he didn't ask why and Libby certainly didn't offer to explain.

Glory waited anxiously in the kitchen twisting her fingers in knots.

"Thank goodness, you found her," she cried. "Libby, my dear, I'm sorry I made such a silly hash of everything."

"Let's eat." Charles began removing the food Glory had placed in the oven to keep hot while he went on his rescue mission. He monitored what went on while he fiddled about with serving dishes and oven mitts.

Libby murmured something to Glory, and they hugged quickly. Glory smiled and said something he couldn't hear, then left the room. Extraordinary how they'd taken to one another in such a short space of time. Libby stood irresolute for a moment then walked across and put her handbag on a chair in the living room.

He couldn't look at her. She'd been crying. Tears had sparkled on her lashes in the streetlight. Those blue eyes had shone luminously and sucked him in. He'd come so close to kissing her it wasn't funny. How were they supposed to live in the same house? Did she have any idea what she did to his nervous system and every other bodily function? Charles slammed serving spoons into the various dishes and reached into the cupboard for bowls.

"Can I help?"

She was right beside him, cool and perfect. Her lips were moist and tentatively parted, inviting. She'd been ready to kiss him. She looked ready now. A girl with her looks would expect it, and she wasn't phased at all by being almost kissed in the street. She'd laughed as though his clumsy attempt was a joke. She could be a tease. He knew nothing about her, what she was really like.

"Take these to the table, please." He gave her a handful of chopsticks and the blue-patterned Chinese bowls Glory liked.

"Charles," she said, without moving, "I won't take this position if you don't want me to. If you find it too—awkward."

Charles kept his attention on the Mongolian Beef. Steam rose in curling tendrils. "Gloria wants you to stay."

"Do you?'

Charles hesitated. He couldn't raise his eyes to her face. His whole body screamed yes. She's wonderful, beautiful, a dream come true. There's no valid reason not to let her move in.

"I suppose we can give it a try." He looked up, couldn't resist. She smiled, and he was lost. "Yes, I do," he said.

"What will Tiffany say?" Her head tilted to one side so he knew she was teasing, but the near kiss was a monster looming between them even if she didn't regard it as anything more important than a hiccup.

"She'll be pleased that Gloria has a live-in companion," he said stiffly. "It's a good solution."

Libby nodded but said nothing. What she was thinking behind that inscrutable little grin? The look on her face made him want to grab her and finish what had nearly started in the middle of the pedestrian crossing. Libby had been receptive, so receptive his body took charge and threw rational thought in the gutter. Her eyes had almost closed in expectation and he could taste the sweetness of the kiss . . .

Charles clunked the lid back on to the beef and bent to remove the Sweet-and-Sour Pork and the Chicken with Almonds from the oven. Libby waited, watching him mess about with the food, making him so self-conscious he nearly spilled the lot on the floor. She grabbed a pot holder and saved the pork.

Her hair brushed his cheek as he straightened up. She was oblivious. And even if she wasn't, even if by some highly unlikely freak of nature she felt a similar, single-minded passion for him, she would be living here, and they couldn't act on it because Glory would know in an instant and the whole dynamic of the arrangement would alter. Instead of an employer/employee relationship it would become an altogether different thing. Where would that leave Glory?

There would be no kisses and no thought of anything beyond at most, friends and housemates. Unless he refused to let her stay, and then they'd be back where they started with Glory upset, and him running down the street chasing the girl of his dreams like a teenager. Ridiculous.

"Are we ready?" asked Glory from the doorway. She walked to the table with a decided limp.

"Why are you limping?" he demanded. Had she been limping earlier? He hadn't noticed. Libby had swamped everything. "Did you hurt yourself at tai chi?'

"Of course not. I had a little fall, that's all." She pulled her chair out.

"A fall?'

"When?" asked Libby. She was frowning, concerned. She hadn't noticed either. "While we were out?'

"I slipped on the step. It's nothing. Just a little bruise. Stop fussing," said Glory. She sat down. "Where's my dinner?'

"Coming up," replied Charles. That settled it. The thought of Glory home alone, injured, in pain . . . Libby had to stay.

Libby placed the bowls and chopsticks on the table and went back for the rest of the food. Charles deposited the fried rice.

"Friday is Gloria's Chinese day," he said as Libby sat down. "She goes to tai chi and gets inspired to be Asian."

He grinned at Glory, and she said, "It'd do you good to do some meditating."

"Tai chi sounds fascinating," said Libby, "But I've never had the time to do anything like that."

"You can come with me," cried Glory enthusiastically. "You might as well join in if you escort me to my class. The exercises would do your arm good and you'd learn to relax properly. That would help your playing."

"Exercise?" Libby pulled an alarmed face. "I've never done any sort of sport."

"You wouldn't have had time, would you?" murmured Charles. Her injury was only temporary, that was another thing to keep in mind when temptation became unbearable.

"Do you play any sport?" Libby asked, throwing him a suspicious glance. Charles chewed and swallowed, but Glory answered for him.

"Charles is a very good tennis player," she said. "He plays on Sundays."

"Oh." Libby raised her eyebrows and nodded as if confirming something to herself.

"What?" he said.

"Nothing. I thought you might have surfed or something."

"Why?'

A slight, rosy-pink glow suffused her cheeks. He stared at her in surprise. She was embarrassed about something.

"You look fit."

He met her eye then looked away. She'd studied his physique. As much as he'd studied hers?

Glory began telling Libby about her tai chi class. Charles ate in silence. Glory said, "You can move in as soon as you like. How about tomorrow? Charles can collect you and your things from the hotel. Do you have much?"

"Not really. Two suitcases and my cello. The rest is in storage in Holland until I send for it."

"That's easy."

"Have you two discussed any details?" interrupted Charles. "For example wages, conditions, days off, holidays?"

Glory glanced helplessly at Libby.

"No, we haven't," Libby said. "What do you suggest?'

"I haven't had much time to think about it," he replied tersely, "but I suggest you draw up a contract of sorts."

"I know a lawyer," said Libby. "I suppose we could ask him to do it."

"Do we have to be so formal?" asked Glory. "It all seems straightforward to me."

"Until something unforeseen happens," said Charles. "It's best to be certain where you stand. Both of you."

"What do you think, Libby?" asked Glory.

"Whatever Charles thinks is best."

"I think it's best to have everything clear beforehand, before you enter into an arrangement," he said. "Don't want any nastiness down the track."

"There will never be any nastiness between Libby and me. She hasn't a nasty bone in her body," declared Gloria. "I know a good sort when I see one and you should too, Charles. You have to learn to trust your instincts more."

Charles said nothing. If he did what his instincts demanded Glory would be shocked to the soles of her sensible shoes.

Libby moved in the following Tuesday morning. She arrived by taxi to discover Gloria in a flutter of excitement.

"I made sure Josie gave your room a good clean yesterday, and she made the bed even though she's not a housemaid."

"I could have done that, Gloria." She certainly didn't want to put the cleaning lady's nose out of joint and have to do the cleaning herself.

Gloria flapped a hand dismissively. "I want you to feel at home here. Is this your cello?"

"Yes."

Libby placed the well-traveled solid black case on the floor of the living room. The taxi driver carried her suitcases in for her. Gloria came back from closing the front door behind him.

"You can leave it down here in the corner. It's a real conversation piece with all those travel stickers." Gloria ran her hand lightly over the "fragile" sticker, studying the blue Reykjavik patch.

"Yes, it was my first professional position. Will Charles mind if I leave it here? I know he hates anything to do with classical music." The last thing she wanted was to antagonize Charles. He seemed to have quite decided mood swings. One moment he was charming, then obnoxious, then almost kissing her. The next, helpful, then businesslike and reserved.

"How about settling yourself in and we can have a cozy chat over lunch," said Gloria. "Can you get your bags upstairs?"

"I have some washing in one of them. Perhaps if I unload in the laundry I'll be able to carry it more easily."

"Leave the other for Charles," said Gloria.

"How's the leg you bruised?"

Gloria frowned, clearly baffled.

"You had a fall. Remember?" Libby prompted. Gloria's short-term memory mustn't be too good although she showed no signs of that limp.

Gloria burst out laughing. "I made that up," she cried.

"The fall?"

"Yes, Charles needed a bit more persuading to let you stay, I thought."

"Gloria! You terrible fibber!" Libby laughed despite her astonishment at such blatant and unrepentant manipulation.

"Not really. I hadn't told him about the real fall I had the week before so it was simply a slight delay in communication. Now, you get yourself settled and I'll start lunch."

Libby loaded the washing machine and thought. Gloria had neatly sidestepped her remark about Charles and classical music. There had to be a story there. Gloria was sure to know what it was.

Gloria chatted happily as they ate soup. "Let's go

shopping in Chatswood for a new teapot this afternoon," she said. "I'm going to enjoy having you here so much. To tell you the truth I was a little bit lonely. I moved here from Maitland a couple of months ago. Charles insisted I couldn't manage on my own any longer. He worried about me. The house was rather large and difficult to manage. But all my friends are there." She sighed and nibbled at a piece of toast.

"But you go out to the Seniors' Club, don't you?"

"Yes, I go along a couple of times a week and every so often they have evening functions. We had a trivia night just last week and the night before that something else . . ." She frowned, remembering. "A concert by the local community band."

"Was that good?"

"No, they're shocking. No wonder I couldn't remember it. I'd blanked it from my mind."

Libby laughed at the expression on Gloria's face.

"But it gets me out of the house."

"You must have made some friends there at the club, though?"

"Yes." Gloria leaned forward even though they were alone in the house. "There's one person in particular I like very much."

Libby smiled slowly as Gloria's meaning filtered through. "A man?"

"Oscar. Charles doesn't know about him." She sat back with a secretive little smile.

"Wouldn't approve?"

Gloria shook her head. "Dear Charles, he worries too much. About everything."

“Gloria, surely Charles would be pleased to hear you’ve made new friends. I’m sure he only wants you to be happy.”

“He does, of course, he does, but he doesn’t think I’m functioning on all cylinders now I’ve hit eighty. He wants me wrapped up in cottonwool and placed on a shelf.”

“Are you Charles’ only relative?” Libby asked.

“In Australia, yes. He’s English, but you’d know that.”

“How long has he been here?’

“About seven years. Henry, my husband, was an Aussie. I met him during the war.” Another sigh accompanied by a little private smile. “We came to live here permanently when Henry retired and Charles followed after he’d finished his studies.”

“After Vienna,” said Libby. “What about his parents? He seems . . . not very keen on them.”

Gloria screwed up her mouth. “No. And he hates me to talk about it to anyone but . . .” Libby waited. She spooned up more soup. Gloria would crack. “Charles had a difficult childhood. Henry and I became more his parents than they ever were despite our being his grandparents’ age.”

“What about them?’

“His grandparents? Two have passed away. The other two, unrelated to each other, are in England. Both in homes for the aged. Neither knows what’s what. My late sister Deirdre was Charles’ grandmother. Her daughter, Irene, is his mother.”

Libby put her spoon down. “Why were you more his mother than his mother?” she asked directly.

Gloria appeared to have forgotten Charles' embargo on discussing his family because the information poured out in a determined flood. "Irene wasn't interested in having a child. Henry and I were never blessed with children. Charles was such a sad little lonely chap. I adored him and it seemed as if I was the only one. My sister lived in Switzerland at that stage. Charles's other grandparents were in Scotland. We were in London. His parents traveled all the time with their careers, then they divorced. Neither appeared to want him. Henry and I did and we were right there for him all the time he was growing up."

"No wonder he loves you and worries about you," said Libby gently. What sort of monsters were those parents? "Why do people bother having children if they don't want to care for them?"

"Heaven only knows. Especially when others would give anything to have them. It doesn't seem fair, somehow. In Charles' case his mother went so far as to tell me, once, he was a mistake."

"A mistake? What a despicable thing to say. Did she say it to him?"

"I don't think she had to. It was quite clear what she thought. What they both thought."

"They must have had very important careers," said Libby scathingly.

Gloria bit her lip and studied Libby's face before replying. "You be the judge," she said. "Irene Temple and Gerald Hogarth."

Had she heard that correctly? Surely Gloria wasn't having delusions. Everything else she'd said was sane.

"But they're . . . that's . . . I played under Gerald Hogarth in Rotterdam. He was Guest Conductor for a season." Libby drew an amazed breath. "He's a fantastic musician, an amazing man! And Irene Temple? She must be the best mezzo soprano alive today. That's incredible. Charles' parents?"

Gloria nodded. "Don't, whatever you do, let on that I told you. Charles would be furious and very upset. He hates gossip."

"I can't believe it. I didn't know they'd been married to each other and I certainly didn't know they had a child."

"No, they barely knew, either."

"Do they communicate at all?"

"Not that I'm aware of. I get the occasional letter from Irene, and Christmas and birthday cards, of course. Nothing from Gerald, but I wouldn't expect to. He's remarried."

Libby vaguely remembered a quiet Italian woman accompanying the Maestro occasionally.

"That's unbelievably sad. What a waste of . . . everything." She'd been going to say opportunity and talent, but Charles wouldn't see it like that and neither would Gloria. She herself would give her eye teeth to have those genes. "Is Charles musical at all?'

"As a little boy he sang constantly and he played the piano. He'd sit for hours doodling about making up his own songs. Then he'd sing them to me. But I couldn't be there all the time. I had my work and my husband to care for. Charles had a series of nannies and then went off to boarding school. He came to us for the holidays and he gradually became more and more bitter about his parents' neglect. He expressed it by openly shunning everything they held dear—namely music."

"No wonder," Libby murmured.

"No wonder what?"

"Oh, Charles makes it very clear that he doesn't like musicians and I wondered why he felt so strongly. It seemed quite irrational. Now I see it wasn't."

"No, but I think he should accept the fact that they are what they are and move on."

"Very hard for him, though."

"That's why he should meditate," said Gloria. "It gets things in perspective. He's a very bitter, tense boy. I wouldn't be at all surprised if he developed stomach ulcers."

She stood up and began to clear the table of their empty bowls. Libby followed her to the kitchen and helped stack the dishwasher. To leave behind a childhood like that, really leave it behind, would take years of Gloria's meditation, and the real test would be facing those two people in the flesh and forgiving them. Not a course she could see Charles embarking on in the near future. He'd traveled halfway round the world to avoid them.

But now she was armed with information that made his incomprehensible behavior, comprehensible. She must have made his life hell in Vienna. She'd been the epitome of everything he detested, living right upstairs and oblivious to everything but her own passion.

What a self-centered monster! She'd boasted about

playing Elgar in the Town Hall and been offensive instead of reassuring him when he told her he felt guilty about his girlfriend. And now here she was popping up in his house reminding him about his past—in his own home, which, quite rightly, he treasured.

"I'll just go and rest for half an hour before we go shopping," said Gloria.

Libby wandered out to the back garden. More of the strongly scented purple flowers grew out here. Hyacinths, Gloria said they were. She stood in the middle of the lawn trying to sort out the new Charles.

She had to get this in perspective if they were to live together civilly, in this house. Charles had a deep-seated antipathy to his parents because of their careers and, by extension, to her as a professional musician with the same driving passion. Okay.

How did that affect her? They hardly knew each other, it needn't affect her at all. It shouldn't matter one way or another what he thought about musicians. But it did. She had to admit to herself it did. He'd made it affect her.

He'd invited her to dinner despite having a girlfriend already—Tiffany, the dinner service. He'd had second thoughts, he had a conscience and that was by and large a good thing even if it was rather overdeveloped to the point of almost prohibiting a casual dinner between old acquaintances.

But he'd almost kissed her. Surely she hadn't imagined that and it hadn't felt from where she was standing as if it would be an old chum's peck on the cheek. Now that they were under the same roof and he was in effect her landlord, any further overtures would have to come from him and if any moves were made they'd have to be nipped in the bud.

She wanted to recuperate and establish a new life, not give herself an emotional meltdown. She certainly hadn't come back to Sydney looking for a doomed affair with an already spoken for man who hated musicians and had all sorts of emotional problems with his family. Even if that man made her heart pound and her knees collapse, and whose lips had nearly met her eagerly awaiting mouth in the middle of a pedestrian crossing, in a busy street that to them had become suddenly invisible.

Charles didn't have dinner with them that night. When they returned from shopping he'd left a message saying he'd be home late. Gloria didn't comment. Libby wasn't sure whether to be pleased, relieved, disappointed, or jealous. She'd thought he might have dinner with them as it was her first night, but there was no reason why he should. He was free to do what he liked. Go out with Tiffany, go out with anyone. Stay out all night. Ironically, her presence allowed that.

He left early for work the next morning. Libby heard him in the kitchen while she dressed, but by the time she came downstairs he'd gone, leaving no trace of himself beyond the electric jug filled with hot water.

She made several phone calls, leaving her new phone number and address, and one of the talent agencies surprised her by saying they had a job she might suit.

"It's a TV ad for something—potato chips, I think,"

she reported to Gloria. "They need people to walk by in the background."

"How exciting. You can do that."

"Yes, I've been walking for many years now." They both laughed.

"All by yourself, too," added Gloria. "When is it?'

"Sunday, this week. I have to turn up at eight A.M at this address in the city. They're closing off the street."

Charles wondered if he should eat out again. Two nights in a row might suspiciously seem as though he was avoiding Libby. It may even appear rude and he didn't want that. He'd prefer distant and cool, busy and totally unaffected by her presence. Natural.

Tiffany would happily meet him at another restaurant, but last night's meal was not a success from his point of view. As they ate Japanese food crosslegged on the floor at low tables he realized that she and her friends talked about such boring things. It was all right for her. She did alarming things at a gym every other day before work, but he didn't. His legs were frozen in place after the first course, and he'd never taken to raw fish and seaweed.

The conversation centered on power hungry people whose lives revolved around backstabbing and manipulation. He'd never known, or quite honestly cared, until he met her, just how vicious the fashion industry was. Not that he cared now. Tiffany and company did, it appeared, because they all got quite worked up about the nefarious activities of someone called Pablo.

He'd always taken a superficial interest, but suddenly

neither the dubious delights of Japanese dining, nor the machinations of Pablo, nor the numbness in his legs was sufficient to focus his attention.

His mind had kept wandering. To Libby. Had she moved in as planned? Did she like her room? Could she get her suitcases upstairs by herself? What were she and Glory doing right now? What had they eaten for dinner? Not raw fish, he'd bet.

"Don't you think?" Tiffany had asked in the middle of this daydreaming, and he'd stared blankly, which made her snappy and cool for the rest of the tiresome, knee-crippling evening.

He didn't want another meal like that. He didn't want more Tiffany-style chat or more chilly Tiffany glances. He wanted to stay at home.

Libby answered when he rang Glory in the afternoon. He wasn't expecting her voice in his ear, so intimate and close.

"Hello." With a lilt as though she'd been mid laugh when she picked up the phone. She sounded happy and carefree.

"It's Charles," he said sternly because his throat had choked up and he had to force the words out.

"Hello." The lilt had gone. Wary.

"I haven't seen you since . . . did you move in all right? I saw your cello downstairs."

"It's not a problem there, is it? Gloria said it would be fine, I'll move it," Libby said all in a rush, with the words tripping over as they fell into the receiver.

"No, no, it's fine, it's okay. Leave it." He sounded

like a pompous prig berating a waiter for spilling soup. "I'll be home for dinner tonight."

"All right." Pleased? Impossible to tell. "We planned Spaghetti Bolognese. Gloria's going to teach me to cook more than my three staple meals, starting tomorrow."

"What are they?"

"Tuna Casserole, Spaghetti Bolognese, and Spanish Omelet."

Charles grinned. "I can see why. Glory's a very good cook."

"I'm not very domesticated. I'm really not much use . . ." She stopped and Charles held his breath as her voice trembled slightly on the last phrase. A pause.

"I'm sure you are," he said eventually, almost whispering, as though she were next to him. He realized he'd reached out his free hand to comfort her. Blimey!

"I'm only good at playing the cello and now I can't even do that," she said.

Charles gripped the receiver tightly and firmed his voice. "You will."

"No." The vehemence startled him, dismayed him. "No," she cried again. "I may never play again. The doctor in Holland told me. And I know two other people, orchestral players, who had to give it up completely. If I can't ever play again, I don't know what I'll do. I'll die." She paused. "I'm sorry." It was almost grudging, and now her voice was hard. "I know you don't care."

"Of course I care." Was that true? Really true? Or was he just a little bit pleased?

"Sure." Libby obviously didn't think so. Her voice

changed. “What time will you be home?” Bright and bubbly. He pictured her smiling mouth with the full lips almost caressing the receiver as she spoke.

“About six.” And he couldn’t wait. “Maybe five-thirty.”

Chapter Five

Charles smelled garlic bread followed by the rich aroma of Bolognese sauce when he pushed the door open at ten to six. Music wafted down the hallway. One of Glory's New Age things. She'd taken to them with a vengeance since the tai chi fever had gripped her. If that was the correct terminology—probably a bit too aggressive for what he gathered tai chi was all about. It certainly made her irritatingly serene.

No one had heard him come in. Charles detoured to his bedroom, stripped off his suit and work shirt, and hurled his tie on to the bed. A quick splash in the en suite bathroom, and on with jeans and black longsleeved T-shirt. Much better. He swept a brush through his hair and studied the result. Not bad. Maybe a shirt would be better? He began to pull the T-shirt off, but stopped with his chest exposed. No! For heaven's sake! He let it fall, tucked it back in with a scowl, closed the door carefully, and walked with tense nonchalance through to the rear of the house.

Libby sat reading a book on the couch with her feet curled up under her. She had on white slacks and a greeny-blue top. Calm and lovely. A curtain of dark hair fell across her cheek as she read and she raised a hand to drag it slowly back. She looked up and smiled when she heard him come into the room.

Charles paused, engulfed by déjà vu. What if she always sat and smiled at him like that when he came home from work? What if she lived in his house permanently? She looked so comfortable and happy. She fit perfectly. He'd fit perfectly next to her.

"Hard day at work?" His daydream fell in a heap at his feet. She was joking. Mimicking a loving housewife. Something she'd never want to be. Like his mother. She'd never so much as made herself a cup of tea, let alone cooked a meal. Servants were there to do those sorts of things—cook and clean, put out the garbage, iron clothes, drive the car, mind the child.

"Not bad." He went to the fridge for a glass of juice. "Would you like a drink?'

"No, thanks." She put her book on the coffee table, and, as he joined her on the couch, he saw it was one from his shelves. She followed his glance. "Hope you don't mind if I borrow that. I've never had the courage to tackle *War and Peace* before."

Charles laughed. "Good luck. I got as far as page four hundred eighty-seven. You can tell me what happens."

"I'm only on page sixteen so you'll have to wait a

while." She gave him a little grin, then looked away quickly as their glances collided and tangoed briefly.

Charles asked abruptly, "Where's Glory?"

Libby pointed out the full-length windows to the back garden. "Picking flowers."

"She loves the garden," he said. Glory came into view with an armful of pink blossoms, then disappeared behind the garden shed. "She's doing flower arranging at the local Community Center."

"She's very active, isn't she?"

"Yes, but she's getting forgetful. She boiled a saucepan of water dry last weekend; luckily I was home, but it worried me. And I shudder to think what she'd do if she fell and hurt herself badly." Charles studied the juice in his glass. "I'm glad you're here," he said in a low voice then added quickly, "that there's someone with her."

"I'm glad I'm here too." Charles turned to look at her in a kind of wary, half-hopeful surprise. "I was getting desperate for somewhere to live. And a job," she added.

He took a mouthful of juice. It ran chilled and sweet down his throat.

"Libby, I don't mean to pry, but what are your long term plans?" he asked in as cool a voice as he could muster. "I mean, obviously you don't want to be a companion to the elderly for the rest of your life."

Libby exhaled heavily. "I might not have a choice," she said. "What I said on the phone was true. I'm no use, I can't do anything except play the cello and now I can't do that."

Charles was horrified to see a tear run down her cheek. She didn't appear to notice because she made no move to brush it aside, she just sat with her face in profile staring blankly at *War and Peace* lying on the coffee table. He glanced down. Napoleon, on his rearing gray horse, stared back at her, pointing the way forward. Out of the picture, out of view.

"It's all I ever wanted to do." Her voice came low, dragging his attention away from the novel. The sadness in it made his heart turn right over. "I heard a cello on the radio when I was three, and I can clearly remember thinking it was the most wonderful sound I'd ever heard. I made my parents buy cello recordings for me, and as soon as I could I started lessons. And I was good at it. I *am* good at it." She turned toward him. Other tears had followed the first, leaving shiny tracks over the smooth skin.

"I know you are," he murmured. "I've heard you play."

He reached out his hand and gently smoothed the moisture from her cheeks with fingers aching to grasp and hold and pull her toward him. He wanted to breathe in the luscious scent of her, bury his face in the smooth hollow of her neck.

"I'd better check my sauce." Before he could react she was on her feet, heading for the kitchen. "What are you designing at the moment?"

The brightly voiced question threw him for a moment, tangled as he was in her scent. "Umm—we're working up the plans for a new wing on St. Vincent's Hospital. It's my project, but a few of us are involved.

We have to consult with the medicos all the time, of course. I was over there today."

"Wow."

He turned to her with curiosity, surprised by the awe in her voice. "Why wow? The firm has lots of big projects like that. This one actually isn't all that big," he amended, but he was pleased by her reaction. She looked pensive as she stirred her sauce. She sighed. "What?" he asked.

"What you do is so useful. What I do is nothing—worthless—by comparison. You're building a hospital. What do I do?" She flung the spoon on to the bench where it landed with a clatter.

Charles shook his head. Her egotism was extraordinary, hardly unexpected but still surprising, bursting out this way when he wasn't prepared. They'd been discussing his work, not her. He frowned and she must have read his expression as disgust because she cried, "I know you agree, don't bother denying it. Musicians are a waste of space and effort."

"Rubbish!" Charles stood up, stung by the sharpness of her attack. Too close for comfort but not truly accurate now that he was forced to examine the statement. Not all musicians—just some—two to be precise. "I didn't say that. The world needs music and musicians just as it needs all the arts. I can't imagine a world without music. Calm down, for heaven's sake!"

The bubble burst almost as quickly as it had inflated. One slim hand covered her mouth while wide blue eyes stared desperately at him over the top of her fingers. "I'm sorry, Charles. I'm so . . . so stupid."

"You're not stupid," he said stolidly. "Sometimes you just pretend to be."

Libby came round the bench toward him. Charles sat down so as not to meet her face to face. Her underlying apprehension was too naked. She was terrified he was going to kick her out. He drained his glass of juice.

Libby said in a much calmer voice, "It's irrelevant anyway because technically I'm not a musician any more. I am a lady's companion." The last words were stated in very prim, precise, rounded tones that made him smile and glance at her. She was smiling demurely, but her eyes sparkled as she met his gaze.

A shadow outside, coupled with the scraping of feet on the mat, returned him to reality. "And here comes the lady herself," he said softly, tearing his eyes from hers with effort.

Glory came in through the glass side door with her arms full of pink-and-white blossoms.

"Hello, dear," she said. "Spring is in the air. Aren't these wonderful?"

"Yes, lovely."

"Dinner smells very nice. Libby says Spaghetti Bolognese is her pièce de résistance."

"Let me take these, Gloria." Libby held out her arms for the flowers and laden, disappeared through the laundry door.

"Can't do too much damage to spaghetti," said Charles when she was out of earshot.

Glory swatted a hand in his general direction. "Be nice."

Charles grinned. "I am, Glory. I'm glad you two are

getting along, and it's a very good solution. I should have thought of it myself."

She smiled one of her wise old-lady smiles, which had been given an added veneer of inscrutability by her recent intense and sincere, as far as he could gather, interest in things Chinese.

"Libby is a beautiful person. I'm growing very fond of her already," she announced, and went away to help Libby with the flowers.

After slurping spaghetti and devouring garlic bread and salad followed by fresh fruit, Libby and Charles cleared the table while Gloria stacked the dishwasher. Charles began making coffee, but Gloria declined the offer.

"I think I shall leave you two now," she said, giving the benches a final swipe with a yellow sponge. "One of the drawbacks of growing old—waking up very early and nodding off early as well. Good night. I shall take myself to bed with Hercule Poirot."

Charles carried a tray with the coffee things to the living room. Libby sat on the couch and watched him fiddle with teaspoons and sugar. Was he as nervous as she was? He didn't appear to be, but she never had much of a clue as to the workings of his mind. Did that haughty and sometimes disdainful expression hide deep and extreme emotions that he allowed to erupt only occasionally, then hastily squashed? Or were they just in relation to the hatred of his parents and all they stood for?

"Would you like to watch television?" he asked.

"Not especially. Unless you do."

"No."

Libby cast her mind about frantically for some safe topic to discuss. What did friends talk about? All her previous friends were the musicians she worked with and they never lacked for conversation, usually bagging or praising the conductor or the soloist. Except Gerald Hogarth. They'd universally applauded Gerald Hogarth. She could hardly discuss him.

She peeked at Charles surreptitiously, trying to discern some resemblance. He had the same hairline as his father and the same arch of the eyebrows, although Gerald's thick hair had gone a spectacular silver gray. The face shape perhaps came from his mother. Libby wasn't as familiar with Irene Temple; she hadn't ever worked in an orchestra accompanying her. Irene Temple mainly performed opera, but Libby had never played in a pit orchestra in Europe.

Charles looked up suddenly and heat prickled her neck as he caught her studying him.

"Milk?" he asked as he poured coffee.

"Thank you."

He added a dollop from a small white jug. As Libby took the mug her fingers nudged his. He drew his hand away quickly and turned to his own coffee, dumping in sugar, stirring intently.

"I hope you don't get bored. Here with Glory all day."

"Gloria said it would be all right if I did part-time work now and again. I won't leave her alone much and she has her own activities." Libby hesitated. "It'll be a big change for me. I've always worked and when I wasn't at rehearsal I practiced."

Charles nodded. "Had you thought of retraining? Going back to study?'

Libby shook her head. "I haven't. Nothing really interests me and I'm very limited as to what I can handle." He obviously had no idea at all how she felt.

"You could do the teaching degree—teach high school music."

Libby placed her mug carefully on the table. Her hand was shaking suddenly with rage at the denseness and insensitivity of his remark. Teaching was a vocation like anything else. She'd never, ever, considered classroom teaching. She was a performing artist.

"Charles, being a musician, or any artist for that matter, isn't something you can just turn off! I could no more teach in a school than climb Mt. Everest. I've only been unable to play for a month and already I'm going mad. It's so frustrating. I want to practice. I wake up in the morning and the first thing I think is 'what shall I work on today' and then I remember and it's like a kick in the stomach."

She stopped and clamped her mouth shut, aware that her voice, which had started out fairly controlled, had risen in volume and pitch and now resembled the screech of a seagull circling a dead fish. Charles's face had undergone a corresponding change but had moved from polite sympathy to that of a man faced with a dead, rotting fish—that is, disgust.

Libby sat with her mouth tightly closed, her hands gripping each other to prevent them from waving about wildly as they had moments before.

Charles said in a clear and precise voice, "Libby, plenty of people have to change the way they live their lives. People suffer terrible accidents and disasters and losses and they deal with it, make changes, and cope the best they can."

His English accent had assumed an intense life of its own and made him sound like the headmaster at his old boarding school. The one he'd detested and scorned as an insufferably pompous git.

"Without becoming hysterical, you mean?" she said caustically.

Charles pursed his lips.

"There are other equally fulfilling ways to earn a living." Somehow he just couldn't stop it. The wretched man had invaded his speech patterns at an impressionable age.

"Not for me," Libby cried. That priggish, self-righteous voice of his made her want to thump him on his well-bred nose.

"How do you know? You freely admit you haven't tried anything else." He was looking down said nose at her now—the way he'd regard something nasty smelling on the sole of his shoe.

"What do you suggest? Building a hospital?'

"There must be lots of things," said Charles. He ignored that stupid hospital crack she'd wished she hadn't made as soon as it left her mouth. "Some women are fulfilled by raising their families."

Libby ground her teeth. "True. *Some* women are and all power to them. About the only thing I *can* do is have babies, but in case you'd hadn't noticed I'm unattached. Surrogate mothering—is that what you're suggesting? I hadn't thought of that. I'll look in the classifieds tomorrow."

Charles glared at her with unconcealed exasperation. "If you want to, sure, why not? Anything's better than sitting around in despair and complaining and saying you'd rather be dead than not play that wretched cello."

Libby leapt to her feet, endangering the coffee table and its coffee paraphernalia. "I did not say that! And don't you call it a wretched cello! How dare you? You know nothing about me at all. You've no idea how it feels to have the one thing you love in life torn away. Music isn't just an occupation, it's a . . . a passion."

Charles had risen as well during this tirade and he faced her now, towering over her, equally furious, his cheeks a dull red.

"I know exactly how this obsession works," he hissed. "Exactly! It excludes everyone else. It feeds on the over-inflated ego of the victim until they think nothing else in the world matters except themselves and their so-called art. Nothing matters to them unless it can, in some way, enhance the brilliant career. Woe betide anyone who gets in the way."

Libby nearly choked as she saw the pain on his face. She swallowed the next angry retort, which had all but escaped and which involved his parents. Thank goodness she hadn't blurted it out. Charles would be devastated. So would Gloria. She'd be banished from the house, and rightly so.

Libby held her breath for an unsteady moment. She said very formally, "I apologize for my hysteria, Charles. I know you don't like displays of emotion."

He stared at her briefly before whirling about and charging from the room. His footsteps thudded on the hall carpet, the front door slammed. Libby collapsed on to the couch and sat trembling, breath coming short and erratic, heart pounding. Had Gloria heard?

Libby strained her ears. Silence. A couple of minutes later the toilet flushed. Doors opened and closed softly, but no further sounds indicated Gloria's presence.

She carefully stacked the empty coffee cups on to the tray and lifted them with her right hand, steadying the load with her left. Even that small pressure hurt. Her hopeless arms! She was useless. Charles' ugly words flashed into her head. "Stop complaining—terrible disasters—accidents—people cope" and the ugliest of them all: "obsession."

He made her sound like the worst kind of addict—a heroin junkie or a gambler or an alcoholic. Was he right? The thought almost made her drop the tray. But what was she supposed to do? The doctor had told her—and she'd observed the results herself in colleagues—no playing, complete rest. She'd never be able to do the same work again. The constant repetitive movement at such an awkward angle required by the cello would simply reignite the problem later on.

Libby trudged upstairs to her room. Too early for bed. She pulled aside the slats of the blind and peered down into the darkness of the back garden. Where had Charles rushed off to? He hadn't taken the car. The expression on his face was heartbreaking. How could she have attacked him that way? In his own house. Libby's own face began to glow with the heat of embarrassment. She turned away from the window, catching a glimpse of herself in the dressing table mirror as she did so. Her cheeks were scarlet.

She placed her palms flat against her face and closed her eyes. This was a disaster already. Charles would ask her to leave in the morning. He'd say the situation was untenable, or use some equally clinical expression, and it would be in everyone's best interests that she find another position. And she'd only been here two days.

Maybe if she stayed out of his way tonight he'd calm down and if they didn't run into each other for a day or so he might reconsider.

And Gloria might become the next Australian astronaut.

Libby had a shower hoping the hot water and jasmine-scented soap might wash away the guilt. It didn't. She put on her pajamas, the pale-blue silky ones with teddy bears on them, and climbed miserably into bed. Gloria was in bed with Hercule Poirot, and Libby'd go to bed with a bunch of Russians with complicated names. They'd keep her busy all night and then some.

Drat. The Russians were downstairs where she'd left them. Libby pulled back the covers and opened her door. No sounds from below. Charles must still be out. She darted across the tiny landing and skipped down the stairs in bare feet. *War and Peace* was on the end of the couch where she'd been sitting. She'd moved it so Charles could put the tray on the table.

The front door opened and closed. Libby froze clutching the chunky book to her chest. Charles was coming down the hallway. If she ran now she'd look completely ridiculous—like a big, blue rabbit scuttling for cover. If she stayed where she was he'd catch her in her pajamas. Not that there was anything wrong with that. It just wasn't very dignified.

He stopped when he saw her. His mouth moved. About to say something? But he passed his hand across his face with a gesture of such similar resignation and confusion to that which she felt, Libby said softly, "I'm sorry, Charles. I . . ." But he cut her off.

"No. It's my fault. I'm the one who should be apologizing and I do. I'm very sorry I said what I did. Please try to forgive me."

Libby nodded. "Yes, of course I do. Thank you."

She stayed motionless, unsure. Should she say more or should she make a dignified retreat before another disastrous utterance broke this truce? Charles didn't move or speak either. He gazed at her through eyes that became gentle. Libby shifted uncomfortably. A quick embarrassed little smile flicked on and off her lips. Her bare feet were cold. The hair on the back of her neck, damp from the shower, had created a cold wet patch on her pajama collar.

"I forgot my book. I mean, your book."

His gaze flicked down to *War and Peace* and lingered. Libby's cheeks began to glow again. Why was he staring? Surely she'd done up all the buttons properly. The top one wasn't revealingly low placed.

She turned to the staircase and climbed a couple of

steps. Stopped. A question that had bothered her since the conversation with Gloria about his parents clamored for an answer. Charles was still standing there, watching as if mesmerized.

"Charles," she said tentatively. "Have you ever felt passionately about something? I mean in a positive way not . . . you know . . . against. Is there anything you love to the exclusion of all else? The way I do?"

For a moment he looked so startled and boyishly open she wanted to fling her arms around him. But his lips firmed into a tight line. He shook his head. "Architecture, I suppose. I love designing something from scratch. Organizing space . . . but it's not something I'd . . ." He gestured vaguely. "It's not like your cello is to you."

"What about a person," she asked softly. "A woman?"

He stared at her. "I know what it's like to love someone I can't have, who doesn't feel the same way."

"Oh." The Tiffany dinner service? Given the harshness of his tone, Libby wasn't game to ask.

His expression lightened. "But there's Glory. I love her."

Libby smiled back, relieved. Charles and his passions weren't a topic she should be investigating, she'd already decided that. Prying into other people's love lives wasn't her forte. She'd only asked to discover if he felt passionately about anything at all.

She was sure that's why she'd asked such a question.

"I'm beginning to love her too," she said.

The smile didn't seem to want to leave her lips. She couldn't tell if Charles was genuinely smiling at her, or laughing privately at how stupid she looked standing there grinning at him.

"I like your pajamas," he said.

"They were a gift." A shiver convulsed her.

Charles moved towards her. "Cold?"

"A little," she managed to whisper as he stepped on to the bottom step. His head was level with hers. Hazel eyes searched her face, linked with her own gaze briefly, and slid sideways. Up one more step. Closer.

He reached out a hand and flipped open a small white panel on the wall by her shoulder. "I can turn on some heating if you like, but there's usually no need at this time of year."

"No!" The word burst from her lips like a small explosion. She'd lost control of her vocal delivery. Words either got stuck in her throat, crept out furtively like spies, or exploded like hand grenades.

"No?" Charles's mouth, inches from her cheek, curved in that smile that made her equally want to kiss him and kick him. Kissing him began to win the tug of war of senses over sense. His breath feathered her cheek gently. His lips were tantalizingly close and he rested his hand on the wall beside the panel so that he almost enclosed her in his embrace. All she had to do was lean forward very slightly. All he had to do was drop his arm to her shoulder and hold her against his body. All he had to do was kiss her.

Libby's knees began to shake. She shivered again despite the warmth radiating from his body and the heat building in the depths of hers.

"You should go to bed," he said.

"Yes," she murmured, her gaze fixated on his mouth so near she was melting. Boiling. Melting. Boiling.

Charles stepped back slowly.

"So you keep warm."

"Ohhh." The sound escaped in a long drawn-out sigh.

War and Peace crashed to the floor and bounced off the bottom step on to the polished wood under Charles feet. He bent to pick it up, flattening the cover into place and smoothing the crumpled page corners. Libby watched, mortified. At least it hadn't split open and strewn all nine hundred and eighty odd pages of itself over the living room and surroundings.

"You missed my foot this time." He handed it to her.

"Thank you, yes, sorry. It's not damaged is it?" Babbling fool. Libby gripped *War and Peace* tightly so as not to lose it a second time.

Charles shook his head. He had that smirk on his face again.

"I'll go to bed," she blurted. "And read."

"Good idea. Good night." Charles turned away toward the kitchen.

"Good night." Libby escaped to bed.

Gloria took Libby to her lunchtime tai chi class on Friday. They arrived at the Community Center hall early so Libby could meet the instructor, Alice, an enthusiastic Chinese woman who, when told of Libby's tendon damage, thrust a pamphlet about acupuncture into her hand.

"See this doctor," she said. "He'll fix you."

Libby smiled politely and glanced skeptically at the paper. Acupuncture involved needles. Needles weren't her friends.

"If you enjoy the class you should come along to one of the regular sessions," said Alice. "This one is geared toward the seniors."

Alice went off to the front of the hall to hang up a banner with tai chi written on it in English and, presumably, the same thing in Chinese characters. Soothing music flowed from a CD player on the small stage.

Libby studied the leaflet about tai chi she'd picked up on the way in. Slow, gentle, low impact, strengthening tendons and joints. It sounded good. She'd watched Gloria practicing in the garden and liked the way the movements flowed. They also did something called *chi kung,* which she gathered was a form of meditation. The general idea appeared to be to enhance the flow of chi in her body. She hadn't known she had any chi to start with.

"Libby," said Gloria in such an odd voice Libby looked up from the pamphlet in surprise. "I'd like you to meet Oscar Babic."

Ah-hah! The secret boyfriend.

A round-faced elderly man in a navy-blue track suit and white jogging shoes stood beaming in front of her. She had a brief image of Bob in twenty-five years time. Same shape, same hairline, same jovial expression. He extended his hand and pumped hers vigorously up and down.

"Gloria didn't tell me you were a beauty," he exclaimed loudly.

"Oscar, shush." Gloria's cheeks, to Libby's amazement, turned rose pink. "He's a terrible flirt," she added.

"Apologies, Libby, if I embarrassed you." He gave a solemn little bow.

Libby grinned and glanced at Gloria who was smiling like a schoolgirl. "You didn't embarrass me, Oscar. Thank you for the compliment."

"Good news, my love," Oscar boomed. "I've just come from talking to Meredith in the office and a place has opened up on the Floriade trip. Old Toby's going into hospital for an op. Sorry for him but I put your name down straight away. So fast, Meredith hadn't even finished telling me."

"Oh, Oscar!"

Libby had never seen Gloria at a loss for words. Or so pink in the cheeks.

"What is it?" Libby asked. "The Floriade trip."

"A bus tour to Canberra for the flower festival. For a week. Marvelous jaunt, we go every year," cried Oscar. "Gloria missed a place because it was booked out before she even arrived in Sydney. Now she's in."

"Sounds wonderful. When do you go?'

"A week from Monday, nine A.M. Returns the following Sunday at four. You'll need to pop in and give Meredith the A-okay and a check after class."

"Oscar, I can't," said Gloria, uncharacteristically flustered. "So soon."

"Why not?" Libby and Oscar said together, then laughed at their impromptu chorus.

Gloria looked from one to the other and shrugged. "I don't know. Should I, Libby?'

"Would you like to go?'

"Yes."

"Then go. There'll be someone along to supervise, won't there Oscar? A guide type person?"

And someone to count them and make sure they all took their medications and got back on the bus on time and had all their belongings. Like a school trip. Charles would want to know these details and many more she hadn't thought of. But heavens! Gloria was an adult. A mentally competent, experienced adult. And she had Oscar who, Libby was positive, wouldn't let Gloria out of his sight.

"Of course. Two chaperones. Pam and Mike," Oscar said to Gloria. "Meredith has all the paperwork and information in the office. Hotel address and so on. It's very well organized."

"I don't suppose there's any reason not to, is there?"

"Absolutely no reason at all," he replied. "You're coming along and that's that."

Senior citizens in tracksuits and jogging shoes began entering the hall in chattering groups of twos and threes. Libby was the youngest person in the room by at least forty years, not counting the instructor. Gloria proudly introduced her to them all, and by the end of the class she'd gained fourteen new friends and half-a-dozen invitations to tea.

Plus she loved tai chi and decided to join Alice's Saturday morning classes.

Charles received the Floriade news over their Chinese takeout that evening with a calm exterior hiding an inner turmoil. He and Libby would be alone in the house for a week. Had she thought of that when she so blithely encouraged Glory to go on the tour?

Not that there was anything wrong with the excursion. Floriade was right up Glory's alley—tulips and pansies all over the place and a busload of people her own age. He'd thoroughly read the brochure Gloria had thrust into his hand. Everything seemed very well organized. One of the accompanying guides was a nurse, he knew the hotel they'd be staying at, and there didn't seem to be any reason to try to dissuade her. Not that he could stop her with that pair against him.

But Libby here with him? Alone? If she paraded around in her pajamas again he wouldn't be accountable for his actions. Charles gave a snort of despairing laughter, earning curious looks from the two women who were busily discussing what Glory should pack.

"Take an umbrella," he said. "And a warm jacket. Canberra can be cold in spring."

They eyed him suspiciously but continued their conversation.

"Perhaps I need a warmer jumper," said Glory. "I've never needed anything other than lightweight knits."

"Ooh yes, let's go shopping," said Libby. "Have you got a hat? It can get very windy in September. I had a student friend who came from Canberra. We used to visit his parents."

Charles' ears pricked up. He couldn't help himself. A boyfriend? Of course it would be. He suspended a piece of chicken delicately between his chopsticks, feigned disinterest.

"A boyfriend?" asked Glory. The chicken slipped from his suddenly awkward grasp and landed on the table next to his bowl. For some reason when he glanced first at Glory then at Libby, both women shared the same secret-concealing, private smile. And he wasn't included. They hadn't even noticed his eating mishap.

"No. Simon was, or rather is, gay." Libby's eyes flashed to Charles for an instant then returned to Gloria. "Is it all right if I go to tai chi on Saturday mornings?"

"Of course, dear. You should go too, Charles."

"No, thanks," he grunted.

Gloria began enthusing over the health benefits and the possible effect on Libby's injured tendons. Charles returned to his thoughts and his Chow Mein.

This living together-but-not-together arrangement had been hard enough with Glory in the house. For that week it would be worse. He'd come home from work to find Libby with dinner prepared then spend an evening making conversation and trying to keep his hands off her. And she'd sit there looking like every man's dream come true but totally oblivious and immune to his desire, thinking he was a man prone to violent outbursts about his parents. Which wasn't strictly true. He avoided thinking about them as much as possible. He'd succeeded until Libby arrived like a bombshell in his life.

What would happen, however, if he did make a move on her?

Charles spooned more rice into his bowl. She'd either accept him or reject him. If she rejected him he would spoil everything, for all three of them. If she accepted him—well, there'd be all sorts of problems, and he'd already gone over them in his head when she moved in. And come to a decision. The right decision. Hands off Libby.

The thing was, how long could he stick to it?

The following week flew by. Libby and Gloria went shopping and found a stylish pink fluffy hat and a thick white-knitted jumper. On Tuesday they went to Gloria's dental check-up. Libby sat reading magazines until Gloria reappeared to report, "My teeth are perfect. The dental nurse said, 'Gosh, Mrs. Bennett is eighty-one and still has all her own teeth' so I said, 'Who else's teeth would I have?' "

She insisted Libby make her own appointment. "You don't want to be needing someone else's teeth when you're my age," she said sternly.

On Wednesday Oscar invited them both to lunch at his self-contained unit in the retirement home complex to eat vegetable soup he'd made himself. Watching the way they interacted reinforced Libby's initial impression that here was a budding romance. It was also quite clear Gloria was very familiar with Oscar's home, and this wasn't her first visit.

On the way back to Willoughby on the train Libby said, "Shouldn't Charles meet Oscar?"

Gloria pursed her lips. "Not yet."

"Why? Oscar's a friend of yours. Of mine now too." Libby grinned and received a pleased smile in return. "It's not a good idea to keep secrets from Charles. Not necessary."

"I suppose not." Gloria frowned. "It's just that I . . . I don't think he'll approve."

"Approve? He's not your father, Gloria!" Libby laughed aloud at the total unexpectedness of the remark, but when she looked at Gloria she wasn't smiling. Her laughter faded. "You're serious."

Gloria nodded. "Silly, isn't it? I'm scared Charles will say I'm too old to . . ."

"Fall in love?" said Libby softly. "Oh, Gloria . . ." Her throat suddenly clogged. She gazed into the gentle, elderly face helplessly.

"What is it, dear?"

Libby shook her head. "Nothing. It's nothing . . . I think I'm envious."

Gloria smiled. "You'll find someone special. You never know. It may be sooner than you think."

Libby sighed and stared out the dirty window at the rooftops and trees flashing by.

"I've never seriously thought about falling in love or marrying," she said. "I was always so focused on music there was no room for anything else."

"When you meet the right man those won't even be considerations," said Gloria. She was wearing her calm, inscrutable face.

It was all right for her, she'd found two good men to love. Gloria had always had the love and support of husband and family. Charles stepped in when the first husband died, and now Oscar appeared to be taking over.

"What if I don't meet the right man and I don't have my music either, Gloria? What then?" She tried desperately to keep the hysteria from her voice.

Gloria took Libby's limp hand in hers and squeezed.

"Never say die, Libby. Don't give up. Go and see Alice's acupuncturist."

Libby nodded half heartedly, but it didn't convince Gloria because she said in the same stern tone she'd used on Charles that first night, "Libby, there's far more to you than your cello. You have more than one string to your bow . . ." She paused and when Libby looked at her expecting the rest of the sentence Gloria was grinning.

"That's a terrible pun, Gloria," she said.

"Sorry. I can't help myself sometimes." Gloria stood up and grasped the pole for support as the train slowed. "Come on, we get off here."

Charles took Glory to the Community Center on Monday morning. She bubbled with excitement and introduced him to a fellow named Oscar who materialized the moment they rounded the corner from the car park. Oscar supervised the stowing of her luggage and helped her mount the steps of the bus. Charles saw him through the window fussing with Glory's coat as she settled herself in a window seat. She waved to him and mouthed something like "take care." Then she blew him a kiss, which he returned.

He waited impatiently while the old folks dithered about with their suitcases and their carry-on bags, clambered on and off the bus calling to each other about saving seats, and shouted "Have you seen Beryl?" and "Where's my ergonomic pillow?" while the couple in charge tried to check off names and count bodies.

Eventually the driver closed the door on them all,

and the bus lumbered away with a roar and a noxious cloud of diesel exhaust. Charles continued to his office consumed with thoughts of Libby and how he would survive the next seven days.

Libby sat at the table with a cup of tea and the newspaper. The "Positions Vacant" columns were just as depressing as they had been three weeks ago. True, now she had a place to live and a job, but she really had nothing to do. Especially with Gloria away.

Josie was vacuuming vigorously in the front part of the house. There wasn't even dusting.

The only thing she had to look forward to was the potato chip advertisement next Sunday. That would be mildly exciting and interesting, but not something to be relied upon for steady work. There was plenty of volunteering available. The Community Center noticeboard was full of cries for help. Perhaps she should become a home visitor for the elderly or visit people in hospital. They were all worthy and necessary occupations.

But she didn't want to do any of it. She wanted to play her cello.

Libby walked to the local shopping center later and bought various bits and pieces to prepare for dinner. Dinner for two. Her and Charles. How would that work out? So far so good, as far as she could judge. They hadn't had any major upsets or rows. They'd both been on their best and most polite behavior since the night Charles had flung out of the house and returned to find her running about in her pajamas.

She'd managed to resist the almost completely devouring need to kiss him when he asked about the heating and thus saved herself from even more humiliation. He, of course, had regarded her with the same supercilious amusement he seemed to reserve for her alone. Better to amuse him, she supposed, than have him treat her with the contempt he showed for musicians in general.

If they continued to treat each other with the same respect they should manage quite well this week. After all, they were like housemates. And plenty of people shared houses without anything developing between them. Platonic relationships.

Libby shook her head and headed for home with her shopping, and the first night alone with Charles looming like a storm cloud on the horizon.

Chapter Six

Libby cooked Wiener Schnitzel for dinner. Charles wasn't sure whether to comment or not. Had she consciously chosen a quintessential Viennese meal and, if so, what did it mean? Vienna might not have happy memories for her, at least where he was concerned.

"Did you ever go to that restaurant down the street from our building in Vienna?" Her tone was casual, conversational. She passed him a small plate with lemon quarters. He took one and squeezed it over the crusty golden veal while his mind calculated rapidly. Take it at face value. Surely there was no hidden trap in *that* question?

"The one with blue tablecloths?"

"No, the other side of the street. The woman who ran it looked ferocious but was incredibly kind. She thought I was a starving student so she gave me extra *bratkartoffeln.* It had a blackboard menu on the footpath."

"I remember her. Hilda. She never gave *me* extra anything," he said indignantly.

Libby smiled and ate. Wiener Schnitzel had been a calculated risk, but it looked like it was working. Gloria had given her a few tips on its preparation before she left, plus the hint that it was one of Charles's favorites. Now they could chat about Vienna without any problems. It was the only thing they had in common apart from Gloria.

"Hilda made the best chocolate cakes I've ever tasted," she said.

"There's a place I know in Glebe that does a pretty good cake," Charles said. "We could go for afternoon tea one weekend and give it the Hilda test." He cut schnitzel studiously while he waited for her response. "This is very good."

"Thank you," said Libby. "And thank you, yes, that would be fun. I can still remember her Black Forest Gateau after eight years. Will your place measure up, I wonder?"

Charles smiled. "Sometimes memory plays tricks and enhances the value of things."

"True." Libby sighed. "But I like to think of Hilda's place as a chocolate cake paradise."

They finished the meal in companionable, idle chat. Charles cleared the table and stacked the dishwasher while Libby prepared coffee.

"I think I'll go for a walk around the block," he said. "Been stuck inside all day. Won't be long." He paused. Libby glanced across at him.

"Would you like to come?"

"No, thanks. You go. I walked to the shops today. Coffee will be ready when you get back."

"See you soon."

He strode down the hall, whistling as the front door closed behind him. Libby smiled. Very nice. No problems. This week would be a breeze. Platonic.

Just so long as he didn't keep smiling at her like that because when he did he was liable to be on the receiving end of some uncontrollable passion. He might have to lock his bedroom door or stick a chair under the handle. Libby giggled as she wiped down the bench top. If he knew what was going through her head he wouldn't be so cheerful, he'd run a mile. But it was a fantasy, Charles would never let himself become involved with her even if he was attracted and available and all the things he wasn't, for one simple reason alone—he thought she was a hysterical, single-minded, egotistical musician. And he was right.

The phone rang.

"Hello," she said, expecting Gloria to be reporting in after her first day of tiptoeing through the tulips.

A woman's voice said, "Who is this, please?"

"Who are you?" retorted Libby, instantly annoyed by the peremptory tone.

"I'm calling Charles Hogarth," she snapped. "Is this the correct number?"

"Oh, yes, sorry. He's just gone out. Can I take a message?" Some demanding nuisance of a client, no doubt. What a pest, phoning Charles at home.

"Tell him Tiffany rang. No message." The girlfriend? Whoops.

"Do you have his mobile number?" asked Libby, reaching for the card with his contact details.

"I do but it's switched off."

"He won't be long. He's gone for a walk." A post-prandial perambulation, they called it in the orchestra.

"Excuse me for asking but exactly who are you?" Tiffany asked, obviously striving for a polite way to ask a delicate but burning question.

"I'm Libby. Gloria's companion."

The relief in Tiffany's voice poured through the phone. "I'm sorry. I must have sounded terribly rude," she gushed. "I didn't realize Gloria had a companion. What a good idea. She's a dear old lady but getting just a little senile."

"I haven't noticed." Senile, Gloria was not. Occasional forgetfulness didn't make a person senile. If it did, half the population could be accused of senility.

"No doubt we'll meet soon, Lizzy," said Tiffany. "Don't forget to tell Charles I called." She must think forgetfulness was catching.

"I won't. I'll write it down. Goodbye," said Libby and hung up.

Tiffany was no bimbo despite the name. Tiffany was a forceful, modern woman who knew exactly what she wanted and what she wanted was Charles.

She had Charles. Charles had told Libby himself. Lizzy.

Libby settled on the couch to watch the news on television. Depressing as ever. Wars, train wrecks, floods, babbling politicians. Charles reappeared just as the weather report was finishing.

"Rain in Canberra," Libby called. "Good thing Gloria took her umbrella."

"Can't begrudge anyone rain these days," observed Charles. "It's been so dry everywhere." He went to the kitchen and returned with the coffee tray. "Who's this Oscar character?"

Libby sat up straight. "Ha ha! I'm not sure how serious things are, but Gloria is like a schoolgirl when he's around."

Charles stared at her in astonishment. "What do you mean? She's got a crush on Oscar?"

"Maybe. He's certainly taken with her."

"That's disgraceful!'

"It is not," cried Libby. "It's lovely. Falling in love is wonderful at any age. Don't you think Gloria is capable?"

Charles grimaced. "I can't imagine. Glory? She's eighty-one."

"And he's younger, she told me. He's seventy-nine and acts thirty. I like him."

"You would," he said. "And Gloria's not your responsibility."

"Charles don't begrudge Gloria this excitement. You sound a real old curmudgeon. Gloria's not an idiot, she's not senile, and she knows exactly what she's doing. Oscar has a unit in an aged person's complex and he's very comfortably well off. He owned a factory that made taps and plumbing fittings and things."

"How do you know so much about him?'

"We had lunch at his place on Wednesday."

"Nobody told me."

"Why should we?" Libby frowned and reconsidered. "Actually, I think she should have mentioned him to you ages ago."

"Thank you very much for your consideration," he said sarcastically.

Libby snorted in disgust. "Gloria didn't want to tell you about Oscar and now I know why. She knows you better than I do."

He didn't reply. Libby said more gently, "They really like each other, Charles. More than just friends."

"You sound as if they're thinking about getting married."

"Would that be so terrible?" asked Libby but before Charles could explode with an answer to that she said, "Tiffany rang and wants you to call her."

"When?" Startled and not particularly pleased. Lover's tiff?

"Just now while you were out." Libby drank her coffee. Not her business. Charles' relationship with Tiffany or any other woman was not her business.

Charles picked up his coffee and stared at the TV. Libby had muted the sound when he came home, now she was aimlessly flicking about the channels.

"There's a movie coming on soon I want to see—somewhere," she said. "I can't remember which channel and all I'm finding is ads."

"Read the guide," said Charles.

Libby got up and found the day's paper with the new guide in it.

"Prime," she read out.

"What is it?'

"*Hilary and Jackie.*"

"Never heard of it," said Charles.

"You won't like it."

"Won't I? How do you know?"

"Because it's about Jacqueline Du Pré." Libby sat down, keeping her face averted.

Charles knew who that was, she didn't need to explain but she didn't even start. He finished his coffee and got up. He wasn't about to make a scene about a movie.

"I've got some work to do on the computer. Enjoy the film."

"Don't forget to ring Tiffany," she said as he headed for the stairs.

"I won't."

He used the phone in the upstairs room he'd arranged as an office, next to Libby's bedroom. Tiffany answered immediately.

"Charles, I haven't seen you for ages. Is everything all right?"

"Yes. Just run off my feet at work and there've been a few changes here at home."

"You've hired a companion for Gloria. What an excellent idea." Her voice dropped and she purred into the receiver. "Now you can stay out all night. How about—tonight?"

"I can't, I'm sorry. I've just come upstairs to do some reports."

"Boring," she cried. "But all right. Tomorrow instead. I'll taxi to you from work and we can go on to my place in your car."

"No, don't do that," Charles interrupted firmly. "I'll pick you up later. I need to talk to you, Tiffany."

"Fine. I'll see you tomorrow. Bye darling."

There was a crisp-sounding click in his ear followed by the dial tone. Tiffany never wheedled and persuaded, that was one of her attractions. Charles hoped that surgical attitude would stretch to being told their alliance was terminated. She held no allure for him any more. He'd barely given her a thought since the excruciating Japanese dinner, and the thought of spending more time with her left him decidedly cold.

He spent the next two hours doing his homework and then, yawning, went downstairs to find Libby curled up asleep on the couch, the credits of her movie rolling on the TV. She'd turned off the main lights and left a lamp on. The room was swathed in shadows from the soft golden glow of the single bulb.

He gazed down at her, unashamedly drinking in the sight. She was more than simply beautiful, she was perfect. He knelt beside the couch and delicately brushed a strand of silky dark hair from the smooth curve of her cheek. Her chest rose and fell gently. Fast asleep.

Charles couldn't resist. He leaned forward and kissed her ever so softly on the mouth. She stirred, and he sat back quickly, but she didn't wake. He bent his head again and placed his lips lightly on hers and this time she did wake as he drew back. Her eyes opened, blinked once or twice, adjusted to the situation.

Charles froze. Their faces were inches apart.

"Charles?" she murmured. She smiled sleepily. "I

dreamt . . . did you . . ." She shook her head. "No." Her face flushed pink as she met his gaze.

She sat up. Charles rocked back on his heels and stood up.

"You were snoring." He picked up the remote and clicked off the TV.

"I bet I wasn't." She laughed, a soft little sound.

He looked at her and wanted to kiss her again, now while she was awake so that she'd know she wasn't dreaming. While she was all soft and relaxed from sleep, warm and sexy.

"I should go to bed."

She stood up and stretched her arms over her head, yawning. "Don't know why I'm so tired. Must be all this doing nothing."

Charles stepped forward and put his arms around her so that when she lowered hers they went around his neck before she realized.

"I'm sorry," he whispered, "I just can't resist . . ."

His lips brushed hers. He'd meant to just steal a tender kiss, one that wouldn't alarm her and wouldn't signify anything much, but she didn't pull away and she didn't remove her arms from his neck.

Then she was kissing him the way he'd imagined and dreaded and dared to hope she might. Her lips parted under his insistence and she melted against him as though she'd longed to be this close and wanted even more. He drowned in the perfume of her and the taste of her and he wanted more and more. He wanted all of her and his hands reached for the curves and hollows and planes they'd always longed to explore.

Then, through the sheer exhilaration that she wanted him the same way, some sort of sanity began to filter into Charles's mind. They mustn't do this. It would spoil everything. He'd already decided that.

He dragged his mouth reluctantly from hers and gazed into a pair of violet eyes wide and luminous, shining with passion and wonder.

"We mustn't," he whispered. "Libby, we can't."

To his vast amazement and shock she slowly extricated herself from his embrace and straightened her T-shirt, nodding.

"No, you're right," she said in a voice almost Tiffany-esque in its clarity. "You're already involved and we're totally unsuited."

Charles said quickly, "That wasn't what I . . . I'm sorry. I shouldn't have kissed you, it's my fault. I took advantage of you when you were half asleep."

"Let's forget it happened," suggested Libby, watching him thoughtfully.

"Yes, right."

"It would mess up everything," she added. "With Gloria, I mean, and me living here."

"Yes, it would be too awkward, especially when . . ."

"When what?"

"We broke up."

"We're breaking up already and we haven't got together yet?" asked Libby with a tense smile. "Not that we would—or should. We shouldn't."

Charles grinned and it felt like a grimace. "Yes. It saves time and emotional turmoil."

"I see." But she didn't look as though she did.

Charles ran his hands through his hair and turned away. He couldn't stand to be so close to her and not be kissing her. He groaned aloud and swore under his breath.

"That was such a stupid thing to do," he said through gritted teeth.

"Yes. Now I'm not going to get any sleep at all," she replied.

He spun around.

"Aren't you?'

She shook her head. "That's a difficult thing to put out of one's mind. But we've decided."

"Yes."

"It would be a disaster. And I'm not looking for a disastrous relationship. I'm not looking for any sort of relationship but especially not a disastrous one."

"But you kissed me," Charles blurted as she turned for the stairs and her bedroom. "And you liked it."

Libby paused with her back to him.

"Yes," she said and hurried upstairs.

She didn't get much sleep that night, and even though she was wide awake when Charles started moving about preparing breakfast the next morning, Libby stayed in her room until the front door clicked shut and she could go downstairs and try to energize herself with a pot of tea.

A day that had started very early and badly became worse suddenly when the potato-chip-ad people rang to tell her she would not be needed for the shoot on Sunday.

"Thank you," Libby said, and added, "For nothing," after she'd replaced the receiver.

It rang again almost immediately. Gloria.

"How are you? How's the tour?" cried Libby with unfeigned delight.

"Wonderful. The gardens are beautiful, even in the rain. We're having a ball. How are you getting along with Charles?"

"Fine. So far. It's only been one day."

Fortunately Gloria missed the hesitation and stiffness in her response, which, to her ears, was staggeringly obvious. "I know. I just hope Charles won't be difficult, he can be moody."

"I don't see him much." And would see him even less from now on, probably. "Guess what? The potato chip thing is off. For me, anyway."

"What a shame. Have you found something else to do?"

"No."

"Oscar says you could do very well as a live-in companion to the elderly. He has a friend in a similar situation to me except he's still living in his own house."

"But I'm happy here with you," said Libby in astonishment. "You're not giving me the sack are you?" She clutched the receiver tightly as a shiver of alarm ran down her spine.

"No, of course not. It's just that . . . well . . . I might, Oscar and I might . . ."

"Might?" Libby held her breath.

"Oh, I can't tell you anything on the phone. Wait till I get home. I should tell Charles as well. First." And

Gloria actually giggled. An eighty-one-year-old school-girl.

"Gloria? You and Oscar?"

"When I get home," Gloria said firmly. "I must dash now, the coach is leaving for the gardens. We're having lunch at Old Parliament House today, then going through the galleries there in the afternoon."

"Sounds wonderful. Enjoy yourself. And Gloria, say hello to Oscar from me."

"Bye-bye dear."

Libby hung up with a big smile on her face. She knew it! Gloria and Oscar. Maybe they'd get married. Lovely. But where would that leave her? Companion to Oscar's old friend? She couldn't possibly stay here if Gloria moved in with Oscar. The smile faded and she began to pace up and down the room. Then she flung open the glass doors and paced up and down the back garden.

She had to get a job! A proper job. Why hadn't those other people rung back? She'd left messages about translating German and teaching theory. None of them had even bothered to call and say the position was filled. That was so rude.

Lame Duck. She was a Lame Duck. Single with not a relative to her name to fall back on. She closed her eyes in despair and saw herself heading for a future in which she moved from one elderly person's home to another, staying until they either died or were beyond her inexpert care, as she became dried up and resigned and bitter about her career that could have been and the love that couldn't. And being invited to Bob and Betty's for Christmas dinner.

The phone rang again, and she went inside with a heavy tread and an even heavier heart. It was Charles and she nearly dropped the phone. Charles the unobtainable. Charles who had dramatically displayed how he felt about her last night but just as dramatically had held her away when she was ready to forget the consequences. Charles who had patrolled ceaselessly in her head all night and with whom she thought perhaps, disastrously and hopelessly, she had begun to fall in love.

"Libby?"

She fumbled and juggled and finally brought the receiver to her ear. "Yes, I'm here," she gasped.

"Can you go upstairs to my study, please, and find a name and number? It'll be on my desk on the top of a letter. The handwritten number."

"Okay." Clutching the handset Libby ran up the stairs. "Gloria just called," she said breathlessly as she reached the top step. "She's having a ball, she said."

"Good."

"With Oscar."

"What?'

"She's having a good time."

"How good a time?" he asked and Libby snorted with laughter and said before she could stop herself, "A better time than we did, I hope."

Charles exhaled loudly. He sounded angry when he said, "Have you got that name and number?"

Libby pushed the study door open and peered at the papers on the desk. “Roger Green and Sons?”

“That’s it. Thanks.”

She read out the details. When she’d finished, she waited for him to say good-bye and go back to work but he didn’t. She heard him breathing.

“How are you,” he asked in a low voice that wasn’t angry.

“Tired.”

“No sleep?’

“No.”

“Me neither.”

“Charles maybe we could . . .”

He interrupted briskly. “I nearly forgot. I won’t be eating at home tonight. I should have told you yesterday. Sorry.”

“All right,” she said softly.

“Friends?” he asked after a short pause.

“Friends,” she said. There would be no more kisses.

Libby took her cello out of its case later that afternoon and sat down as she had a thousand times in her previous life. She heard the notes soaring in her mind before she raised her right hand and stroked the bow across the strings, tuning carefully, bending her head to better hear the intonation.

She began with some slow scales. The fingers of her left hand felt stiff and unwieldy after weeks without practice. The tone was still rich and full, but after about ten minutes shooting pains began in her forearm and spread rapidly to her shoulder. She dropped her weak, useless hand to her side while tears streaked down her cheeks. The bow fell to the floor by her feet. It was no better. There was absolutely no improvement at all. Her career as a cellist was finished forever.

The sound of the front door opening and closing jerked her back to awareness but before she could rise and pack away the now redundant, beloved instrument, Charles appeared in the doorway. He stopped short when he saw her and his expression changed from surprise to mild alarm when he realized she was crying.

"I can't play," she wailed. "I'll never play again."

Charles came toward her. He dropped his briefcase on the floor and grabbed a tea towel from the kitchen as he passed.

"Here," he said and shoved it into her hand. He watched while she mopped her eyes. "Give it time."

"It's had a month," she cried. "More. I might as well sell my cello. It's no use to me. At least if I get rid of it, it won't remind me all the time."

"For heaven's sake!" Charles snapped. "Don't be so hysterical. Have you done anything about treatment? Have you found a doctor?'

Libby shook her head and buried her face in the tea towel. "It's no use," she mumbled.

"Rubbish! How can you be so hopeless? How can you just give up? I would've thought that if cello was so important to you, you'd try anything and everything to get better." Charles was virtually shouting at her now, and Libby raised her face in astonishment.

"The tai chi teacher said I should try acupuncture."

"Well, try acupuncture," he yelled.

"Do you think it would work?"

"How would I know?" Charles threw his arms in the air in exasperation and, as he did, the plate glass window facing the garden exploded with the sound of a pistol shot.

Libby spun around, horrified to see big cracks radiating out from a jagged central hole. Pieces of glass dropped to the floor.

"What on earth was that?"

Charles rushed to the window. His feet crunched on glass fragments. He stopped and moved carefully to the side door. Libby placed her cello in its case and joined him outside.

"It was a bird." He pointed to a couple of feathers lying on the paving stones.

"Where is it?'

"Gone. With a headache," said Charles.

"And a bent beak. That gave me an incredible fright." Libby wandered about peering into bushes and behind trees looking for any sign of a stunned, kamikaze bird. "I thought we'd been shot at."

"Probably a magpie or a currawong," said Charles. "The reflections on the glass fool them."

"Wow."

"I'll call a repairer."

Libby followed him back into the house, and while he read the Yellow Pages and telephoned she carefully swept glass into the dustpan. What had brought Charles home at four-thirty instead of his more usual six? Charles joined her and picked up one of the larger pieces.

"Two hours," he said.

"That's fast."

"They boast immediate emergency response in their ad. Ow!" A shard of glass crashed in to the dustpan and Charles held a bleeding hand out. Scarlet blood poured down his wrist.

Chapter Seven

Libby grabbed the tea towel she'd been crying into and mopped as best she could.

"Come to the bathroom." She led him, with his hand swathed in the Wildflowers of New South Wales tea towel, to the bathroom Gloria used. "Does it hurt? How deep is it?"

"Yes, it hurts," he said in an oddly strained voice. "I think an artery is severed."

Libby glanced at him, sure he was joking, but the set look on his face made her swallow the giggle. "I doubt it. Not in your finger."

"It's cut to the bone."

"Let me see."

Libby removed the blood-soaked tea towel and turned on the cold tap. She held Charles's hand under the running water and studied the wound.

"There's no glass in there. It doesn't look very deep, just enough to bleed a lot. Got any bandages?"

"I'll need stitches."

"No, you won't."

"Are you sure?" Charles stared at his damaged hand, horror on his face.

"Does the sight of blood bother you?" He'd gone pale.

"No, yes. A bit."

"Hold this on it." She handed him a clean handtowel from the vanity unit, then unearthed cotton wool, disinfectant, and a roll of sticking plaster.

Five minutes later the hand was clean, disinfected, and securely wrapped in a sterile bandage.

"Go and sit down. I'll make you a cup of tea," she said. Charles obediently parked himself in an armchair, holding his injured hand gingerly on his lap.

"Better if you hold it up," she called. He raised his hand obediently

Libby watched him as she pottered in the kitchen. How bizarre. Marina, in Holland, had told her men were bigger babies than babies, but she hadn't believed her until now. She grinned to herself as she poured hot water into the teapot.

"Maybe I should retrain as a nurse," she called to him.

He grunted something. Libby carried two mugs of tea to where he sat.

"I've just saved your life after all." She couldn't stop the laugh from erupting and had to put the tea quickly on the table to prevent spillage.

"What's so funny?" he said crossly.

"I've never seen such a display," she managed to gasp between snorts. "Severed artery. Almost amputated finger."

"I didn't say that!'

"Cut . . . hahahaha . . . to the . . . hahahaha . . . bone."

Libby collapsed sideways on to the cushions on the end of the couch and laughed till her stomach ached. Charles sat stiffly sipping his tea as if it were poison.

"Come on, Charles," she said eventually, when she could speak. "It's only a tiny cut."

"I don't see you laughing about your injury. I don't laugh about it either."

"That's a completely different thing." Libby jerked up straight with indignation.

"And I didn't burst into tears." He placed his mug precisely on the table.

"You nearly did." The laughter erupted in a burst, and she clasped her hands over her mouth, gazing at him with shaking shoulders.

Charles picked up the nearest cushion and hurled it at her. Libby shrieked and hurled it back, narrowly missing the tea mugs. He glared at her and stood up. She thought he was going to storm off the way he had the other night, but he suddenly grabbed the cushion and, with a fiendish laugh, threw it at her again. Libby bolted for the cover of the hallway just making the doorway before another cushion thudded into the wall.

"Missed," she yelled. She crouched down and snaked her hand around the corner to grope for the cushion.

"You can run but you can't hide," he said.

Cackling with laughter Libby stood up and hurled the

missile at him before scuttling down the hall to look for more ammunition. She darted into the bathroom and grabbed a couple of towels and the bathmat. Backed up against the hand basin, she waited.

Charles was coming warily along the hall. She could hear his soft footsteps. Her heart thudded hard in her chest and she balled the towels up ready to pelt him as he came into view.

The doorbell rang stridently.

"That'll be the glass man," he said from just outside the door. "Truce?"

"Truce." Libby hung the towels back on the railing. Charles opened the door. A man's voice asked if he had the right house.

"Yes. You were quicker than we expected." The two men passed the bathroom door. Charles glanced in, still holding a cushion, and glared at her. Libby stuck her tongue out, and he laughed. The glass man, wearing green overalls with the name Bruce embroidered on his pocket, glanced in as well. "How do?"

"Hello." Libby followed them to the scene of the crash.

"Cut your hand, did you, mate?"

"Yeah, it's nothing." Charles tossed the cushion onto the nearest armchair. "Just a scratch."

"Bleeds like a shocker, though," Bruce said sympathetically. "I get 'em all the time. Whack a Band-Aid on and keep workin'."

"I'll finish cleaning up," said Libby keeping her face as impassive as she possibly could. She didn't dare meet Charles' eye.

"Vacuum's best when you've got up the worst of it,"

suggested Bruce. "You'll be surprised how it spreads itself around. Better not go wanderin' about barefoot."

"Yes," said Libby. "I didn't finish before because of the . . . um . . . injury. I'll do it now."

"Don't worry, love. I'll be makin' a mess when I take out the broken pane and I clean up after meself."

"We'll leave you to it," said Charles.

"Righto, mate."

Charles took his wound up to his study. Libby went to the kitchen and opened the fridge. She'd planned a stir-fry vegetable-and-chicken dinner for one tonight as taught by Gloria. Snow peas, baby bok choy, garlic, an onion, baby corn, almonds, carrot. She began peeling the garlic. There'd be quite a few solo dinners coming up. But that was all right. She'd lived alone most of her life. Learning to cook properly with plenty of preparation time was surprisingly enjoyable.

Pillow fighting with Charles. Who'd have thought it! She hadn't done that since she was ten, on a sleepover, and they'd got into big trouble from Zoe's Mum because their shrieks had woken the baby.

She'd never seen Charles so relaxed. Happy. He'd even started it. He had a crazy, impulsive streak—a wild streak he kept tightly suppressed. And that thing about the cut. What an absolute hoot. And coming over all macho in front of Bruce. Libby giggled. What a complicated man he was.

She pulled the vegetable drawer open to find bok choy and snow peas, wincing as pain shot up her arm. Maybe she should see that acupuncturist. Couldn't hurt. It wasn't supposed to anyway. But how could needles stuck into you not hurt?

The doorbell rang again. Nuisance. Libby went to answer. A tall, slim, blond woman stood on the step wearing a snug fitting gray pants suit—the female version of a man's business suit. A real estate salesperson? Libby had already spoken to one earlier that day. According to Gloria, Willoughby was a sought-after suburb, and according to the earlier visitor, there were hordes of buyers anxious to move into this very house.

"I'm sorry." Libby forestalled the inevitable spiel. "We're not selling and we're not buying."

The woman raised two immaculate eyebrows. "My name is Tiffany Holland. Is Charles at home?"

"Tiffany, I'm sorry. I thought you were a real estate person. I'm Libby."

The eyebrows rose even farther. "Gloria's companion?"

"Yes. Please, come in. We're in a bit of a mess. A bird flew into the window and broke it."

"Goodness! What a shock," said Tiffany. "I hope Gloria wasn't in the room when it happened."

"No, no," said Libby leading the way down the hall. "Gloria's in Canberra at Floriade. I'll tell Charles you're here. Sit down, please."

"I think I'll stand," Tiffany said in a cool voice, taking in Bruce and his attack on the window, keeping well away.

Libby ran up the stairs. So! This was the Tiffany dinner service. Very classy. Elegant and refined to the utmost. That pant suit wasn't a run of the mill design. Nicely cut jacket. Suited Tiffany perfectly.

Would Tiffany throw pillows at Charles? Would Charles throw pillows at Tiffany? All couples had private jokes and shared moments. Libby gulped. That thought caused pain. Unbearable pain.

"Charles?" She tapped on the study door.

"Yes?"

"Tiffany's here."

Charles opened the door. Frowning. "Here?"

"Downstairs. Watching Bruce."

"Why?'

"He's interesting? She does glazing in her spare time? I don't know."

Libby went into her room, closing the door with a decisive click. The atmosphere positively vibrated behind her.

Charles closed his eyes briefly. Air hissed between his teeth. Tiffany and Libby under the same roof. How could his well-ordered existence have become so emotionally fraught in such a short space of time? Everything had been running along so smoothly until that evening at Bob and Betty's. He drew a deep breath and proceeded downstairs for the second half of the encounter.

But Tiffany wasn't as emotionally volatile as Libby. She knew the deal. No strings. No uncomfortable intimate entanglement. Their relationship was based on partnering each other when necessary and a mutual understanding of the bottom line. Suited them both. When it ran its course, it was over.

Now it was over. Didn't make breaking off any easier, though.

Tiffany stood with her head slightly tilted reading the spines of the CDs on the shelf above the stereo. She turned and smiled but it wasn't a happy smile. A certain tension about the eyes didn't bode well.

"Hello, this is a surprise," he said.

"Is it? I thought we had a date tonight."

"We do but . . ." Charles looked at his watch. "Good heavens. I'm sorry. I had no idea." He waved his arm in the direction of Bruce surrounded by glass and framed in the open window like an artist's rendition of a working man. "This happened and I cut my hand. I didn't realize the time."

"Are you all right?" Tiffany indicated the bandaged hand.

"Yes, it's fine. Libby took care of it."

"Shouldn't you go to a doctor?"

"No, it's only a scratch. Bleeds a lot though."

"Had plenty of 'em meself," offered Bruce from the window. "He'll survive."

Tiffany glanced across with a wintry smile, which slid straight around Bruce leaving nary a mark on his implacable good cheer.

"Are you ready to leave?" she asked Charles.

"I don't think I can. I'd better wait for Bruce to finish up."

"Give us forty minutes," said Bruce right on cue.

"Won't Libby be here?" Tiffany turned her back slightly, so her face angled away from the eavesdropper.

"Yes, but I don't want to leave her with it," Charles replied. He didn't want to leave her at all.

"I don't see why not, she works for you, doesn't she?" Tiffany's voice had developed an icy edge all the more effective because of her deliberately low volume level.

"I'm sorry, I should have thought to phone you," said Charles, retreating into his formal, upper class schoolboy manner. Thank goodness she wasn't a screamer. Bruce would've dined out on that exhibition for weeks. "Tiffany, I need to . . ."

She cut in sharply, "Can we talk somewhere else?" She spoke through stiff lips but her eyes sent laser-like rays toward Bruce. They swung back to Charles. This wasn't going to be as easy as he thought.

He took her through to the rarely used front sitting room, which was in the old part of the house and where he'd put a big, formal, heavy wooden dining table and eight straight-backed antique chairs. Tiffany stood resting her hand on the smooth tabletop. She ran her fingers lightly over the polished surface as if testing for dust.

"You didn't tell me Gloria's companion was a very beautiful, young woman," she said in a voice straight from Antarctica.

"Does it matter?" This was it. He had to say what he'd been intending to say right now. Enough of this shameful prevaricating.

"And you didn't tell me you were living here with her alone. That Gloria was away." Tiffany's eyes had become ice picks.

"I don't think that's at all relevant," he said in a voice

as frozen as hers. "Wasn't our understanding no complications, no involvement, no strings attached?'

"That might have been your understanding, Charles, but it wasn't mine. I always knew you were basically a cold fish, but I didn't think you were a cheat and a liar."

"I haven't lied or cheated, Tiffany. Libby is employed by Gloria and their arrangement has nothing to do with me—or you, for that matter. As it happens Libby and I met years ago in Vienna and again quite by chance, just recently, but I resent the implication that I would lie to you. In fact . . . and this has absolutely nothing to do with anyone else no matter what you may think . . ." Charles drew a deep breath, "I was going to tell you this evening that I think we should go our separate ways."

"Go our separate ways?" Tiffany turned, took two steps, and then spun to face him. She wasn't ice cool any more. Her face was contorted with anger. "Do you have no feelings at all? Was this simply a convenient escort arrangement to you? I have feelings, Charles, you just never allowed me to express them!"

She stared at him with such loathing he suddenly feared she might attack him and try to scratch his eyes out.

"Don't worry. I won't make a scene for you in front of your new girl. We wouldn't want that, would we? Nasty messy emotions everywhere. I put up with your reserve and your haughtiness because I thought maybe one day you'd thaw out, but I don't think you can, Charles. Your emotional savings account has about two cents in it. And I'm glad we're *going our separate ways* because I was beginning to come to the same conclusion myself."

"I'm sorry," was all he could think of to say. He led her to the door and opened it. Tiffany stalked out into the night, head held high.

"For the record," he called. "Libby is not my new girl and she's got nothing to do with this. She's not my type."

Tiffany stopped. She turned slowly and said deliberately, "For the record, Charles, exactly what is your type? A reptile? A cane toad?"

He watched her climb into her sporty yellow car and stood staring down the street long after the tail lights had disappeared into the darkness. A cold fish? A reptile? Cane toads spat venom. Was he frozen inside? His stomach began to ache, the cut on his hand throbbed. He had feelings, Tiffany was wrong about that. At the moment those feelings were a tangled and confused mess.

"Scuse me, mate," said Bruce behind him. He stepped aside. Bruce headed for his truck. He carefully lifted a pane of glass off the side and came back to the house. "Nearly finished."

Charles closed the door and followed him through to the rear.

"You've got it good, mate," said Bruce. He propped the glass against the wall. "Two lookers like that." He shook his head in admiration. "One living in."

"Libby is in the employ of my aunt and I resent that remark," Charles snapped in his most pompous tone. "Not that it's any of your business, but I do not have relationships with the hired help."

"Okay, mate. Don't get your knickers in a twist." Bruce shrugged.

Charles ground his teeth. He headed for the stairs and the privacy of his study. Two steps up he stopped, frozen. Libby stood at the top staring down at him with an expression similar to that recently worn by Tiffany. She proceeded down the stairs, brushing passed him without acknowledgement. Bruce began whistling tunelessly through his teeth as he poked and scraped at the window edging. Charles stood irresolute. What was that all about? Could Libby be upset because Tiffany had turned up?

He joined Libby in the kitchen where she'd started attacking a carrot with a knife. He couldn't help but think she was imagining his neck lay on the chopping board instead of the carrot.

"I'm not going out after all."

Libby sliced the carrot and started on an onion. What did Charles expect her to say? He was standing there waiting for some sort of response. The hired help weren't supposed to speak unless spoken to, surely, and he hadn't asked her a question.

"Is there enough food for me to eat with you?"

Libby paused in her chopping. "Sure."

"Really?"

"Yes."

"Like a drink?"

"No, thank you."

"Can I help?"

"Not with that." She nodded at his bandage.

"Oh, no, I suppose not."

Charles went to watch Bruce, who had finished replacing the glass and was now plugging in a battered-looking vacuum cleaner.

Libby continued preparing the vegetables. She didn't dare look at Charles in case she accidentally threw the onion at his back. Marvelous how therapeutic slicing and cutting was. How the actions took her thoughts away from that most incredible statement—the hired help. She hadn't heard Bruce's preceding remark but on her slight acquaintance with him it wouldn't have been a tactful one. But hired help?

Libby removed the chicken strips from the fridge. She placed them in a bowl with crushed garlic and lemon juice. Realistically, she would have to get used to being the hired help. That's what she was, and if she wanted to keep this position she would have to put up with it. And she would also have to keep any dreams featuring the lord of the manor, Charles, firmly out of her mind.

That kiss was best forgotten. She wouldn't mention it, and he definitely wouldn't. He'd probably forgotten it, too, or maybe he expected to be able to kiss the underling as his right. What was that called? *Le droit de seigneur.*

"See you later," called Bruce. Libby looked up to see him pocketing a check as he headed out the side door held open by Charles.

"Thanks," she called.

Charles strode back across the living room straight to where she stood trying to break up thick, yellow *hokkien* noodles in a sieve under the hot water tap.

"Ready in ten minutes," she said, keeping her eyes on the noodles and wishing he wouldn't stand so close.

"Libby?"

She didn't reply, just leaned past him to grab the wok and place it on the burner.

"Tiffany and I broke up."

"I'm sorry."

"I'm not."

"Oh." She lit the gas and poured oil into the pan. "I hope I get this right I've never used these noodles before."

"Do you want to know why?" Charles asked.

Libby dumped the chicken pieces into the hot oil and jumped when they sizzled and spat. Charles turned the gas down and grabbed, a spatula to toss and stir vigorously.

"No. It's none of my business." She snatched the spatula away from him.

He picked up the chopping board laden with sliced vegetables and began adding onions to the chicken.

"Better to do the onions first," he said.

"Go away," cried Libby. "Go away and sit down somewhere and wait. This is my dinner. I'm cooking!"

Charles pulled a surprised face but did as he was told. He sat on one of the stools facing her over the bench. Not quite what she'd meant by go away, but better than hovering over the cooking area.

"I broke up with her because we never had any fun."

Libby kept her mouth firmly closed. Poor Tiffany, if she was expecting Charles to be fun.

"She's a nice woman," he said, "but we had nothing

in common. It was more of a relationship of convenience for both of us. She wasn't interested in architecture and I'm certainly not interested in the fashion industry."

"Charles, I'm really not interested in hearing about it," said Libby tersely.

"Just so as you know," he insisted.

"I do, now."

Libby stirred the chicken and scraped in the rest of the vegetables. Chunks of carrot missed and landed on the cook top. Charles made her nervous. He obviously knew how to handle a wok, while this was the first time she'd ever even touched one. Why should she care that he'd broken off with Tiffany? What made him think he should tell her?

But the curiosity was overwhelming. "How did she take it?"

"She said I was a cold fish and called me a reptile and a cane toad."

Libby nodded but said nothing. That wasn't a bad summation, all round. Both she and Tiffany had been on the receiving end of his ice cubes. Charles peered over the bench.

"Keep tossing that," he said. "It has to cook quickly and evenly."

"It's no fun being dumped," she said. "Poor Tiffany."

"What should I have done?" exclaimed Charles. "Strung her along? Pretended I cared when I don't?"

"It's none of my business," said Libby.

"You seem interested."

"Only because you insist on telling me and I'm polite enough to listen." Libby tossed her spatula energetically. Vegetables and chicken flew out of the wok on to the floor.

"For goodness sake let me do that. If I'm eating it I want to make sure it hasn't been scraped up off the floor."

Charles jumped off the stool and charged around the bench to elbow Libby out of the way. He grabbed the bottle of hoi sin sauce she had standing ready and dolloped in a large amount.

"Isn't that too much?" she protested.

"Have you done this before?"

"No, I said I hadn't."

"Just clean up that mess you've made and let me do it properly."

"You just can't get good hired help these days, can you?" Libby shot back from the floor, where she was picking up carrot and onion.

Charles switched off the gas and plonked two bowls on to the bench. He spooned steaming hot food into them without a word and carried his to the table.

Libby washed her hands and took her own bowl and a fork to the opposite end of the table.

"I'm sorry you heard that," he said. "Bruce said something offensive. I was actually defending your honor."

"Why, thank you."

She stabbed a piece of chicken and tasted it. Bit chewy but not bad. Now she had four easy meals plus her gourmet Wiener Schnitzel.

Libby deliberately avoided looking the length of the table at Charles. His attitude amazed, confounded, and infuriated her. What did he think? She'd be open to his advances because he'd broken up with his girlfriend, and the fact that he thought of her as an employee wouldn't matter? They'd already reached the conclusion that friends was the best way to go under the circumstances, now here he was telling her about Tiffany as if she'd been the only obstacle to a flourishing romance.

"How's your hand?" she asked. "Finger still attached? No gangrene?"

Charles chewed and swallowed. He took another mouthful and chewed and swallowed again. She thought he wasn't going to dignify that crack with an answer, but he said, "When I was six I was sent to boarding school. I went home for the holidays, but sometimes my parents weren't there and I stayed with Glory and Great Uncle Henry, which I much preferred, or if they couldn't have me, my parents hired a nanny. I always had nannies before I went to school, but they employed someone to look after me in the holidays. Always someone different."

Libby put her fork down carefully. She didn't say a word, frightened he would stop talking if she interrupted the flow.

"I fell once, down the steps to the house and cut my knee quite badly—banged my nose as well. There was blood everywhere. I was terrified. I couldn't breathe. It hurt and I cried." He gave a small self-deprecating laugh that made Libby's eyes moisten. She almost held her breath. "The nanny I had at the time was grim. She didn't stand for any nonsense, any weak, sniveling tears. I had to be a man, she said. My nose bled for ages and started again in bed, and she was cross because I woke her up in the middle of the night with my carrying on. I'll never forget the blood all over my pillow when I turned on the light."

"How old were you?" whispered Libby.

"Seven." Charles resumed eating. "Thank you for being polite enough to listen."

"I'm sorry I laughed." Libby ignored the jibe, recognizing it for what it was, an attempt to cover his embarrassment at such an intimate revelation. An apology.

"Don't be." He met her eyes. "It was a long time ago. I'm not seven any more."

Libby smiled. "Aren't you?" In many ways he *was* still that defensive frightened little boy.

"No, I'm not," he said. But he added, "I still don't like the name Ruth though."

"Nanny's name?'

"Yes."

"I can't stand people called Julie," announced Libby. "Every Julie I've ever known in my whole life has been horrible starting with Julie McSomething in Kindy who pinched me all the time, and ending with Julie Molinaro in the Rotterdam orchestra who whined nonstop and had BO."

Charles burst out laughing. "That's pretty extreme."

"It's a fact of life."

"One of my Sunday tennis group is a Julie."

"Is she nice?"

"Yes, and she serves with a mean topspin."

"See," Libby said triumphantly.

"Which is great when she's my partner." He grinned at her and scraped up the last of his noodles.

The rest of the week passed relatively calmly. Libby played at being a housewife by cooking dinner each evening. She filled in the days visiting Betty twice; seeing her lawyer about her financial status and in regard to the Turramurra house, which she thought she might have to sell; shopping; and job hunting.

Even with these activities there were vast stretches of empty time. She went to the garden and swung her arms about practicing the tai chi movements she could remember from her two or three classes. As exercise went, it was definitely her kind of thing. Calming. Trying to remember which hand went where and when which leg stepped there took her mind off her larger problems. And her body always felt looser when she'd finished. She suspected bits of her were moving that had never moved before.

The meditation part of the training was the hardest. Her brain was too busy, too full of thoughts. After a couple of unsuccessful attempts she gave up the practice at home and only did it in class. She knew that was a cop out, all her experience as a practicing musician told her—just because something was difficult wasn't justification for giving it up. Alice told the class repeatedly they'd gain the most benefit from meditation.

"We are trying to tame the monkey mind," she said. "Allow your thoughts to slow naturally. No force." But

Libby's thoughts wouldn't slow, and there were so many of them all sloshing about in her head like clothes in a giant washing machine. At least the co-ordinated movements of the sequence made her focus on something solid and physical.

Her cello sat silently and reproachfully in the corner. Never before had she gone so long without playing. In a fit of despair she considered putting it out of sight in the garden shed but quickly dismissed that idea as ridiculous. The instrument was far too valuable and needed a regulated temperature. She carried it to the dining room and left it in the far corner.

On Friday, for something to do, she went to Glory's senior tai chi class. Alice reminded her to visit the acupuncturist, but by the time she got home the determination had fizzled to nothing. What was the point?

Charles observed Libby during their evenings together. The determined, confident, life-tackling girl he'd met in Vienna had been replaced by a mature, experienced woman, but this Libby had an inner disharmony, an underlying depression, and gradual decline in purpose. Something inside her was slowly dying. Hateful as it was, he had to admit it was because she couldn't express herself any longer through music.

She didn't listen to the radio or the stereo. The reminder was too painful, perhaps. Part of him wanted to shrug it off as a stupid, melodramatic reaction typical of her type. Charles remembered all too vividly when his mother had a bout of flu and lost her voice for a day or two. Two recitals had to be cancelled and the ensuing dramas would have done credit to a Shakespearean tragedy. He was thirteen, home for Easter holidays, but may as well have stayed at school for all the notice she took of him, lying in her bed with scarves and hot water bottles—the room reeking of eucalyptus oil, ringing a bell constantly for attention and fussing from her minions.

The memory of that collapse into helpless clamoring despair made him furious. His mother wasn't one to suffer her hardships alone or silently. He had no patience with it then and a large part of him had no patience with such behavior now.

"Get off your backside," he wanted to scream, standing outside his mother's door with his fists clenched in impotent rage. "Get up and get on with it. It's only a stupid cold, not the Black Death. You didn't care about me when I was sick."

The marriage was in its death throes by then too. His father wasn't even in the country. Charles couldn't remember, if he ever knew, what tour the famous conductor was on at the time.

To be fair, Libby wasn't as bad as his mother. Libby had become quiet. Too quiet. Another, smaller, part of him wanted to comfort and cheer her. But where would that lead? To a rekindling of passion, that's where.

Any indication of tenderness from him could be wildly misconstrued by Libby, which would cause more problems than it solved. Any tenderness from him would be difficult to keep under control, especially if it involved physical contact, however slight.

Thank goodness Glory would be home on Sunday

evening. She was a chaperone, whether she realized it or not. Best of all, Libby would have company during the day.

Charles shook his head at the irony. The whole point of Libby coming to stay was so that he didn't have to worry about Glory home alone. Now he was worried about the minder being home alone.

Libby looked up from *War and Peace*. She'd made headway with it and had covered about a quarter, he estimated. "What's funny?"

"Nothing." He picked up the architecture magazine he'd been flipping through and started reading an article on the Harry Seidler–designed buildings in Canberra.

"What?" she insisted.

Charles smiled. She was watching him with a quizzical expression on her face and those deep, violet-colored eyes shone warm and inviting. Charles's smile widened. Libby was gorgeous and she was sitting here in his house the way he'd never imagined she would. He'd never believed he would even see her again after Vienna. It was a miracle, a staggering, wonderful miracle.

"What page are you up to?" he asked.

"One hundred and ninety."

"Only about eight hundred to go."

"It's very small print," she said defensively.

"Shall we go for that afternoon tea tomorrow?" Charles asked casually.

"Yes, please. I'm going stir-crazy home all day alone."

"You don't have to stay home."

"I know but I don't have anything else to do, Charles."

Instead of the usual rise to hysteria and anger her voice stayed flat and level. She opened her book and resumed reading. Charles watched for a moment, frowning. He found his place and continued with his own magazine.

"It's just that I'm not used to it yet," she murmured.

Chapter Eight

The café Charles had discovered in Glebe was set back from the road in a paved square. Tables sat outside on the pavement sheltered from the bright spring sunshine by big green shade umbrellas. Giant tubs of brightly colored petunias marked the boundaries.

Classical music wafted across the space through the open door. Mozart. Innocuous enough. Libby glanced at Charles half expecting him to baulk at the dreaded sounds but he didn't.

"Inside or out?" he asked.

"Out," said Libby. An obvious choice given the perfect weather.

She sat with her back to the sun leaving Charles in half shadow facing her across the small table. This afternoon she would make sure nothing upset the relaxed atmosphere between them. Charles had been whistling earlier as he pottered about the house, tidying in preparation for Gloria's return tomorrow.

Libby picked up the laminated menu. Charles watched her reading it with a tiny frown creasing her perfect brow, marveling for the hundredth time that it was really Libby opposite him, amazed she'd cheerfully agreed to this expedition and that, so far, things were running naturally and smoothly.

Today she was wearing a navy-blue, ruffled, cotton skirt and a white scoop-necked blouse. Everything she wore effortlessly became stylish and elegant. Even those pajamas . . .

Charles reined in those thoughts abruptly. This outing—outing, not date—was a natural, ordinary thing to do. Easy. Casual. Just as an outing with a friend should be. Housemates. Perfectly normal.

"Cappuccino for me, please," said Libby, suddenly looking up and catching him staring. She handed him the menu. "You choose the cake."

A chirpy young waitress suggested they go inside to select their cakes from the display.

"We know what we want, thanks," said Charles. "Black Forest Cake for two, flat white, and a cappuccino."

"Do you have two types of chocolate cake?" asked Libby quickly, before the girl left.

"Yes. We have a chocolate-fudge mud cake as well."

"We'll have one of each, please." Libby grinned at Charles. "Have to test properly if Hilda's reputation is under pressure. Do you mind going halves?"

"No." Charles adjusted his sunglasses casually. Mind?

She hadn't looked so happy for weeks and she'd thrown herself into the spirit of this jaunt with more enthusiasm than he dared hope. "You could have one of each all to yourself, of course."

"Gosh, I'll be hard pressed to finish one if it's anything like Hilda's. Her cakes would harden your arteries just looking at them. But when you're twenty-two that's the last thing you think about, isn't it?" Her smile was as bright as the sunlight glinting off the gold chain nestled against the warm skin of her throat.

Charles nodded. He'd seen the carefree twenty-two-year-old Libby. If only he'd been more . . . what? Brave? What could life have held for them both if he'd not been so tongue–tied and gauche in that Viennese stairwell?

He leaned forward. "Libby, tell me about your family. I don't know anything about you."

The smile faded. He said quickly, "I'm sorry, I know they died in an accident, that's not what I meant. What were they like? What did your father do?"

The smile returned, but softer now, as she remembered. "Dad was a lecturer in Australian history at Sydney University. Mum was a doctor's receptionist. They told me they fell in love at first sight." She laughed and glanced at him from under silky lashes. "You'd think that was ridiculous. But they both said the same thing."

"Where did they meet?" Would she notice how choked his voice had become? He may have once, but he hadn't thought love at first sight ridiculous since a cold winter's day eight years ago in Vienna.

"On the Manly ferry. They were both going to the beach for the day with friends. One of Mum's girlfriends knew one of Dad's mates and the two groups hooked up."

"You were lucky to have parents who were so happy together."

"I was." Libby's eyes blurred. Charles spontaneously stretched out a hand to cover her fingers. She returned the pressure briefly, sending a thrill of electricity along the nerve endings. "I still miss them."

"Of course you do," he murmured. What hope had he of filling that void? He couldn't possibly. For a start he didn't know how. Loving families weren't within his life experience.

"G'day, Charles," said a voice.

A shadow fell across his face and chest. Libby snatched her hand away. Charles recognized the speaker with a sag of dismay.

"Drew. Hello." Wearing sports gear, white shorts, jogging shoes, a designer logoed T-shirt, and baseball cap. A thin beading of perspiration lay across his brow. Muscular thighs and shoulders bulged. Fit and tanned. Show–off.

"What brings you to this part of town?"

Drew's pale-blue eyes were fixed on Libby. They would be. She was Venus and he thought he was Casanova. Of all the people to catch them out together, Drew was the worst. Already he was giving Libby his seductive smile along with an extended hand. Probably slimy with sweat from whatever sport he'd been engaged in. Disgusting.

"Drew Barwick," he said not waiting for an answer to his previous question because Charles had obviously ceased to feature on the radar screen. The smarmy idiot's voice had dropped several tones. Surely she was too smart to fall for his clichéd moves.

"Hi, I'm Libby." She smiled up at the pest with her usual charm. She was a polite girl. Charles watched to see if she surreptitiously wiped her palm on her skirt. She didn't.

"Libby is an old friend," Charles said quickly. "From Vienna." He didn't dare look at Libby's expression to see how she took that claim.

"We're testing the chocolate cake," she said brightly, causing his head to turn immediately. "Charles tells me it's as good as the one at our favorite Viennese restaurant."

She threw him a quick little grin. Relief made his insides go weak. She said "our" as if they'd shared Austrian experiences, eaten schnitzel and strudel together, talked and laughed. Been friends. He fell in love with her all over again.

"The food's not bad here," said Drew, resting a hand on the back of the spare chair. "But I can take you somewhere even better. The chef is Austrian."

The "you" definitely meant Libby alone, Charles not included. Typical. That attitude made him the least likable of anyone Charles had had to work with.

"Do you two work together?" asked Libby into the gaping silence that followed Drew's remark.

"We did. I moved on. Run my own business nowadays." He said it with such insufferable pride and the implication of others' inability to branch out, Charles's fingers involuntarily curled into a fist. Drew "moved on" because he was such a pain in the neck no one wanted to work with him.

"How's business?" Charles asked. The music had changed. Opera. Music he detested. The perfect accompaniment to a man he disliked.

"Picking up nicely," Drew said with what Charles assessed as deliberate vagueness. He'd heard via the work-related grapevine that Drew was having a tough time of it. Not that he wanted the man to go bankrupt. Not really.

He just didn't want him chatting up Libby.

"Do you live here or are you visiting Sydney?" Drew asked.

Both his hands were on the chair back now. Charles prayed with all his might Libby wouldn't suggest he join them. Even a man as self-confident as Drew wouldn't sit down uninvited.

The waitress arrived with a tray and began unloading coffee, cake, napkins, glasses of water, and cutlery.

"Thank you," said Libby. She returned her attention to Drew. "I've just come back from overseas. I intend to live here."

"Perhaps I could give you a call. We could investigate the other chocolate cake place," he said, adding as an afterthought. "That's if I'm not stepping on any toes." He raised his eyebrows at Charles, who had no choice but to shake his head.

"Entirely up to Libby," he forced through gritted teeth. A woman had begun singing. Her rich voice cut through the ambient noise. He'd recognize it anywhere. Now the disaster was complete.

Libby shot him a swift glance, but he couldn't tell if

she'd recognized the vocalist or whether the glance was connected to his terse statement. But of course, she didn't know who his parents were. She said to Drew, "I'm in a position as a live-in companion so my evenings aren't entirely my own."

She sounded doubtful, perhaps a hint of regret underlying the statement of prior duty. Charles' stomach contracted. His mother's voice soared, reminding him . . . he hadn't heard her for years, had no contact. He reached for his coffee. Act casual. Libby can do what she likes, with whomever she likes. Even Drew Barwick. Though why she should want to. . . .

"I'll take my chances," Drew said. "If you care to give me your phone number."

"I'm staying with Charles," Libby said.

"I see." Drew turned to Charles with an unmistakable smirk. "Live-in companion is a new one."

"No, you don't see," snapped Charles. "Libby is companion to my great aunt Gloria."

"I didn't know you lived with your great aunt, Charles."

"She lives with me." Charles emphasized the word order so Drew got the point. "But she needs someone with her during the day. Hence Libby."

Libby unwrapped her dessert fork with studied care. If only this obnoxious man would leave them alone. What a pain. He was almost drooling over her. And those shorts were too short and way too tight. Showing off those bulging thighs like some steroid-ridden bodybuilder. He looked as though someone had attacked him with a bike pump. His eyes gave her the creeps too, pale blue and intense. Serial killer eyes.

How rude was he, asking her out when she was enjoying herself with someone else? He was supposedly a friend of Charles'—a colleague, at least. Wouldn't have too many friends if that's the way he treated them.

Charles didn't like him either, she could tell. His face and voice went all stiff and he became ultra polite. Surely he didn't think she was interested in a creep like Drew?

"This cake looks yummy," she said directly to Charles.

"It will be," he said. "Which are you having first?"

"Mud cake, please. Let's cut it in half."

Charles shuffled the plates about. Libby bisected the mud cake roughly with her fork while he did the same with the Black Forest. Thick chocolate icing and whipped cream globbed in all directions as the transfer from plate to plate was attempted. Libby giggled and licked her fingers.

Drew was still standing there leaning on the chair as if he expected to be invited to join them. He must have a hide like an elephant not to get the message.

"It was nice to see you again, Drew," said Charles. "Good luck with the business."

"Thanks, Charles." He finally released his grip on the chair. All indications were promising he was about to move on. "Goodbye, Libby. I'll call. Soon."

"Nice to meet you, Drew," she replied as sweetly as she could with such a threat looming in the near future.

When he'd left, neither said a word. Libby forked up several delicious mouthfuls of cake allowing each one to linger, overflowing the taste buds with sinfully rich sweetness. She sighed with pleasure and was surprised from her reverie by a laugh from Charles.

"You look absolutely blissed out," he said.

"I am." Libby ran her tongue around her lips collecting the stray cream and chocolate crumbs.

"So. Am I right? Better than Hilda?"

"Very close," Libby admitted.

"Come on, be fair," Charles cried. "That was eight years ago. You know memory plays tricks."

"True." Libby smiled. He seemed so intent on making his point, taking this whole cake thing very seriously. "All right. Equal. That's as far as I'll go in deference to Hilda's skill."

With a satisfied smile, Charles picked up his fork and ate some more cake. He swallowed. "Will you go out with Drew?"

Libby hesitated before replying. Charles was studiously scraping crumbs and cream off his plate. Not looking at her.

"He might not call," she said.

"He will. Will you?" He stared directly at her for a moment then his eyes shied away. "Sorry. None of my business who you go out with."

"No," she said. "I won't go out with him. I didn't like him at all."

"No?" The relief in his face and voice was so plain Libby longed to reach out her hand and stroke his cheek.

Tell him she wanted to be with him and him alone. That men like Drew had annoyed her all her life, and she'd turned every one of them down.

But she didn't because this was an outing between friends, and Charles had made his position very clear. She'd be crazy to upset the balance they'd achieved.

Had he recognized his mother's voice in the background? He'd given no sign. Perhaps Drew had distracted him, in which case he hadn't been a complete waste of space after all.

Libby went with Charles to collect Gloria on Sunday afternoon. The jolly Floriade travelers stepped carefully down from the bus and milled about in a chattering, grayhaired flock. Oscar helped Gloria descend. Surrounded by the others in the group, Gloria gazed about, spotted the welcoming committee and waved vigorously. Charles hurried forward.

Oscar kissed Gloria's cheek but eager relatives surged in between and by the time Libby and Charles reached them, Oscar had disappeared.

"I'm so looking forward to a lovely hot cup of tea," Gloria said as she returned hugs and kisses enthusiastically. "Then we have something to discuss."

Charles caught Libby's eye over the top of Gloria's smooth gray hair. He raised his eyebrows fractionally. Libby shook her head and mouthed, "No idea."

He scooped up Gloria's suitcase from the baggage being unloaded from the underbelly of the bus.

"The car's just around the corner, Glory."

"We'll be home in no time. I baked muffins," said Libby proudly.

"Ooh, clever girl." Gloria squeezed Libby's arm.

Charles strode ahead. Libby and Gloria followed more slowly. They rounded the corner to the parking area. Oscar was marching further down the street dragging his own bag on wheels. Odd that Glory hadn't asked Charles to give him a lift home although his complex was only a matter of two blocks walk from the Community Center. Odd he hadn't stayed to ensure Glory was safely in Charles's care, given his fussing at departure time.

Had they grated on each other in such forced proximity? But Libby had spotted him kissing Gloria goodbye. Strange. Was Oscar the topic of the forthcoming discussion? Very possibly.

"How's Oscar?" Libby asked.

"He's popping in later so you can ask him yourself," said Gloria. Her cheeks had turned pink.

"Popping in at home?"

"Yes. Now how did you and Charles get on while I was away?" Gloria glanced up at Libby with her Miss Marple expression.

"Fine. Very well. We went to Glebe and ate chocolate cake yesterday. Then, because we took so long over afternoon tea, it got late and we went to a place called The Vanguard for dinner and listened to a jazz group." Libby paused for breath. She saw the amusement on Gloria's face. "What did you expect? That we'd murder each other?"

"No, quite the opposite," said Gloria and laughed. She hugged Libby's arm and patted it with her free hand.

Libby said with forced casualness, "Gloria, Charles has a girlfriend, remember?" Gloria sniffed but said nothing. Libby was compelled to add, "Though . . . as a matter of fact . . . that blew up the other day . . ." She stopped, pulling the sides of her mouth down in a guilty grimace. "I shouldn't gossip. Charles ought to tell you himself."

But Gloria's delighted reaction encouraged her. "What's-her-name's really gone?"

Libby glanced ahead at Charles who was stowing Gloria's suitcase in the boot of the car—out of earshot but she lowered her voice none the less. "Tiffany, yes. I felt sorry for her. She seemed nice and she's very pretty. I don't think Charles did a very tactful job of breaking up, not that I heard what was said . . . but she called him a cane toad, apparently."

"Oh, dear. Did he tell you that?"

"Yes."

"Mmm." Gloria nodded, smiled to herself and gave a general impression of being well-satisfied.

"Come on, you two," called Charles, so Libby, unfortunately, was unable to extract any more interesting comments.

Libby answered the door to Oscar after dinner. His balding pate reflected the porch light and wisps of white-gray hair stuck out at erratic angles. He'd donned a cricket club tie, navy-blue sports jacket and smelled of Old Spice the way her grandfather used to.

"Hello, Oscar." Libby stepped forward for a kiss on the cheek. "Come in. Did you have a good trip? You darted off so quickly earlier I didn't get a chance to ask."

"Yes, I know. Wanted to get home and spruce up a bit, you know?" His pale gray eyes regarded her anxiously. "Before coming round?"

Libby nodded although she didn't know at all. Oscar stood on the doormat as though some magic barrier prevented him from entering. Libby grabbed his hand and pulled.

"Come in, Oscar. Come and meet Charles. I'm so glad you've finally paid us a visit."

Oscar stepped inside but as Libby closed the door, he said softly, "To tell you the truth, Libby. I'm a bit nervous, you know?"

"I can't imagine why," said Libby with an astonished laugh. "Charles won't bite. If he does, bite him back."

Oscar chuckled, squared his shoulders. "Lead on, McDuff," he said in a much more familiar voice.

"It's McNeill, actually," replied Libby dryly, making Oscar laugh even more, as she'd hoped.

Charles and Gloria were sitting in the living room discussing the design of Canberra's National Museum.

"It's got a great big red handle thing over the top like a basket," Gloria was saying.

Charles rose, puzzled, as Libby entered with the visitor. Glory's friend. No one had mentioned he was coming. Libby was smiling from ear to ear. Glory leapt up faster than he'd ever seen her move. These two females were in cahoots again already and Glory had only been home a matter of hours.

The fellow strode forward with great confidence, booming, "Charles, how very pleased I am to finally meet you. Oscar Babic."

He shook Charles's hand vigorously, gave Gloria a peck on the cheek, and slung his arm around her.

"How do you do?" murmured Charles.

"Would you like a drink, Oscar?" asked Gloria appearing, to Charles' surprise, extremely comfortable with this intimate gesture.

"No, thank you, my dear. By the look on young Charles's face you haven't told him a thing."

"She hasn't," said Charles. "And I'm very intrigued as to what it could be." Not to mention extremely suspicious.

His eyes moved from Oscar to Glory, taking in the solidarity of their stance. United against a foe, real or imaginary. Himself? Why did he feel under siege before anyone had uttered a word? And Libby wasn't helping, standing there grinning. She must have known Oscar was on his way here tonight. She could at least have warned him.

"Sit down, Oscar, please," Charles said.

Oscar remained standing with Gloria beside him.

Libby stepped forward. "I think, perhaps, I should leave. This is obviously family business—excuse me."

"No," cried Charles at the same time Glory said, "Please stay, Libby."

Libby sat down on the nearest chair, which placed her next to Glory. Charles wished she'd aligned herself closer to him. This way they were all facing him waiting for his reaction to whatever it was they were going to spring on him.

Oscar said, “Gloria and I have known each other now for several months—ever since she moved to Sydney to live with you. We met at the Seniors’ Club and believe me, it was a golden day for me when she walked into the room. The place came alive.”

Charles stood unmoving, his gaze swung from Oscar to Gloria to Libby and back to Oscar. The smile hadn’t left Libby’s face since she’d answered the door. Charles could feel his own features assuming a look of disbelief as Oscar’s meaning began to emerge through the fog of his incomprehension.

“We’ve become very close over the last months. I can tell by your face you think we oldies can’t feel things the same way as you youngsters, but you’re wrong. We’re both experienced adults. We know what we like and don’t like and we’re too old to put up with any rubbish from anyone telling us what we should or should not do. So with that in mind, and the fact that neither of us has a great deal of time left, we’ve decided to join forces and end our days together. We’re getting married.”

Chapter Nine

Charles couldn't think of a word to say. Not one single word. He looked at Libby but she was no help, she was beaming at Glory with a soppy look on her face, and as his mind groped to make sense of what Oscar had just told him, Libby launched herself off her chair with a cry of delight.

"Congratulations! How wonderful."

She hugged Glory and kissed Oscar on the cheek. They all turned toward him expectantly. A slew of conflicting emotions whirled through his head as he gazed at Glory's worried face. Shock was winning at the moment, but beneath that came a flicker of relief, and after that disbelief, and then the realization she would be leaving to live with another man. And what about Uncle Henry?

"Be pleased for me, Charles," she said and he didn't have the heart to say what he really felt: that she was leaping into something without thinking it through, that she was too old to be in love, that she should remember the husband she'd adored for over fifty years.

"I know what you're thinking," said Oscar gently. "But I love Gloria and I'll take care of her. We'll be very comfortable together."

"His unit is specially designed for seniors, Charles. No stairs, big light switches, easy door handles, safety bathroom. I'll be much happier there."

"I didn't know you weren't happy here," he said, aware of how miserably self-pitying and childish that sounded.

"You know what I mean," said Glory. "It was dear of you to take me in but I was in your way. I know I'm getting forgetful and silly."

Charles stepped forward and wrapped his arms around her, her small body fragile in his arms. She was old, he knew that. Her fingers were arthritic, she tired easily, her memory failed her more and more. The day might come when she would need constant care. But to him she was Great Aunt Glory, his savior and the only rock in his life to which he could cling.

"You'd never be in my way," he said hoarsely. "How could you be in my way? But whatever you want. As long as you're happy."

"Thank you, my dearest Charles," she whispered.

"Celebration time," cried Libby. "Pity we don't have any bubbly."

She bounced up and down clapping her hands with what to Charles sounded like overwhelming relief. Had she expected fireworks from him followed by "Leave this house and don't ever darken my doorway again"?

"We do. Sparkling grape in deference to my elderly

liver," said Oscar. "I left it on the front step in case things didn't go too well."

"I'll get it."

Libby sprinted for the front door. The looks on Gloria and Oscar's faces were indescribable. That they loved each other was plain as could be. She flung the door open and spied Oscar's brown paper-bagged bottle nestled against the house wall out of the sight of any casual observer opening the front door. Tears popped into her eyes at the thought of him placing it there hoping against hope that his interview with the prospective bride's family went well. At seventy-nine.

Charles had assembled four champagne flutes by the time she returned. He expertly popped the cork on Oscar's bottle without losing a drop. Gloria handed Libby her glass, the pale gold liquid frothing with rich white bubbles.

"To my dear great aunt Gloria," said Charles raising his glass. "And to Oscar. May you have long and happy lives together."

"Here, here," said Libby. "Gloria and Oscar."

"Thank you," murmured Gloria. Delicate crystal tinkled as the four glasses touched.

"When will you marry?" asked Libby.

"As soon as possible," said Oscar. "Not much point waiting about at our age."

"Oscar wants me to move in straight away," said Gloria. "But I'd rather wait."

"You could stay with Esme while we arrange things. Much easier having you close by. Much more fun too." Oscar squeezed Gloria's hand and said to Charles,

"Esme lives next door. Her husband died recently so she's a bit down. Gloria would cheer her up no end."

"Sounds like a good idea," said Libby.

Oscar took Charles, who had been remarkably quiet since his toast, aside and began an earnest discussion, which Libby gathered revolved around finances how Charles needn't worry about Gloria's standard of living, and how her own money would remain hers.

"Libby, I'm terribly sorry to have sprung this on you," said Gloria quietly. "I'll give you the proper severance pay, of course, and I'm sure Charles won't insist that you leave immediately."

"Oh!" Libby nearly choked.

Reality stuck its ugly nose in amongst the froth and bubbles. Of course she would have to leave. She couldn't possibly stay here alone with Charles. She wasn't part of this little family group no matter how much she felt she was and no matter how warmly they welcomed her into their lives. She must keep reminding herself she'd only met them recently.

"Don't worry about me at all," she said.

"I'll ask Oscar about his friend, the one who wants a companion. I think he lives in Double Bay."

"Goodness, very upper class. Much more my style." Libby raised a grin that apparently fooled Gloria because Gloria smiled and glanced across at the two men still deep in discussion.

"How do you think Charles took the news?"

"Surprised—but he shouldn't have been completely because I told him I thought there was something going on with you two."

"Oscar's a special man."

"You're very lucky, Gloria, finding someone to love you and vice versa. Twice."

"You will too. Maybe not twice but once can be enough for a lifetime. It would have been for me if Henry had lived."

"I haven't really looked for anyone. I always loved my cello more than any man I met."

"Maybe now's the time to change your approach," said Gloria. "That cello won't keep you warm at night."

Gloria's words chased each other around in Libby's head that night as she lay in bed. For the first time in her life her cello was in the background. Was that why she thought she might have fallen so hard for Charles? Because her main love had been forcibly removed and he was the first man to come along? Was she like a duckling that attaches itself to the first object it lays eyes on after hatching?

He certainly wouldn't have been her first choice if she'd thought about who she would fall in love with. As a dreamy teenager she and her girlfriends had speculated, the way girls do. Libby had always specified an artistic nature, preferably a musician, but any of the arts would suffice and where her friends had insisted upon money she honestly hadn't thought it important. Enough to live on was plenty. She and her perfect man would eke out a living together. Somewhat along the lines of Mimi and Rodolfo in La Bohème. Without one of them dying of consumption.

If she'd had such daydreams as an adult, she still

wouldn't have chosen Charles. Charles hated musicians and was annoyed by her teariness and despair and emotional outbursts. She would have chosen a fellow musician who understood her passion and strove, as she did, for perfection in her art. Someone she could discuss her professional problems with and who she would support in turn.

Did anyone choose who they loved?

What did she know about love? Did she even know what love was? Libby turned over restlessly. She knew desire. She knew she craved the touch of his hands and the kiss of his lips. She knew she wanted to be with him. Was that love? She thumped her pillow and turned over again.

How did people recognize love when it came? Did it creep up behind you and yell "surprise"? Did it sing? Did it cry? Did it laugh? She hadn't a clue.

She was tired, she was sleepless, she was confused, she was raving.

Charles desired her body. Most men did. Like Drew with those creepy eyes. He'd be all over her in two seconds flat if she gave him the slightest encouragement. The way she had with Charles. She'd given him enormous hints and he'd understood. But Charles had stubbornly suggested they remain friends.

Gloria was leaving. The problem of an affair under her nose and the ensuing complications went with her. But it still left the problem of compatibility.

Plus there was the renewed problem of homelessness.

She hadn't had a chance to talk to Charles about staying on as a boarder. Why would he want a boarder and where would her rent money come from? If she sold the Turramurra house she could pay off the remaining mortgage and buy herself a unit with what was left. She'd have somewhere to live but no income.

Libby sat up and pushed the covers aside. Too hot. She got out of bed, stumbled barefoot in the dark across the room to push the window wider. A figure was standing in the garden. A man. Charles. He turned at the scraping sound and looked up, his face pale in the moonlight. Libby stared down. Her heart thudded hard in her chest. Romeo, Romeo, wherefore art thou, Romeo?

He didn't move.

No balcony. No ivy to climb up. No urgent desire provoking him to climb up.

Libby retreated slowly and sat on the bed for a moment. She stood up, put on her long, red-and-white cotton Japanese robe, tied the belt securely around her waist and thus demurely attired went barefoot out the door and down the stairs. He'd left one table lamp on. The soft yellow light spilled across the paved area but didn't reach the grass. Was Charles still there?

Yes. Libby stepped softly across the lawn to stand beside the still figure. The night air, fresh and cool, bathed her hot skin. A million stars twinkled above. She breathed deeply tilting her face to the sky. The moon shone strongly above the house casting silver dust over the shrubs and trees. Perfume from Gloria's flowers clung to her nostrils. Charles stared into the darkness.

"I'll miss her," he said eventually.

"Yes. But she'll be living close by."

"Is she doing the right thing?" he asked suddenly, grasping Libby's arm, startling her.

"I think so," she said. "As far as I can tell."

He sighed, released his grip.

"Charles?" Libby asked tentatively in the ensuing silence. "Would it be all right if I stay on for a while? Until I find somewhere else to go?'

"Stay?" His voice made her jump, the word came so loudly in the quiet of the night.

"Yes, please. I'll start looking for another place tomorrow. Oscar has a friend who's thinking of taking on a companion so I might be lucky."

"You want to move out?" he barked.

"No, I don't want to move out, but I can't stay permanently after Gloria moves, can I?" He was silent. The moonlight etched shadows under his eyes rendering them dark and mysterious. His mouth was a darker slash. A straight, tight line.

"You can go back to how it was before you invited Gloria to stay," she said. "Except . . ."

"Except what?"

Libby was going to say, "except without Tiffany" but she amended it to, "You won't have to worry about Gloria at all because she'll be living happily with Oscar."

Charles stuck his hands firmly in his pockets. If he didn't they'd reach out all by themselves and pull Libby against his body. Seek to draw comfort and succor from her.

Go back to how it was before Gloria? He'd thought, occasionally, after a few weeks of Glory that's what he wanted—his independence again. But now he'd glimpsed another sort of life. Mainly since Libby moved in and mostly in the last week. Living alone with Libby. It was fraught with a wonderful and exhilarating kind of danger, but it also felt wonderfully right.

"Why can't you stay here with me?" he asked.

Libby's head whipped around. She'd been stargazing but that stopped her abruptly. "Because I haven't got a job and I can't pay rent." Her eyes bored into his belying the matter of factness of her tone.

"Is that the only reason?"

"What other reason would there be?"

"I don't know. *I* don't see another reason."

"But . . ." She frowned, confused.

"Stay here with me, Libby," he said softly.

"What exactly does that mean?" she whispered.

"I want you to stay here with me."

"Why?"

"We got on well together last week. I think we'd make good housemates."

"Oh." She turned away. "Maybe we would. Until I start practicing again."

"But you can't play, can you?" Too quickly. The words came too spontaneously.

"Would it bother you if I could or is the only reason you're making this offer because you think I won't ever play again?"

"You think yourself you won't play again," he cried. "What I think is irrelevant. You certainly take no notice of my opinion."

"Why should I?"

"No reason. No reason at all."

Libby looked up at the moon again. Nearly full, just needed a little filling out around the top edge. What was he asking her? Stay with me? Was that a "live with me?" Did he even know himself?

"Why do you want a housemate?"

"You need a place to live. You're already here. It's working well."

"No. Why do *you* want a housemate?'

"I thought you'd be pleased," he cried. "Fine. Don't stay if it's that much of an issue."

"I don't think I can, Charles. Not unless we're clear about why I'm staying."

"Aren't we? I thought we were."

"And what sort of arrangement it really is," Libby added. Nothing was clear in her mind. Nothing at all.

"Housemates. Friends sharing," he said defensively. "What else?"

"Indeed."

"Are you suggesting I might try to seduce you? That's exactly what Bruce hinted at." And she'd heard Charles' response to Bruce.

"No need to make it sound such an unpleasant prospect. The way you kissed me implied you might like to. I don't want to live with you on those terms, Charles."

"And I don't either. I don't want to just live with a woman. When I choose a partner I'll marry her."

"If I'm sharing the house, won't that cramp your style? And mine, when it comes to dating? Tiffany didn't like it much." She paused and added, knowing it was malicious, "Drew didn't seem to mind, though."

Charles stared at her. He didn't want to date other women. He wanted Libby. She wanted him to make some sort of acknowledgement of a change in their relationship, but he couldn't bring himself to make that big commitment. Neither of them was ready. They each would expect completely different things.

He couldn't tell her he wanted her waiting for him each evening like a loving housewife, and he'd be glad never to see that cello in her hands again. It wasn't her. That existence would destroy her. He couldn't do that to her. He couldn't marry her even if he was brave enough to ask.

She didn't love him the way he loved her. She'd made that very clear just now by talking about dating. Other men. Drew.

What was the problem with her staying on? They'd been happy this past week. Why couldn't they continue on the same way?

Charles said, "Don't worry, Libby, we'd never succeed in a marriage, so there's no point even pretending we would. You're not the sort of girl I want on a long-term basis."

Where had that come from? Sometimes words leapt out in patterns and meanings he had no control over. Like a kind of Tourette's Syndrome where what came out wasn't obscenity as such, but instead was stiff and cold and ultimately cruel.

"But short term would be okay?" Libby said scathingly. She turned away and muttered, "And I thought I was falling for you. What an idiot."

The words exploded like skyrockets in his head,

blasted him from his emotional bunker. She was falling for him? When all the time he'd thought his love was one sided and her kiss was experimental. When she'd just told him she didn't want to live with him as a lover. She had, hadn't she? And he'd just insulted her with his cold fish impersonation, spat poison like a cane toad.

He stepped close behind her, gently turned her to face him. Moonlight glinted in her eyes and on her hair.

"I fell for you the first time I saw you," Charles blurted. Libby gasped. Her hands flew to her cheeks in shock. Her eyes glistened and she blinked rapidly. A single tear escaped, melting his heart. "Love at first sight," he whispered.

He gently pried her fingers away from her face, and holding them captive, bent forward and brushed his lips carefully against hers.

Libby closed her eyes as a shudder rippled through her body.

Now she knew. Love creeps up in the warm dark of a spring night.

"Have you changed your mind?" he asked softly, and kissed her again before she could reply. This kiss was tender and soft and gentle and warm and loving and strong and Romeo and moonlight and starshine and the perfume of flowers on cool night air and breath halting and kneebuckling and heartstopping. She sagged against him so he had to release her hands to hold her up. He laughed softly into her mouth, and she sighed and straightened up.

"No," she murmured. "I think I need to find another place to live."

"But I want you to stay," he murmured. His hands ran over her hair and down her cheeks to cup her face.

"So I can love you and cook dinner for you each night?" Libby whispered. She kissed him gently on the mouth. "I'm not going to live with you and be a Susie homemaker. I can't. I have to find something I can do myself. If all I'm fit for is companion to the elderly so be it, but I won't be a housewife."

"Is that the only alternative you see?" He put her away from him softly but firmly. "That's so typical of you. You go from one extreme to the other. What on earth makes you think I want you to sit at home and play housewife? I didn't say that."

He took three determined strides away from her then stopped and flung his arms wide in a frustrated gesture of resignation.

Libby called after him, her voice strident in the still night, "You didn't say it, but I think that's what you really want, Charles. You might love me, but you want a woman who'll stay home and keep your house clean and tidy, have dinner ready when you come home, raise your children, and have no opinions and no passions except you. I don't know if that woman exists, but I know I can't be that woman and I can't help it if your mother wasn't that woman either."

Charles spun around but Libby charged on. "Your mother has a wonderful talent and a brilliant career. She gives joy and pleasure to millions of people. So does your father. You can't re-create your childhood, Charles. It's happened. Deal with it!"

"Just what do you know about my parents?" he shouted. "My childhood! What do you know?"

Libby quailed in the face of his rage, but it was now or never. Seize the moment.

"I know what Gloria told me," she said quietly. "And before you go and abuse Gloria, what's the big deal? So I know you had a tough childhood. So what? It sounded terrible but don't blame me for what happened to you. Your parents are two people who by the sound of it should never have had a child. That can happen in any profession. Plenty of people offload their kids on to childcare of one sort or another."

"But they love their children," hissed Charles. "Do you know what it's like to grow up knowing you're not loved, not even wanted? If it hadn't been for Glory and Henry I don't know what I would've become."

"I'm sorry, Charles I don't know what that was like. I can't imagine it but just because I'm a musician doesn't make me some kind of selfish, egotistical monster who eats children for breakfast."

"No, I know, but I don't think I could handle it, Libby. I think I love you. I'm *sure* I love you, but I can't take on life with a professional musician. I'm sorry. I want a wife who puts me ahead of the other things in her life. And I don't want my children to suffer that either. I don't want to play second fiddle to a cello."

He didn't even smile at the grim word "play." Libby was beyond laughing at anything, and the elation provided by the admission that he loved her fizzled miserably the more he spoke. What sort of almost love was that? Cane toad love?

"Well," she said harshly. "Who's talking about wives? Who's talking about taking on life with anyone? Hadn't we already decided neither of us wants that type of commitment? I'm not after a husband, I don't know what gave you that idea, but if I was I'd want one who loved music with as much passion as I do, not one who resented and detested my vocation."

Libby stalked to the pool of yellow light spilling out through the sliding door, marched across the living room, climbed the stairs, and entered her bedroom all on remote control.

And that's how love parts on a warm spring night.

Charles didn't see Libby alone for the rest of the week. She and Glory fussed about organizing the packing and transfer of Glory's things to Oscar's unit. He went to work early.

Dinner was eaten amidst either polite chat or intense discussion of weddings. He smiled and nodded and agreed with what they said, but it all floated by. Even the Saturday he drove Glory to the retirement home for the last time, hardly registered.

"Charles," said Glory as she hugged him. "Cheer up. You can get on with your life now and stop worrying about me."

Charles kissed her. "It's not you, Glory. I'm really happy for you both. Really I am," he insisted as he saw her skeptical frown. He cast about for another valid reason for his glumness, one she would swallow without awkward questions and embarrassing revelations on his part. "We've problems at work—going over budget."

Oscar clapped him on the shoulder. "There's never enough money. Clients expect the best of everything, but they won't pay for it. Don't know what they want the poor devils at the coal face to do."

"That's right," agreed Charles. "Absolutely."

Glory beamed. Oscar glanced down at her. "At least you won't have to worry about this little lady here." Glory tucked her arm in his.

"I know," said Charles. His throat tightened. For the first time he saw what Libby had seen immediately. These two loved each other. Lucky Glory. She deserved every moment of her happiness. Stupendously lucky Oscar.

He waved an arm out the window as he drove away. Glory was right. As usual. She would be better off living there. The facility had a tennis court, swimming pool, recreation room, activities for the able-bodied, and a nursing home–style wing for residents no longer capable of caring for themselves.

Glory would get on with her life but could he get on with his?

How did people manage this falling in love business? Glory and Oscar had sailed right into their love without the slightest wave or rock spoiling the cruise. They made it seem easy and it wasn't. It was impossibly hard.

He'd thought he was being honest with Libby when he told her how he felt. He thought she'd appreciate and understand his honesty but she was scathing. Plus he'd made a dreadful mistake thinking she returned his love.

But what else was he supposed to think? "Thought I was falling for you," she'd said, and he'd leapt eagerly to the conclusion that she had completed the fall, but he was wrong. Totally and utterly wrong. And he didn't know why.

The answer appeared to be that he was completely wrong for her. It was pointless to even think about what might have been, given the chance. She wasn't prepared to stay and see.

Libby sat reading the paper at the table when he arrived home. She had a pencil in her hand.

"Find anything?" he asked casually. He took his jacket off and threw it onto a chair. She seemed determined to move out, and he didn't know what to say to stop her. She didn't have to go, they could live harmoniously enough together, couldn't they? Platonically live separate lives? He sat down across the table and read upside down. Accommodation Vacant. She'd ringed various advertisements.

"No," she said. "I'll have to sell my house and buy a flat."

Charles covered his astonishment. A house? "Where's the house?"

"Turramurra."

He couldn't conceal the surprise at that. "Whew! Worth a tidy sum."

"There's money owing on it that's why I need a job," she said tersely. "At the moment it's paying itself off, but if I sell it I think I could afford a reasonable flat somewhere like Drummoyne."

Charles nodded appreciatively. "Nice."

"At least I'd have a place to live."

"Libby, you have a place to live. Here."

"We've already discussed that." Libby stood up.

"Why won't you accept help from me?"

Libby paused. She sucked in her bottom lip, considering. "Because," she said eventually, "it would make me dependent on you and I've never been dependent on anyone. I don't like to sponge off people."

"Staying here for a few weeks while you get sorted out isn't sponging," he cried.

"I'm already going to stay a few weeks. I'm not leaving this minute, Charles. I'm talking indefinite staying with no reason other than I have nowhere else to go. It wouldn't be helpful to either of us."

"Okay, okay." He pulled the paper around and began reading idly while Libby went out into the garden. She'd circled and crossed out various rooms for rent in share houses and bedsits. Miserable sounding places in outer suburbs where she would subside gradually into a dried up husk of her former joyous self.

He turned the pages. More circled advertisements, this time in Positions Vacant. One in particular had a heavy ring around it. Movement from outside caught his eye. She was practicing tai chi with intense concentration on her face as she moved slowly through the sequence. Anything she undertook she did to her utmost. She was going to work at those movements until they flowed perfectly. It was the same attitude she had to her cello. He'd heard it through his ceiling eight years ago. Would he ever hear it again, that beautiful, rich tone conveying her passion and love for music? Inseparable from her.

Charles went to the CD shelf. He ran his finger along the spines searching for the one he wanted, found it, and slipped the disc into the player.

Elgar. The cello burst into the room growling and snarling, demanding attention.

Libby froze. She glared at the window. He wasn't sure she could see in from outside with the bright sunlight reflections on the glass, but she charged toward him and flung the door open.

"Turn it off," she yelled. "Turn it off."

Charles cut across as she headed for the CD player. He stood in front of her and grabbed her upper arms.

"Why don't you do something about it, Libby? Have you been to that acupuncturist?" he shouted into her startled, angry face.

"No, I haven't. You know I haven't." She wrenched herself free.

"Why not?"

The cello soared around them, passionate and throbbing.

"It'd be no use and I hate needles."

"Is that all? Is that the best you can come up with? I hate needles?" he barked derisively. "Why don't you go? You never know, it might help."

The phone started ringing. Charles ignored it. So did Libby.

"Nothing will help, Charles, don't you understand? Anyway, I thought you'd be pleased. One less self-obsessed musician, isn't that what you want?"

Violins and woodwind plunged in to support the

cello as it plummeted to the depths. The answering machine mercifully silenced the phone.

"You're being just as self-obsessed now except it's twice as unhealthy."

"I'm being realistic."

"Then why have you circled this ad?"

Charles grabbed the paper and pointed to the heavily outlined advertisement. "If you can't play ever again, what's the point of applying for this?'

Libby gazed back at him, white-faced. Elgar thundered around the living room. Charles placed the paper precisely on the table. The words in bold black stared up at him. Lecturer in Cello, Sydney Conservatorium of Music.

"I think you should apply," he said quietly.

"Really?" It came as a whisper as the cello quivered and cried in the background.

"Yes."

"I've never taught."

"But you've learnt and worked and practiced and you've been taught by the best teachers."

"They'd want me to play." She sat down heavily.

"They'd know you can play, you've got a résumé as long as my arm. You're a graduate of theirs, aren't you?"

"Yes." She gazed up at him with a flicker of hope in her eyes. "Do you really think I should?"

"Yes. They'd be crazy not to snap you up."

"I could teach without doing much playing and my arm would gradually get better. They might understand."

"Apply," he said and walked out of the room as the cello strove for the heights.

She'd get the position, he was positive. She'd sell her house and buy an apartment. She'd slip into the life of a professional musician with ease, she'd renew old acquaintances, she'd begin to play and perform, she'd meet new people—men with the same passions she had. She'd fall in love, for real, with a colleague. She'd forget him and he'd slip easily out of her life the way he had in Vienna. Just a shadow, which materialized briefly then faded away.

But she'd be happy and whole and that, strangely enough, made his heart glad.

Libby sat, listening. Rapt. She knew every note of the music swirling over her. A wonderful concerto. Marvelous. Her eyes strayed to the light flashing on the answering machine, but she waited until the cello and orchestra had come to rest before rising with a sigh to press the PLAY MESSAGE button.

"Hey there. Message for the lovely Libby from Drew Barwick. Interested in meeting sometime? Give me a call. Mobile 0434 . . ."

Libby stabbed her finger on ERASE before he'd finished.

First thing Monday morning Libby made an appointment to see the acupuncturist on Wednesday. Then she rang the number in the advertisement for the lecturer in cello and was told she could either collect the application forms herself, download from the internet, or they'd be posted out. She set off for the station immediately once she'd locked up the house.

The Sydney Conservatorium of Music had undergone renovations and extensions since her day but the distinctive white, castle-like facade remained in its magnificent inner city, waterfront position. Libby approached the building through the Botanic Gardens, enjoying the spacious green lawns and the spectacular views of Sydney Harbour as she strolled under the massive Moreton Bay figs lining the path. She'd walked here as a student, carefree and happy, the future stretching golden before her.

Standing in the foyer waiting for someone to finish asking the receptionist about a recital, Libby gazed around. A group of scruffily attired young men carrying brass instruments wandered past, laughing. An intense-looking girl strode by with a violin case and a folder of music. A soprano sang somewhere in the distance. All so familiar.

A dumpy, gray-haired woman came through the main door, glanced at her, stopped to peer more closely. "Libby McNeill?"

Libby smiled. Harmony and orchestration classes. Write an invention in the style of Bach, arrange this piano piece for string quartet.

"Hello, Jocelyn."

"What are you doing here? Last I heard you were in Germany."

"I was, three years ago. Then I went to Rotterdam. Now I'm here. Been back about a month."

"Playing?'

Libby shook her head. "RSI."

Jocelyn sighed with a sympathetic grimace. "Shame. Becoming more and more common. We should be training our students how to care for their bodies so this sort of thing doesn't happen. Have you seen anyone? There's a very good doctor. I'll give you his name." Jocelyn rummaged about in a copious handbag, produced a card, and gave it to Libby. "Remember Frank Jones? Viola? He had the same thing, but this chap fixed him. He has to be careful but still . . ."

Libby took the card. "Thanks. I'm seeing an acupuncturist on Wednesday."

"Good idea. Try everything you can. You don't want to give up, Libby, don't let the black dog of depression take over. You're too young and far too talented for that." She placed her hand on Libby's arm. "You know the cello position is vacant?"

Libby nodded. "That's why I'm here."

Jocelyn leaned in. "Tom Hanson had to leave. Became a little too touchy feely with his female students." She straightened. "I have to keep moving. Lovely to see you. Good luck with the application."

Libby studied the form on her way home on the train. Applications closed very soon. She needed references. Not difficult. A few people in Europe would fax something. Charles had a fax machine in his study, next to her bedroom.

Teaching experience. She'd tutored at a German summer school for musically gifted children. That was it.

They'd sift through and invite possibles in for an interview in early November. The teaching year started next February, late in February. If she kept scrupulously away from her cello, had acupuncture, saw Jocelyn's expert, surely there'd be some improvement by then? Nearly five months away.

Libby stared out the window as the train rattled across the Harbour Bridge. She could teach. She could nurse her arm and only play with students in their lessons. There was a glimmer of light at the end of the tunnel. Don't get depressed, Jocelyn had said.

She had been depressed, terribly depressed, she could see that now. Suddenly cast off and alone in a hitherto secure world turned uncaring and unfamiliar. That's why she'd fled for home—Australia—forgetting, or not realizing, the extent to which that home had changed in her absence.

But she wasn't alone. Betty and Bob, Gloria with Oscar in tow, and of course, Charles, all offered support.

Even if she didn't get this position there'd be others, and sometime next year she could freelance if Jocelyn's miracle man did his thing, and her arm was up to it.

As soon as she got home she'd ring the estate agent who was letting her house and ask for an appraisal. Then she could start seriously investigating apartments for sale. Then she could move out.

Her heart contracted sharply. Move out. Away from Charles. He said he loved her. She knew she loved him. He kissed her as if he meant it but when it came to a definitive statement of commitment he couldn't provide it. He didn't love her enough to ask her to stay as his wife. Simple as that. If he had, she more than likely would have seriously considered saying yes despite the barrage of words to the contrary she'd thrown at him.

Libby crossed her legs. Marriage. Here she was

contemplating marriage when the idea of marrying anyone had never entered her head except to be scoffed at and discarded as highly undesirable. She and Charles didn't know each other anywhere near well enough to be even thinking of the word let alone the concept. He was entirely correct to dismiss the notion. She could manage on her own as she always had.

The estate agent was delighted with Libby's decision to sell the Turramurra house and even more delighted with her intention of buying. He could barely contain his glee as he discussed her options. "Which area?" he asked.

"Close to the city. Ground floor." If she was able to play again she didn't want to lug a cello up stairs. "Two bedrooms." If she got the job at the Conservatorium she could practice there. Neighbors might not like cello playing. Charles hadn't, in Vienna.

He gave her a colored brochure listing properties.

"I have to sell Turramurra first," she said.

"No problem. It'll go very quickly."

When Charles opened the front door that evening a tantalizing aroma wafted down the hallway borne on the lyrical strains of Keith Jarrett's piano playing. He followed his nose to the kitchen.

"Hello. I didn't know you liked jazz," he said.

"Hi. We went to dinner at a jazz club," Libby said. "Had you forgotten?'

"Of course not. I just didn't think you'd choose to play it."

"I like most music." Libby wrinkled her nose. "Except I really can't listen to rap and that techno computer generated stuff with not a genuine musician in sight."

Charles grinned. "What's for dinner?" Judging by the mess it had many exotic ingredients.

"Curry." A worried expression replaced the smile. "My first attempt. It's got all sorts of things in it I've never heard of. I had to ring Gloria for help."

"Smells fantastic."

She stirred the curry with a fixed expression, gearing up to say something important. Charles waited, heart pounding.

"I picked up the application form for the job at the Conservatorium," she said. "Could I use your fax machine please? For references? I'll phone people tonight."

"Of course. Good." He turned away knowing she was watching him, expecting more.

"I saw the real estate agent today and he said the house will sell quickly."

"Of course it will in that area," he said. "If the price is right. Better not be too greedy."

"He's getting back to me with the valuation. Will you check it, please?'

"I haven't seen the house," he said. "His figures won't mean much to me. It'll be a reasonable quote."

"I suppose so. Yes."

He wandered in to the living room and picked up the TV remote to switch on the news. Politicians came on-screen talking about superannuation, some shots of an accident on a highway somewhere, flooding in Europe. None of it sank in. None of it was the slightest bit interesting. Libby was on her way. She may not get that job but even if she didn't she would try elsewhere. Her spirit had returned. She'd collapsed momentarily, but now she was up and fighting again. She didn't need him. What could he do but let her go? Charles wouldn't plead with a woman. Libby knew how he felt about her. If she wanted him she only needed to say so.

As if on cue she came and stood in front of him. He couldn't help it, his pulse leapt as he looked up at her. Libby, with those beautiful big blue eyes and skin that felt like silk under his fingers, that mouth crying out to be kissed. Why couldn't she love him? Did she realize he loved her enough for them both with some left over? Could he live with her once she returned to her old life?

"I ran into one of my old teachers today. She gave me the number of a specialist who helped a viola player we know."

Libby didn't smile but the tentative hope lit her eyes. Charles swallowed and cleared his throat. "Have you made an appointment yet?"

She shook her head. "I want to thank you, Charles."

"I haven't done anything."

"You gave me a kick up the bum the other day and you believe I can get this job. That's important to me."

"Is it?" He glanced up, and away again quickly.

"Yes." He thought she'd finished, but she remained standing in front of him. "I was surprised, actually. That you said I should apply."

"You need a job and it's obvious you can't do anything else."

"No." She laughed a forced sounding laugh. "No. I'm not very useful, like I said before. Anyway, thanks."

"You're welcome." He stared at the TV. A woman came on talking about the arts, and all of a sudden his mother's face filled the screen.

Libby turned in surprise as rich contralto tones flowed into the room. Her eyes flew from the screen to Charles who, blank-faced, watched his mother.

"Has she written her memoirs?"

"First I've heard of it," he growled but he listened until the report ended. "*My Voice, My Life.* That sums her up pretty neatly."

"How long since you've spoken to her?"

"Four years." The answer came back short and sharp as a pistol shot. "She had a car accident. Glory told me and I called just in case . . . you know."

"Yes, I know. Exactly," said Libby. She'd never forget that other, terrible, accident.

"She said, 'How lovely to hear from you. Thank you for ringing,' " he mimicked sarcastically. "After a bit of chitchat, the doctor arrived and she had to go. I might have been some anonymous fan—although she'd probably have spent more time talking to me if I had been."

He stood up abruptly and aimed the remote at the TV. Into the sudden silence he said, "I think your curry needs attention," and strode out to the garden.

Libby dashed to rescue her culinary masterpiece, poured in a cup of water, and stirred madly. She filled another pot with water for rice and started clearing the debris left after the preparations.

That book of his mother's would make interesting

reading. She sounded horrible and what she'd done to Charles was inexcusable. Messing up the child and then the man's life like that. Mothers had an incredible responsibility. Libby paused mid-wipe. What sort of mother would she make? Time was passing rapidly as far as baby producing went. At the rate she was going her children, if any eventuated, would have a geriatric parent.

Practicing, rehearsing, and performing while rearing children must be fiendishly hard. Something would have to give. A husband would need to be very understanding and put his own career on hold to accommodate that lifestyle. If not the child would be like Charles—farmed out to minders.

Babies had never featured in her world—like seniors. Now suddenly the two extremes of life had entered her consciousness. Had she really been so preoccupied with herself and her career? Like Irene Temple? Impossible. She'd just never put herself in the situation where she had to choose. It was all academic anyway because there hadn't been a man in her life who'd made her choose. There'd never been a man who meant more to her than her cello.

Until now.

The water in the saucepan began to boil. Libby absentmindedly added rice and stirred for a few seconds. She leaned against the bench, spoon still in hand.

Charles didn't want commitment and when—if—he ever did, she had to face the fact it wouldn't be with her. She had to shape her own future. Hadn't she told the truth about wanting a man who loved music with the same passion she did?

References. She'd call the orchestral manager in Rotterdam and her friend Lillian, in Switzerland, who was leader of a chamber orchestra. That should do. Her résumé was up to date and just needed photocopying.

Libby dropped the spoon on the bench and went upstairs to find her address book.

When Charles came back inside she was studying country codes in the phone book. He went to the kitchen for a drink of iced water.

"If I ring Rotterdam now it should be some time in the morning," she said.

"This rice has nearly boiled dry," was his reply.

Libby scrambled for the kitchen, knocking the phone book and her address book to the floor as she went.

"Don't panic," said Charles watching her scrabbling about picking up bits of paper, which had fluttered around and under the table. "I've saved it."

"Thanks." Libby plonked the book on the bench and picked up a wooden spoon to test the curry.

"Tastes pretty good!" Her eyes widened in surprise. "Here, try it."

Charles steadied the spoon she held, brushing her fingers with his. He opened his mouth. Libby watched anxiously.

He reached his verdict. "More, please."

She scooped up another sample. He took the spoon from her suddenly shaking hand and, smiling down into her eyes, offered it to her.

Libby parted her lips to accept the spicy, fragrant mouthful. He withdrew the spoon slowly then reached around her for more, placing a hand lightly on her waist.

She held her breath. He straightened and raised the spoon again to slip it into his own mouth, but his hand stayed on her waist burning the imprint of his fingers on her skin through the T-shirt.

Libby sighed and licked sauce from her lips. Charles dipped the spoon into the curry again, but this time as he held it to her lips he brought his own mouth close and tasted at the same time. His hand increased its pressure, his lips hovered close. He withdrew the spoon gently and placed it on the bench behind her so that he had to wrap his arm right around her body.

Libby smelled the tangy spice of his breath. Hers would be the same—coconut and cardamom, cinnamon, chili, cumin.

"Curry breath," he murmured.

She smiled. "Curry breath," she whispered.

"Can I taste?"

She nodded, mute, as he nibbled gently at her lips, moving across slowly savoring the touch, the sensation, the flavor, with little light kisses that made her insides melt and flow with a heat far greater than anything in the food.

Libby closed her eyes and floated. Her arms hung loosely by her sides, her whole being centered on her mouth and his lips teasing and provoking. He moved his arms to hold her closer but almost immediately pulled away.

Libby's eyes snapped open. His expression was solemn.

"Don't stop," she breathed. She lifted her hands and

caressed his face to pull his mouth to hers again but he resisted.

"I don't want to kiss you, Libby," he said in the most anguished, contorted voice she'd ever heard.

"Are you sure?" She giggled softly. "Doesn't feel that way to me."

"I mean it. I don't want to," he said harshly, but he clutched her hard to his body. Libby froze in his embrace. He gradually released his grip. "Don't you see how torturous it is? Every time I look at you I want to kiss you. I want . . ."

"But you can," Libby said in bewilderment. "I want you too." She slid her arms around his waist and held tightly, but Charles tore himself away to pace around the kitchen, coming to rest staring at her from across the bench.

"It'd be a disaster. We've no future together. I wouldn't be able to handle your career and we'd fight and I'd be devastated."

"You?! You'd be devastated? What about me, Charles? Do I get a say in this or is it all you?" cried Libby. "Why can't we try?'

"Because I'd rather not even have a taste of what I'd be missing for the rest of my life," he said quietly.

"That's ridiculous!" she yelled. "You can't shut yourself away from emotion. You can't pretend you don't feel things and then not express them in the hope they'll go away and not hurt you."

"That's how I feel," he said.

"Scared of being hurt?'

"Maybe."

"I won't hurt you, Charles," Libby said in a low voice. "I love you."

"You won't mean to but you will," he said. "Just by your very passion for what you do. I love you too much to stop you doing what you love most. It's the very essence of you and you shrivel away without it. I don't want that to happen."

"How very noble of you." Libby glared at him then turned her back to switch off the boiling rice. She dumped it into a colander and blasted hot water over it. "What if I shrivel away without you?" she said but couldn't prevent the last word breaking into a sob. She swallowed, kept her back turned to him.

"You won't. You don't need me."

"And it sounds like you don't need me, either," she said bitterly. "Pass me some plates."

Charles ate in silence. Libby sat mute at the other end of table. Had he done the right thing? He'd done the noble thing but was it the best thing? Judging by how he felt now it wasn't and by Libby's reaction earlier she felt the same. Then he remembered his mother and the way she overdramatized everything. They couldn't possibly co-exist for long without some form of major explosion. He wasn't prepared to let that happen to either of them. He had to be strong—for both their sakes.

Charles escaped for a walk after dinner. Libby rang Lillian, in Lausanne, and secured the promise of an immediate and glowing reference. Willem, in Rotterdam, was equally as obliging.

"What's happening with the orchestra?" she asked after he'd agreed to fax her reference.

Willem told her the latest gossipy news and added, "Gerald Hogarth is Guest Conductor in December. We're very fortunate. He had a cancellation in his schedule. He's in your part of the world at the moment—Japan."

"Japan? Hardly my part of the world." Libby laughed but a half-formed idea sprang into her head. "Did you know he has a son in Sydney?"

"I knew he and Irene had a child. A son?"

"Yes, estranged, unfortunately. I wonder, Willem . . ." She paused. Was this altogether too personal? Charles would be furious. "Is there any way of contacting Gerald?"

"I can give you his agent's number."

"Marvelous, thank you."

"Bryant Lloyd." He read out a phone number and an email address. "That's his personal email. Best of luck, Libby."

"Give everyone my love," she said.

When Charles returned she was innocently watching TV.

Fei Yang the acupuncturist didn't attack Libby with lethal-looking needles as soon as she set foot inside the room. Instead, with a gently inquiring smile and a soft, Chinese-accented voice, he asked Libby to sit down and explain her problem.

"I think massage first." He indicated the massage table partially concealed behind a disappointingly plain, green fabric screen. There should have been Chinese dragons or bamboo at the very least. Libby lay on her back while her arm was prodded and probed by a set of very determined fingers.

"Here?" Fei Yang asked occasionally, and Libby either yelped in pain or shook her head with relief.

"I understand," he said eventually, which was mildly encouraging because he didn't sound at all alarmed or defeated by his discoveries. "This is very bad injury but can be fixed, no problem."

"Really?"

"Rest is only proper cure."

"I know, that's what my Dutch doctor said. How long?"

"Hard to say. Sometime different every person. Depends. To day I massage. Next time maybe needles. You must rest arm completely. Okay?"

"Yes," said Libby obediently.

Fei Yang began working on Libby's shoulder. His slender fingers were like iron, but he explained when Libby winced, "Tendons are very difficult fix. No blood to heal. Must work hard to stimulate. I will not do too hard today. Tomorrow you feel more pain but different, from massage. Understand?'

"Yes," Libby gasped.

He continued to pulverize Libby's arm for another thirty minutes. As he worked he chatted happily about his family and Libby's cello, and confided he hated Classical Chinese music but loved Beethoven, Mozart, and Aretha Franklin. Libby sat up quite dazed with her arm feeling like a lump of dough.

"Tomorrow there will be bruises," said Fei Yang. "You

come back next week, we see. Injury very deep, maybe need needles."

"Can I do tai chi?" Needles!?

"Keep this arm low but otherwise tai chi is very good exercise."

Libby rang Gloria when she got home.

"Fei Yang said it will take a long time to heal but it can be fixed."

"Wonderful. See I told you," cried Gloria. "Now, I have some news. We've fixed the wedding date and guess who's coming?"

"Me," said Libby.

"Irene."

Libby almost dropped the phone. "Irene Temple?"

"Yes. I rang and told her I was getting married, and she said she was due here in November on her book promotion tour. Oscar and I set the date so she can attend. She's promised to sing."

"Gloria, how exciting. It'll be the social event of the year. You'll have paparazzi hanging from the rafters."

"Do you think so? Oh dear, I never thought of that."

"I don't think you need worry. Her fans aren't exactly the wild types who mob rock stars. Where are you having the service?"

"That's the thing . . . I'd love to have it there, at Charles's place. I want him to give me away. Do you think he'll mind?"

"He'll be honored. You'll have to ask him about using the house though, Gloria. He was upset when he saw the report on TV about Irene's memoirs. I don't know what he'll say to her being here."

"I think it's time he faced up to a few things," Gloria said sternly. "He's been running away long enough and blaming his childhood for everything he can think up."

Libby sighed. Life was simple in Gloria's eyes. In her day people didn't have psychological problems connected with their upbringing. They just needed to "get on with it and stop moping about." Nobody seemed to realize the stiff upper lip sometimes hid a morass of insecurities.

She said, "I thought about contacting Gerald Hogarth and asking him to talk to Charles. I just found out from a friend he's in Japan at the moment. They should speak to each other—it's crazy, this situation."

"Are you in love with Charles?" demanded Gloria.

"Gloria! Where on earth did that come from?"

"People only go out of their way to do something like that because they want to help a person they love. Otherwise they don't bother." She paused for a moment but Libby was incapable of saying anything. What Gloria had said was inarguably correct. "I think he loves you but he won't admit it. That boy has trouble expressing his feelings."

No use prevaricating with someone as astute as Gloria. In fact, discussing the situation with her would be a relief. She thought a love affair with Charles was a given.

"He expressed his feelings, all right," said Libby. "He admits he loves me but he says we're too different for it to work. He thinks he'll get hurt. He's assuming we'll fight and break up before we've even given it a chance. Perhaps he doesn't love me as much as he thinks he does—or as much as I love him."

"Just as I said. He's running away and it's time to stop. I've never worried about it before because the girls he dated—the ones I met—were so unsuitable. But he mustn't lose you. I think it would be a very good plan to contact Gerald, and if he could get here for my wedding all the better. Shall I do it, or you?'

"Would you? I've got a contact number. But how do Irene and Gerald get along? I don't want your wedding to turn into a Hogarth family brawl. That would really hit the headlines."

"Very well, I think. They've performed together quite often. Gerald remarried years ago. Charles has teenage half-siblings."

"Gosh! Does Charles know?"

"I don't think so. He's made a point of not knowing anything about them at all."

"It's very sad."

"Yes. But you can help him, Libby. Because you're a musician and he loves you, you're the best and only one who can. You understand both sides."

"When he discovers who had the brainwave of bringing them all together he might not be grateful, Gloria."

"But you have to try. If you really love him you have to take the risk."

"You're in this too."

"Yes, but Charles will always be my nephew and he knows I love him. Unfortunately, you have to prove it to the silly boy."

Jocelyn's expert doctor was on leave for the next month and booked up until February. Libby made an appointment just in case nothing came of Fei Yang and his "no problem." She'd know about the teaching position by then, too, having that morning dropped her application into the red mailbox on the corner, sending it off with a secret kiss for luck.

She'd know lots of things by February. She'd know whether Gloria's wedding day had become an all-in brawl, she'd know whether Charles was on speaking terms with any of them but most particularly her. She'd know how much, or how little, he loved her.

But this was now and she had to take charge of her life again. Libby rang Betty.

Charles answered the phone when Gloria called. Libby had been preoccupied and uncommunicative and excused herself to go upstairs as soon as they'd eaten. He supposed she was expecting the faxes from her European friends so she could complete her application. He didn't know how to approach her so he didn't. They seemed to have said all there was to say and would just keep batting the same words back and forth like shuttlecocks. He kept quiet and ate the stirfry she'd prepared.

A penciled name and time glared at him on the notepad next to the phone. She was meeting someone called Alan Reynolds at ten. A musician friend? Someone from the Conservatorium? Someone she could confide in and share her frustrations with, who would commiserate rather than get annoyed, who would empathize rather than antagonize? Someone else. Another man.

He hadn't been listening to Glory at all.

"Charles, are you still there?"

"Yes, sorry, what did you say?'

"Can Oscar and I get married at your house and will you give me away?" she said slowly and precisely.

"I . . . of course, I'd love to, I'd be . . . am honored," he babbled, shaking his head to clear the images of Libby with another man. Kissing another man. "When did you say?"

"Saturday, November the third. I think that's the date . . . just a moment. Yes. The third. I thought in the garden would be lovely. The azaleas and what not should still be out and the roses should be open. Thank you, darling."

Charles pulled himself together. "Glory, it's an honor, I'd be upset if you didn't want to use the house. It's your home too, if you ever need it again."

"If Oscar dumps me you mean?" She chuckled.

"If he does he's a fool."

"Oscar's no fool. We won't have many guests. Just Oscar's son . . . Peter is it? Or Phillip?"

"I don't know," said Charles. "You've never mentioned his name to me."

"Well, whoever he is, he's coming and bringing his family. They live in Newcastle. Four or five of them plus his sister Lucy who lives in Cronulla. His daughter lives in South something. Either Africa or America. And Charles?" Her tone changed. An unusual wariness, odd for Glory. He waited. "Your mother is coming."

"My mother?" A movement on the stairs caught his eye and in the shellshock of Glory's statement he spun about to see Libby watching, intense, wide-eyed. Her fingers twisted around each other.

She knew! He glared at her.

"Charles?" said Glory in his ear. "She's here promoting her book and said she'd love to come. She wants to see you."

He dragged his attention back to the now loathsome conversation. "To see me? Why?"

"I think she's realizing a few things as she gets older."

"Tough," he snarled.

"Give her a chance, Charles, please."

He drew a deep shuddery breath. It was Glory's day, he wouldn't spoil it. "For you. I'll do it for you," he said. "But as far as I'm concerned she's just another guest. A stranger."

"Thank you, darling. I'll call you about the other details. Catering and so on."

Charles put the phone down and turned with deliberate slowness to face Libby. She was still standing on the bottom stair with that look of guilty concern and dread. And well she might.

"You knew she was coming, didn't you?" Even to his own ears his voice sounded like slow-dripping poison.

Chapter Ten

Libby cleared her throat. "Gloria told me earlier."

Guilty and worried she may be, but underneath lay a steely determination made obvious by the firm set to her mouth. Libby didn't give up easily if something grabbed her imagination. Her passion flew regardless of consequences.

"And you didn't tell me?"

"It wasn't my place. It's not my business."

Libby came toward him, but Charles flung himself down into an armchair, away from the danger of her touch, face averted.

"No," he said. "That's right. Maybe you should move out after all." He risked a quick glance. The words were experimental, not really meant. But the shadow of Alan Reynolds hovered.

She came closer. "I am."

If he hadn't been sitting, he would have staggered and crumpled under this blast to the gut. What he had taken for guilt must have been reluctance to announce her decision.

"I decided today. I can't stay here, Charles. You were right. We're just torturing each other. I'll stay with Bob and Betty until I get my house sorted. There's a buyer already."

"Congratulations." All his anger fizzled away into the bottomless chasm of loss.

"Gloria invited me to her wedding," she said.

"Of course. You must come." He folded his arms. "Meet my mother," he added. "You're such a fan. Get her autograph."

"Charles . . ."

"When are you going?"

"Tomorrow. I'll take a taxi."

She stood biting her lip. Charles stared at her. She looked away, then down at the floor, then at him again. Searching for words on a misplaced cue card.

"I'll let you know where I am when I find a place."

"Fine."

"Thank you for letting me stay on after Gloria left."

"Don't worry about it."

"It was good of you."

"I'm a nice guy." He uncrossed his arms.

"Yes, you are," she said emphatically. "You are and I love you, Charles. Can't you see that?"

He swallowed and studied the backs of his hands resting on the arms of the chair.

"I love you too," he said softly. "But I don't think it's enough."

"You don't love me enough?" Her voice caught, but he didn't dare look at her face to see the tears and the anguish he knew were there.

"Oh, I love you enough. How can I not love you? I've loved you ever since I saw you one icy day in Vienna, but you'd end up hating me and maybe, just maybe, I'd hate you the way I hate my mother and I couldn't bear that to happen."

"I see."

"Libby you deserve—need—someone who can go with you in your world, who not only loves you but loves what you love. Maybe this Alan person . . ." He couldn't finish, the name was so bitter on his tongue.

"Alan? Who's Alan?"

He turned his head the bewilderment was so real. "The man you're meeting tomorrow at ten. It was on the pad by the phone."

"The real estate guy? He's about fifteen."

"Fifteen?" Charles laughed with relief resonating in his body.

"Looks it." She smiled but it wasn't her usual smile. This one was wobbly and strained. "I'm assuming he knows what he's doing and isn't there on work experience. He said the present tenants are interested in buying and there are others. I told him to take the best offer because I need to settle as soon as possible. He's showing me some units tomorrow."

Charles met her gaze. Her lovely blue eyes swam with

unshed tears. He looked away, heard her deeply indrawn breath. Soft footsteps headed towards the stairs.

"Be happy, Libby," he said quietly.

"You too, Charles."

Libby settled in with Bob and Betty and it was just as she had imagined. Not simply cast in the role of surrogate daughter, she was surrogate, invalid, Lame Duck daughter. With a broken heart. Except she didn't tell them that tidbit.

Betty wouldn't let her make so much as a piece of toast for fear she'd strain her arm, and when Bob got up in the mornings he appeared in the bedroom doorway with a mug of tea and a cheery grin, asking was she awake as he'd brought her a cuppa.

"Just like the Queen," he chortled. "Queen Elizabeth." And Libby who had smiled at that joke when he first made it fifteen years ago, stretched her lips dutifully again and pretended to be awake at six-thirty.

They almost loved her to death. After three days she rang Gloria in desperation.

"I need another job, Gloria. This sitting about doing nothing is driving me nuts. Bob and Betty are kindness itself, but they won't let me do anything. Can you ask Oscar about his friend? The rich one in Double Bay?"

"Are you sure you want to do that, Libby? What if the job at the Conservatorium comes through? You'll be committed to Karl."

"I suppose . . . I hadn't thought. I'd be letting him down, wouldn't I?"

"Wait until you hear something," suggested Gloria. "Karl is fine for the moment. He has a housekeeper and his daughter coming in regularly."

Which left Libby back where she'd started.

"I can't stay here much longer," she said to Betty, who stood at the kitchen sink peeling potatoes. Libby sat where she'd been instructed—at the table, watching. "I have to get myself settled. It'll take weeks to buy a flat and I should be earning in the interim."

"Such a shame the other thing didn't work out. It was all my fault."

"Rubbish!" Libby shook her head in astonishment. "Gloria is a fantastic woman and I've you to thank for meeting her."

"So inconsiderate taking you on then upping and marrying like that." Betty glanced down at Abraham, twining around her legs. "You don't like spuds, Abe."

Libby laughed. "She's very happy and I'm going to the wedding."

"We did think for a moment you and Charles might hit it off," said Betty. "He couldn't keep away from you at dinner. Perhaps I should have another little party and invite him." She laid down the peeler and wiped her hands on the kitchen towel. Abraham switched his attention to Libby.

"No!" Libby sprang to her feet. She tripped over Abraham but the ensuing tangle of cat and legs didn't deter Betty.

"I'll talk to Bob tonight. Who else can I ask, I wonder?"

Deep in thought Betty headed for the living room where the telephone and address book lived.

Libby attempted to keep her mind off Charles by traipsing about the inner city suburbs all weekend and the next, with Betty and Bob in tow, inspecting flats.

They were kind, and she was grateful for the help and the advice, but they weren't Charles and unfortunately Charles was everywhere but by her side. She imagined his comments on the floor plans and designs, she heard him laughing over Betty and Bob's remarks and adding his own. He was in the reflections from the windows when she stared sightlessly at a view from an apartment; she had held his hand and mopped up blood in a bathroom with similar tiles to this.

What was he doing? Had he renewed his affair with Tiffany or was he as miserable as she? Had he placed her in a sealed part of his mind, the love of his life? He was able to distance himself and detach himself very readily. His parents had a lot to answer for, inadvertently teaching their son he wasn't loved and therefore somehow unworthy of being loved.

Charles just couldn't accept that her love was strong and true and she wanted him there like a rock in her life. He was reliable and caring and had the ability to express deep emotion if he would only allow himself. He'd inherited more than he realized from those passionate, expressive parents of his, whatever their faults and however hard he tried to suppress it.

On the following Tuesday evening Libby took the phone from Bob with a clammy hand. The raised eyebrows and the wink he threw at Betty made no secret of who the caller was. They both ostentatiously removed themselves from the room.

"Hello, Libby."

"Hello," she said or rather, whispered, because her vocal chords had momentarily seized up. Was she imagining he sounded tired and drained? Could it be on her account? Sleepless nights making his voice hoarse? Like hers. Except her hoarseness stemmed from emotion.

She'd forgotten in just a couple of weeks how she adored the timbre and accent of his voice. And the way he said her name now, as though she were a priceless treasure—the way people said Fabergé or Ming or Rembrandt with all the inherent weight of the connotations the word conjured up. She'd never noticed before.

"How are you?"

"I think I've found a flat," she said because it was easier than begin to explain how bad she really was, how terrible, horrible, dismal . . . bereft without him.

"Where?"

"Rozelle."

"Good area."

"Yes."

She waited, giving him a chance to cry "don't buy it, come home to me. Live with me and be my love, my wife," but he didn't. Instead, he said, "There's some mail here for you."

"Thanks. Should I come to pick it up?"

"I could bring it to you."

"I . . . no, don't bother." He'd never get away from

Betty and Bob alive. The humiliation would be soul searing.

"It has the Conservatorium logo on it," he said. "I thought it might be important."

"They're probably acknowledging my application. Open it if you like."

"Do you want me to?"

"Go ahead."

She heard the sound of an envelope being torn, then rustling. He read out, "Dear Ms. McNeill, thank you for your application for the position of Lecturer in Cello. Please telephone the number below to make an appointment for an interview, to be conducted in mid-late November. Please bring any relevant paperwork, résumé, references, and recordings if applicable. Yours sincerely someone whose signature I can't read. Oh, it's Ernest Lovejoy. Director. That's terrific, Libby."

He sounded genuinely pleased for her. Libby was so stunned she couldn't speak.

"Here's the number." He began to read it out. She lurched into action, scrabbling for a pencil and had to ask him to repeat it twice before she got it down properly. "Ring them tomorrow."

"Yes, yes, I will. I can't believe they got back to me so fast."

"They know quality when they see it. I had no doubts."

"I did."

"You're more than qualified for the job."

"I suppose," she said doubtfully. "It's only the first

stage. It depends who else has applied. I haven't had much teaching experience and . . ."

Charles interrupted her rambling. "Don't be so pessimistic. You'll talk yourself out of it before you even do the interview."

"You're right. Thanks."

Libby caught frantic arm movements from the corner of her eye. Betty was doing a vigorous mime, mouthing, "Invite him to dinner, Saturday."

She nodded and smiled. Betty withdrew beaming with satisfaction.

"Betty wants you to come for dinner next Saturday."

"Will you be there?"

"I thinks it's for my benefit. To cheer me up."

"Do you need cheering up?"

Libby swallowed hard. "They think I do," she said, half choked.

"I can't make it, I'm afraid. Tell Betty I'm sorry and thanks." He didn't give a reason or even offer an excuse and Libby wasn't going to ask for one. She knew why he didn't want to come. It would be for both their sakes, he'd say. Better not to see each other. Had Tiffany resurfaced? Or someone else?

"How are the wedding plans coming along?" she asked brightly to cover the intensity of the disappointment. Her body sagged into the nearest chair. Abraham came in from the kitchen, stalked across the room, and disappeared down the hallway. Cats remained aloof from emotional entanglements, walking by themselves. Inscrutable.

"I thought Glory said a small service with a few close friends and now she's invited forty people. It's getting out of hand. I think I'll go out for the day and they can all totter about with their walking frames and wheelchairs and organize themselves."

Libby burst out laughing despite the burden of her broken heart and his reinforcement of the wedge between them. He sounded so bewildered and glum she wanted to rush right over and hug him.

"Just make sure you've got a few oxygen tanks on hand. A nurse might be useful too."

"She and Oscar have invited me over on Saturday night to meet the best man," he said dolefully. "I love Glory and Oscar seems like a good chap, but I don't really need to meet the other fellow and his spouse, do I?"

"I thought Gloria said his son was best man."

"Maybe he is. I don't know. Glory gets things mixed up and all the excitement is making it worse."

"She sounds wonderfully happy," said Libby as her spirits soared. "That's the main thing. Are you organizing Oscar a buck's night? One of my friends got chained to a fountain during his. He sneezed all through the wedding."

Charles gave a shout of laughter. "Thankfully, that's not my job. I haven't heard anything about one and there's only ten days to go. It's probably a few stiff rounds of canasta or bridge. Oscar's a bit of a card shark, apparently."

"I like him, Charles. They'll be very happy, I'm positive."

"Yes. It's just this wedding." He paused, said in a different tone. "And my mother's coming."

"Maybe you could talk to her . . . get some things out in the open. Tell her how you feel."

"What's the point?" he said harshly.

"It might help."

"Or it might just make me angrier. I think it's best if I treat her like the stranger she is. She hasn't even contacted me to tell me she's coming."

"I'm sorry."

"Don't be. I'm not. I don't expect anything from her. Why should I?"

Libby couldn't answer that but her heart cried out a myriad of other reasons to confront his mother and they all had to do with burying the past and allowing himself to love in the present. To love her without fear of losing her or being hurt. She couldn't say any of it. He wouldn't hear it, he wasn't ready, and the sad fact was he didn't love her enough to try.

She said again, "I'm sorry. I loved my parents very much and I've lost them. I just think while you still have yours it's worth trying to salvage something before it's too late."

"Your parents were real parents, Libby, they loved you and wanted you and nurtured you. It's obvious by the way you are now, and you can't imagine what life would be like without that. I can't imagine what life would be like *with* that. It was too late about five minutes after I was born."

"You had Gloria and your great uncle."

"If I hadn't I probably would have become a juvenile delinquent," he said. "Ended up disgracing them and myself by some outrageous act and getting myself arrested."

"I can't imagine that," Libby said. "You're too smart."

"Smart's got nothing to do with it."

And that was another sad fact.

"Goodbye, Libby," he said. "I'll see you at the wedding."

"Goodbye. If you need help, call me," she said quickly, before he hung up, but there was a click in her ear. Had he heard her or not?

Did he know his father was supposed to be coming as well?

The arrangements for buying and selling properties went ahead all in a rush. Settlement in December. Libby would be in her Rozelle residence for Christmas. Her life's paraphernalia, in storage in Holland, had been set in motion and was on its way. Betty had already extracted a promise that she spend Christmas with them. Probably just as well because the boxes might not turn up for six months.

Bob and Betty, of course, had ransacked their house for spare items ranging from a bed and bed linen to a shower curtain and dinnerware. All Libby had to do was wait, which sounded easy but wasn't.

She visited Fei Yang several more times, and when he told her he was pleased with her progress, she cautiously admitted her arm was a little better. She hadn't noticed any pain when she lifted Abraham onto her lap the previous day, and it had surprised her. Fei Yang nodded but warned her to be very careful. He showed her several strengthening exercises to do. Rest, he said, was the best cure.

Libby stood on the path outside Charles's house clutching Gloria's silver-wrapped wedding gift. Apart from the appearance of red-and-white flowers instead of the little soldierly blue ones, the place looked the same as when she'd left it—the garden, that was. Someone had fixed a bouquet of flowers to the front door, which was the only indication a wedding was taking place.

Was she too early? Got the time wrong? Where were the hordes of guests Charles had complained about? Libby looked up and down the road hopefully. Shimmering waves of heat rose from the tar. A perfect day, clear blue sky, bright sparkling sunlight . . . not a soul in sight, although there were a couple of unfamiliar cars parked against the curb. Maybe she should walk around for a few minutes . . .

This was ridiculous! She was a guest, she was on time at the right time, on the right day. She needn't be timid about going in. This house used to be her home. Libby pushed the gate open and took two steps. She needn't be worried about facing Charles for the first time since she'd moved out.

Her feet refused to take her farther. Her hands were horribly clammy. The wrapping paper would be all wet and crinkled. She eased the steely grip of her fingers. Be terrible to crush the gift. She was so pleased with it.

When Libby wondered aloud about a wedding present, Gloria snorted and laughed and said she and Oscar had more stuff than they knew what to do with between them and the last thing they needed was more. Still, Libby felt she couldn't go empty handed so, bearing in mind Gloria's fascination with Chinese culture she spent an afternoon in Chinatown and found a delicate, beautifully painted calligraphy scroll that could be hung on the wall, and whose message in Chinese characters meant Long Life and Good Health.

It wouldn't look good with creases in it. She switched the cylinder to her other hand. She had never had such a knot in her stomach. Not even waiting backstage to perform the Elgar as a student, not auditioning for her first professional position nor playing under the direction of the world's most fiercely distinguished conductors.

Her knees were shaking. She should have worn lower heels, but they didn't show off her legs so well, and she wanted to show off her legs, figure, face, and the rest of her body today. She wanted to hit Charles right in the eye with what he'd turned down. That's what she'd thought while trying on and discarding outfits for hours on end over the preceding week. Blow Charles's mind, short circuit his nervous system, make herself completely irresistible.

In the mirror she was the epitome of elegance. Cool in a simple, sleeveless cream dress from a Paris fashion house, that had cost a bomb on a mad week of shopping last year. Matching shoes on her feet and a silk scarf created a splash of brilliant color at her throat. Elegant and sexy at home, forty minutes ago.

Now that she stood with shaking, weak legs, clammy palms, a tight ache in her stomach, and a sudden need to use the toilet—running down the road and hailing the first taxi that came by was becoming very appealing. Charles obviously wasn't interested in her any more. He hadn't called since that one conversation about her letter.

Tears welled and Libby blinked furiously in case they actually spilled over and wrecked her makeup, to go with all the other disasters she'd accumulated about her person in the space of half an hour.

A car door slammed somewhere in the street behind her. Chattering voices pulled her back to a semblance of sanity. Couldn't go to pieces in public. She squared her shoulders and cautiously dabbed at the underside of each eye with one finger.

"Hello there, excuse me. Is this the scene of the crime?"

She knew that voice! Libby spun around. A shock of silver hair, a broad chest, a commanding presence . . . Charles's nose and chin.

"Maestro," she cried. "You mean Gloria's wedding? Yes, it is. Hello. I'm Libby McNeill. I played cello in Rotterdam when you conducted us last year."

"Of course. I remember. How could I forget such beauty?" he boomed, accompanying his words with a dazzling megawatt smile that blinded in its insincerity. "Did you meet my wife? Cecilia. And this is our lovely daughter Marlena."

Both stood quietly smiling in the shadow of the Maestro. Libby shook first Cecilia's warm, soft fingertips then grasped Marlena's damp, lifeless hand.

"I'm so pleased you could come. Gloria will be delighted," said Libby. "She's very excited by the whole thing."

"*Certo,*" murmured Cecilia. "Weddings are always an excitement. I look forward to meeting Gloria. Gerald speaks very fondly of her."

"Gloria was always a favorite of mine," Gerald said expansively. "Took care of young Charles for us when we were off on tour. Excellent woman."

"She is," said Libby. Was that how he saw the relationship? What about the nannies when they weren't on tour? And hadn't Gloria said he never kept in touch with her?

"Shall we?" Gerald extended his arm toward the house, and Libby was swept along in his entourage, trotting along with his womenfolk two paces behind the great man.

The door was opened by a teenage boy sporting a trendy blue stripe in his dark hair and looking ill-at-ease in a suit. One of Oscar's relatives, probably. He directed them through to the rear of the house, his smile displaying the metal braces designed to control unruly teeth.

"Where's Charles?" asked Gerald loudly.

"I think he's in the garden," said the boy. Gerald forged ahead. Cecilia and Marlena followed obediently.

Libby darted into the bathroom and closed the door hurriedly. She carefully propped the present against the bath tub. Gerald Hogarth was an overbearing, loud . . . words failed her. If he was so fond of Gloria, how come he never sent her so much as a Christmas card? And not one mention of Charles in the present, just a touched up, selective memory of the dear little son of the past.

He had those two women completely cowed. No wonder he and Irene Temple hadn't survived together. The combination of those two gigantic egos would have been enough to blow the roof off. What on earth had she and Gloria unleashed? Poor Charles. Poor, poor Charles. He'd never forgive either of them.

Libby washed her hands quickly and flung the door open. Charles needed her support. She charged out into the hallway and crashed straight into a solid, immovable object.

"Libby."

His warm hand grasped her bare arm, steadying her, the skin tingling and sparking instantly. Libby opened her mouth but no words came out.

"Libby," he said again, voice warm and soft as his hand.

She gazed up into his face. He was smiling. A tender smile just for her. The longing buried deep in her soul, so carefully covered over with practical good sense for the last weeks, threatened to rise Dracula-like and wreak havoc in these civilized surroundings. Libby lowered her eyes to the safety of his neatly tied silver-gray tie.

"Hello," he murmured and leaned forward to kiss her gently on the cheek. "How are you?"

"Uh . . . fine. How are you?" she stuttered. He looked fine. He looked more than fine. He looked so wonderful she wanted to burrow into his chest and make him hold her tight and love her forever.

"I'll be glad when this is over." He sighed. "I must have been out of my mind to agree to it." His hand slid from her arm and unnecessarily straightened his tie.

"It was very generous of you." Had he encountered Gerald and his entourage? Did he know his father was here? Surely Gloria had warned him. He seemed remarkably calm if the reunion had already occurred.

"How long have you been here?" he asked. "I didn't know you'd arrived."

"I've only been here a couple of minutes. I came in with your father, Charles."

She watched the change come over his face the way she imagined that botox antiwrinkle stuff would work. All the character and movement left his expression leaving it flat and hard and lifeless.

"Oh, yes," he said. "Glory mentioned she'd invited him. Heaven only knows why."

"He has his wife and daughter with him. Cecilia and Marlena."

"A daughter," he repeated. His lip curled slightly and he swallowed.

"Yes. She's only a teenager, Charles. Don't be cruel to her."

"Cruel?" He gazed down his nose at her as though from a vast distance. "What do you take me for? She's a stranger. I'll be as polite to her as I am to anyone else I've just met today."

Libby refused to be cowed. That stiff upper lip had to be destarched. "Marlena's your sister. Half of her is. A half sister, I mean."

"Still a stranger," he said almost petulantly, but she

sensed a weakening. He must be curious to meet the girl if nothing else. Hadn't he always wished for siblings? She had.

"You have to face them some time," she said firmly, and slid her arm through his. He squeezed her fingers gently, which she took as tacit agreement. Or maybe, preferably, gratitude for her presence, her support.

Music from the stereo wafted over the house. Elegant Mozart. Perfect for the occasion, providing alternately jolly, vigorous melodies and beautiful, soothing slow movements, never dominating but ever present behind the guests' excited chatter. Gerald and his girls were standing on the patio surveying the garden and the other guests whose numbers increased by the minute.

Most of them were elderly. Libby recognized a few friendly faces from tai chi beaming at her from under flowery hats. Rows of white stackable chairs had appeared on the lawn facing the rear corner of the garden where the biggest flower beds were in full bloom.

Cecilia said something in Italian to Gerald as they approached, catching Libby's eye around her husband's broad expanse and smiling with a tiny nod of recognition.

"Hello, father," said Charles to the black-clad back.

"Charles, my dear boy!"

Gerald spun around and extended his arms. Charles was enveloped in an embrace that would have fooled someone less knowledgeable into thinking this was a reunion of a loving father and son. Except for the fact that Charles stood ramrod straight and his arms remained stiffly by his sides.

Cecilia and Marlena, remarkably alike with pale oval faces and thick, black, wavy hair, smiled politely in the background. Gerald released Charles to draw them forward with one of his extravagant gestures.

"This is Cecilia, the love of my life, and Marlena, the apple of my eye. Our son Bartholomew is at university, studying hard to become a doctor."

Libby held her breath. How could the man make such a stupendously tactless remark? Easily it seemed. From the shadow, which passed across his wife's face, Cecilia realized the wound he'd inflicted.

As if to make amends Cecilia hastily stepped forward and kissed Charles gently on both cheeks, grasping his upper arms with both hands. Her fingers were surprisingly square and strong looking. Not a woman to shirk hard work. A sensible, sensitive woman. Libby revised her earlier opinion of a wife with no mind of her own.

"It is my pleasure to meet you, Charles," she said in soft, Italian-accented English. "For a long time, I have wanted this. Your father is very proud of you."

"Really?" murmured Charles as he submitted to the embrace. His expression would do a marble statue proud.

"Marlena, meet your big brother," cried Gerald oblivious, it seemed, to the tension radiating from his son.

"Ciao, Charles." Marlena dutifully stepped forward and had to reach up on to her tip toes to kiss Charles's cheek because he didn't bend toward her at all.

"Hello, Marlena," he said. "I've never had a sister. In fact I didn't even know I've had one for the last . . . how old are you?'

"Sixteen," she said and pouted a full lower lip. She peeked up at him from under long dark lashes.

Charles turned quickly and gestured to Libby. He extended his hand. She grasped it and squeezed his fingers encouragingly. He clung to her as though she were a life preserver.

"This is Libby."

"Libby and I have met already," said Gerald without waiting for any further introduction or explanation of her function in his son's life. "She's a magnificent musician. Tell me what are you doing now, Libby?"

"I've applied to teach at the Conservatorium." She glanced at Charles.

He was staring at his father with a look of loathing. She was beginning to understand why, despite the praise from one of the best conductor's in the world. Gerald Hogarth would, in all truth, not have much of an idea what her playing was like. He'd only heard her in an orchestral setting. Throwaway praise such as that meant very little.

Especially when it came at the price of his son's well-being.

"But you should be playing! Teaching is for the old. You are far too young to give up such a career to be an academic. You should be making music, giving concerts, sharing your gift with the world."

"Not everyone wants to do that," Charles broke in. "Some people prefer to stay at home with their families."

"But Libby has no family. Am I not right?" Gerald stared pointedly at Libby's unadorned, ringless left hand. "She has no reason to tie herself to one place. She can go where she pleases. A musician must be free to create and express himself. He cannot be tied to the mundane world like other people. The true artist must be unfettered, free to soar with the angels. Is that not right, Libby?'

"To a point," she said, but it was a reluctant admission made all the more difficult because Charles was still holding her hand. And hearing the same sentiments she'd expressed herself so vehemently, coming from a man he detested. But now she *didn't* want her life to revolve around her music and cello. Did he know that? "I'm having treatment on my arms. Repetitive strain."

"Aah, such a shame," cried Gerald.

"I am so sorry," said Cecilia. "That must be very difficult for you."

"Thank you, yes." If only they'd stop talking about her and music and get on to the subject they should be talking about. Charles.

Gerald turned to Charles and grasped his arm. "You're looking wonderfully well and prosperous too." He gestured around the beautifully maintained spacious garden with its screen of trees and flowering shrubs along the fence line, the neat lawn, the flower beds. "A good move coming to Australia. Very good move. I always thought so. Is that not right, Cecilia?"

Cecilia nodded and murmured something. Her dark eyes met Libby's briefly with an unmistakable flash of sympathy and understanding.

Charles said nothing and Gerald added, lowering his voice slightly, "We must have a talk later, my boy. In private. We've a lot to catch up on."

"Do we?" This time Gerald didn't miss the iceberg-sized chunk of ice in the tone.

His expression changed instantly. Intense displeasure. Libby had seen the same narrowing of the eyes and widening of the nostrils numerous times when he was striving for the effect he wanted with the orchestra and not achieving it. Soon after would come an explosion of cataclysmic proportions. She realized she'd taken a small step backward in self-defense.

Charles regarded his virtually steaming father with such glacial contempt even Gerald's heightened self-awareness couldn't miss it. After a long moment Charles said smoothly, "Excuse me, I must check on Glory. I've been neglecting her and it is *her* day, after all."

Gerald's mouth dropped open in astonishment. Cecilia hastened forward and clasped his arm, muttering soothingly in Italian.

"We came thousands of miles out of our way to be here and he can't even spare me a few minutes," Gerald roared. "His own father!"

Heads whipped around and elderly faces turned pale at such a display of paternal rage. Two floral hats moved away quickly, clutching each other's arms.

"*Calma, calma, tesoro,*" shushed Cecilia, stroking the back of his hand with her sturdy brown fingers. The Maestro deflated before Libby's amazed eyes. She could almost see the ruffled feathers settling back into place and the mottled red blotches leave his cheeks.

Patting the back of his hand. So that was the trick! If the orchestra had known that little ruse, Felix, the Concert Master, could have jumped up and averted many a tirade directed at a sweating, humiliated musician.

Gerald kissed Cecilia's cheek.

"My angel," he rumbled. He drew a deep breath and exhaled dramatically. "Charles always was a very self-centered boy. It's such a shame to see he hasn't changed."

Chapter Eleven

"Excuse me." Libby threw a brief smile in Cecilia's direction and darted after Charles who'd barged his way through Oscar's milling relatives and was just disappearing through the French doors.

"Charles," she called at his stiff, gray-clothed back. "Charles!"

He stopped at the entrance to the hallway. "What?"

Libby frowned, biting at her bottom lip. She didn't know what. Nothing she could say would eradicate a lifetime of bitterness and resentment. Charles's lips twisted as he stared down at her.

"See?" he said softly. The pain in his voice nearly choked her. She nodded, blinking back tears of sympathy. She certainly did.

"I do. Very, very clearly. I'm so sorry, Charles."

"It's not your fault," he said. "Nothing's ever going to change him."

"No. I think Cecilia is a better match for him than your mother, though."

"Quite frankly, I don't care." He sucked in a deep breath, striving to correct an equilibrium severely off center. "Anyway. Now's not the time to discuss this. I'd better see how the bride is doing and get this show on the road." Charles touched his fingers to her cheek quickly. "I'm glad you're here."

He didn't wait for a reply but retreated to Gloria's bedroom door where he tapped twice and was immediately admitted.

Libby went in search of Oscar. She found him in the corner of the garden near a white cloth–covered table, fidgeting beside a man she guessed was his son. A vine trailed purple blooms over the fence behind them forming a stunning backdrop to a host of multicolored flowers crowding the beds. The perfume enveloping them all was heavenly.

"Libby, how lovely you came," cried Oscar as soon as he spied her. His face formed into a delighted grin of welcome.

"As if I'd miss it." Libby bestowed a kiss on the smooth-shaven cheek.

"Have you met my son? Pete. This is Libby."

Pete bore a remarkable resemblance to his father. His eyes had the same cheeky, good-natured twinkle and within ten years he'd be exactly the same shape.

"How do you do," he said shaking Libby's hand firmly.

"Pete took over the business," said Oscar.

"Taps and things?" asked Libby.

"Yep. The old feller taught me everything he knows and then retired to live the good life. Lucky devil."

He slapped his father on the back with such great affection tears sprang to Libby's eyes. This was the way fathers and sons should be. Loving. Friends. Proud of each other.

"And I certainly found a good woman to live it with, didn't I, Libby?"

"The best, Oscar, the best."

"My wife, Janey, is in there helping Gloria get ready," said Pete to Libby.

"I remember when I married your mother," Oscar said. "She was in tears most of the time. She said not to worry, they were tears of happiness but I wondered for a while there. You do when your bride suddenly starts sobbing beside you at the altar. I'll always love her you know, Pete." The last was accompanied by a concerned creasing of the brow. "I know, Dad. She and Gloria would have been great mates. I'm sure Mum would be pleased you found someone."

"I never thought I would," said Oscar softly.

"You two are so lucky to have found each other," said Libby.

"We've a glorious day for it, Oscar." The voice had a rich plummy accent and its owner a generously rounded body packed into a puce chiffon concoction. She wore a name badge that said Marsha Romney-Smythe, Celebrant, and carried a small briefcase from which she produced various pieces of paper.

"Is the bride ready?" She glared at a slim gold watch strapped to one plump wrist.

Oscar said, "She promised she wouldn't be late. I told her we didn't have enough time at our age to waste any of it fooling about like that."

He gazed anxiously over the milling guests toward the French doors through which Gloria would appear.

"Charles is checking on her now," said Libby. "Gloria's as keen as you are, don't you worry."

"It must be about kick off," said Pete rubbing his hands together enthusiastically.

Marsha boomed, "Aha, here we go. There's the signal."

"That's Pete's boy, Tony," said Oscar.

Libby glimpsed the young man who'd opened the door waving frantically from the patio. Marsha frowned at Libby.

"If you would kindly join the guests, please," she ordered. Dismissed, Libby gave Oscar a good luck kiss. Marsha interrupted. "Peter, here, please. Stand there, Oscar. Give your bride a big smile when she appears."

She parted her lips to display shining white teeth as though giving him an example to follow, then called loudly to the guests to take their seats. A hush fell over the company. Oscar and Peter lined up obediently. Libby moved across to the side and stood on the patio steps in the shade of a birch tree. Mozart gave way to *Pachelbel's Canon.* Cameras were raised.

A collective gasp sounded as Gloria's bridesmaid appeared. Irene Temple—in glorious peacock-blue satin, dark hair swept up in an elegant twist, silly little net and floral hat perched cheekily on top, diamonds sparkling in the sunlight—composed and demure in her role.

Cameras clicked wildly but were drowned by a burst of delighted oohs and aahs as Gloria followed on Charles's arm, stepping carefully in her new heels, stylish and lovely in her simple pale-blue lace dress, smiling wider than Libby had ever seen her smile before.

Charles's expression was stern. He stared straight ahead only bending his head to assist Gloria down the steps then resuming the steady advance to Oscar who was doing as instructed and giving his bride a big, welcoming smile.

"Welcome, welcome, everyone," cried the celebrant. "My name is Marsha Romney-Smythe and I am legally certified to perform this wedding ceremony under the law in this state." She gazed around the assembled company as if inspecting a military parade, daring anyone to challenge her authority. "And doesn't everyone look wonderfully happy to be here on this wonderful day in this wonderful garden?'

A few titters and nods of agreement rippled about the garden. Marsha, encouraged, continued, "And I know two people who are more than happy to be here on this wonderful day." She paused. Was she going to ask if anyone knew who those two wonderful people were?

"It's a specially wonderful occasion for these two, Gloria and Oscar, for they have found love. They have found that special someone with whom to share the rest of their lives. And you know something?" Another pause while Marsha's beaming smile traveled over the guests like a searchlight. "I envy these two. I really do because Gloria and Oscar have had a second chance at happiness and they've grabbed it with both hands. They're not afraid to make the commitment to each other, they haven't said, 'It's too late' or 'We're too old,' and they're absolutely and wonderfully right. No one is ever too old to fall in love. There are no barriers to true love. Love conquers all obstacles. Love steamrolls right over the bumps and the pitfalls. Gloria and Oscar have proven that to us today and I applaud them for it with all my heart."

Marsha stopped, momentarily overcome with emotion, to dab a lacy handkerchief under her eyes. Libby, standing on the steps had a clear view over the seated older guests to where Charles stood next to Gloria waiting to give her away to Oscar. Marsha appeared to have forgotten this minor technical detail and embarked upon the ceremony.

Oscar reached across in front of her and took Gloria's hand with a clear wink at Charles who stepped aside with a grin. Someone laughed. Marsha frowned but recovered immediately.

Charles, standing a little to one side now that the danger of being inadvertently married to his great aunt by this raspberry-clad caricature of a celebrant had passed, wished the whole thing was over and that everyone would go home.

Love conquers all indeed! That was a joke. If love conquered all he'd be planning his own wedding with Libby. Love wasn't enough to reconcile two diametrically opposed views, both firmly entrenched, both incapable of change. Or at least unwilling to change. Charles realized he was scowling and rearranged his lips into a smile more suited to the occasion.

His mother stood on the other side of Glory, holding the bridal bouquet while the ring was slipped over the bride's arthritic finger. Irene was playing the part of demure bridesmaid for all she was worth.

She knew very well the effect her entrance had made on the guests. Most of them would be tremendous fans and she'd be signing autographs and lapping up the attention for the rest of the afternoon. Probably had a suitcase full of copies of her book for sale somewhere as well.

But Glory was ecstatic. He'd never seen her so happy and when she'd hugged him earlier and whispered, "Thank you, darling" with tears in her eyes it almost made the excruciating day worthwhile.

And Libby was here. His love. Gorgeous as ever. In control, cool and glamorous. Life on track, steaming ahead with her new apartment, new job almost in the bag, arm on the mend according to Glory, her music, her career.

He hadn't seen her for ages. Millennia, it seemed. One brief, tight, unsatisfying phone call. That was all. He looked over the heads of Glory's friends to where Libby stood. He'd kissed her three glorious times.

Wasn't he nearly on the same spot as that night in the moonlight? The night she sent him to the moon by saying she loved him. He'd kissed her almost where he was standing now. Did she remember?

She raised a hand and slid her index finger carefully under one eye. Teary as well. Weddings did that to women. Jane had been dabbing at her eyes as he escorted Glory from the bedroom. Even his mother's excitement and teary-eyed fiddling and gushing over the bride as they prepared her this morning had appeared genuine. But she was good at faking emotion. She probably didn't know herself any more what was real and what wasn't.

The hug and kiss she'd bestowed upon him when she arrived could have passed for genuine too. If you didn't know better.

A gushing torrent of words brought him back abruptly to the matter in hand.

"And now we have a wonderful treat for you all. Irene Temple will sing 'Ave Maria' by special request from her favorite aunt Gloria, our lovely bride. Miss Temple has made it a priority and taken time out from her hectic schedule to be here today."

Ms. Romney-Smythe almost fell over herself to make room for his mother who sailed into the center of attention with a professional smile on her lips. She nodded to her dogsbody, a thin, competent machine of a woman named Esther who had sidled up to a large portable CD player nestled behind the white covered table and now pressed a button. Harp and strings floated out into the fragrant, warm afternoon, delicate and beautiful.

Irene bowed her head piously, hands clasped lightly at her waist. Her audience waited, faces rapt. No one moved. The effect was just as he remembered. Everyone hypnotized—exactly like rabbits under the thrall of a fox, waiting to be eaten alive. Unaware of the nature of the rapacious beast.

He shifted his weight and looked away, found Libby watching him. Their eyes met over the crowd of big hats, and gray and balding heads and she smiled. For him. She knew exactly how he felt. He smiled back at her, and their smiles met and danced in the warm air.

Then the voice began. Pure, clear, and astonishingly lovely despite the advancing years. Charles's throat tightened. He'd deliberately avoided listening to her recordings and hadn't properly heard her sing live since he was a teenager—even then he had tried hard not to be exposed to it. Now, as her voice soared over the garden he heard her as an adult, heard the rich beauty, the talent, and the exquisite gift she gave to the world. Just as Libby had said and he'd vehemently denied.

He watched his mother with a new awareness. Her eyes caressed her audience and she sang the piece as though it was a major performance before massed cognoscenti in London or New York, rather than her elderly aunt's friends at a backyard wedding in suburban Sydney. Glory was overwhelmed, so was Oscar. They clutched each other's hands tightly, shared a little glance that spoke volumes. Love conquers all. Could it?

Charles swallowed. Did he have a chance at such happiness with anyone? Had he had his chance and ruined it? His eyes sought Libby again. Could he share such intimacy with her? She was smiling, happy for Glory and Oscar, reveling in the beautiful sounds. Libby was far more generous in spirit than he, just not where he was concerned. But if a person truly loved another, surely they would be prepared to sacrifice a little of themselves for the sake of the other?

His parents hadn't. Not for each other and certainly not for their child. They'd separated, each interested only in themselves. Charles' hands curled into fists so that the nails dug into his palms. He stretched his fingers. Relaxed them.

The music died away gently. His mother bowed her head humbly before the applause which erupted like the clatter of hailstones. Someone even called "Bravo." She turned to Glory and Oscar, smiling widely.

"Give us another one, Irene," said Oscar.

She hesitated but glanced at Esther who nodded and started the CD again. Charles didn't recognize this tune, some light-hearted folk song about lovers and happiness. As always, she had the crowd in the palm of her hand. If only she remembered whose day it was and didn't take over completely.

But that was old bitterness speaking because she didn't. She stepped firmly to the side after the song had ended. Ms. Romney-Smythe needed no second bidding to resume command. Then it was all over and people were rushing forward to kiss and hug and congratulate. Charles shook hands and kissed soft powdered cheeks and as soon as possible he nabbed a glass of champagne from one of the waitresses who'd begun circulating with trays.

Libby was still standing under the birch tree, and he scored another glass on his way across to join her.

"What a wonderful service," she said with a smiling emphasis on the wonderful. Grinning, he handed her the champagne and she raised the crystal flute to his.

Charles laughed. "I thought for a minute she was going to marry *me* to Glory."

"Perhaps it's her first go."

Libby sipped her champagne. Most of the tension

had left Charles' manner. His shoulders had dropped from parade-ground stiffness. His fingers grasped the glass lightly. He was actually standing next to her smiling as opposed to scowling, which he'd been doing for the first half of the short ceremony.

"Glad it's over?"

"It isn't, yet," he said. "Not until they all leave."

Libby licked her lips thoughtfully. Should she ask? He must have spoken to Irene. She would have spoken to him, at the very least.

"Have you spent much time with your mother?" she asked carefully.

"About as much as with any of the other guests." The relaxed manner disappeared in an instant. The distant, reserved mask dropped into place.

Libby kept her voice low, conscious of people chatting close behind them. "Charles, it's probably the only opportunity you'll have to sort things out with her, with both of them."

"Why, may I ask, are you so interested in me sorting things out, as you put it, with my parents? What is it to you? Why do you care? I can't see that it makes the slightest bit of difference to you whether I speak to them or not." His jaw was rigid now. He stared at the champagne in his glass, swirling it about abstractedly.

Libby leaned closer. "Because you'll be happier if you do. You need to talk to them."

Charles snorted. "Talk to my father? That pompous, over bearing, self-centered, arrogant . . . you saw what he's like, he hasn't changed a bit."

"That's what he said about you," she said. "Maybe

he's right, Charles. Maybe you need to rethink your opinions about your parents. Your father has a new family and he's obviously treating his children quite differently this time. He's learned. He's changed, Charles. He's willing to talk to you, but all you do is wallow in the past and the wrongs done to you."

Would he walk away and leave her standing with her unpalatable opinions? She had no idea, although from the expression on his face when Irene sang he may be having second thoughts. She clung to that small hope.

He said grimly, "I don't even know why Glory invited him. It's not as if he ever contacts her and he's not even related."

Didn't he understand anything? Libby exhaled loudly. Couldn't he see the opportunity the wedding afforded for a reconciliation? No wonder he frustrated Gloria. Her own patience was wearing thin.

"We were trying to help you. That's why I suggested she contact him. For you."

"*You* suggested it? It was your idea?"

"Yes, so sue me!" Irritation at his stubbornness overcame tact. "And sue Glory as well. You might as well add in your parents while you're at it, for ruining your life for you. Stop whinging and grow up, Charles." She glared at him.

Charles's lips tightened into a thin, straight line. "Why don't you leave me and my sorry excuse for a family alone," he hissed. "You know nothing about me. You think you do but you've no idea."

Libby gritted her teeth. Her breath came in short, hot bursts and she knew if she spoke she'd say something even more inflammatory. From the corner of her eye she spied astounded faces turning their way.

Charles's face was the color of white marble. He suddenly snaked out a hand and snatched the champagne glass from her fingers. He thrust it and his own at a passing waitress and grabbed hold of Libby's arm. Startled guests fell aside like the bow waves from a supertanker as he charged her through the living room and upstairs to the room she'd used. He pulled her inside and slammed the door.

Libby stood by the bed watching Charles pace about the room. Had she overdone it? Had she pushed Charles too hard and too far? She was no psychologist . . .

She'd certainly never seen him react so spontaneously, with so much uncontrolled emotion. Strangely though, she wasn't frightened. His rage wasn't directed at her. During the impassioned flight from the garden the motivating fury had dissipated, replaced by something else. His contorted face revealed less anger than anguish.

"Now!" he exclaimed impotently. "Now."

Libby waited. Charles stared at her. He opened his mouth but nothing more emerged. Her heart went out to him in his mute incapacity. Deep emotion was a new country for Charles and he didn't speak the language. If only he'd allow her to teach him.

He walked to the window and looked down into the crowded garden. Esther had pressed another of her buttons and Spanish guitar music came floating up borne on the gabble of voices.

"Love conquers all," he said bitterly with his back toward her. "Do you believe that?"

Libby hesitated. "I've never thought about it before," she said honestly. "But it should, I suppose, true love."

He turned. Libby forced herself to stay motionless. If she embraced him the way she desperately wanted to nothing would he solved. He'd either kiss her or push her away. They'd done that before. Both ways.

"You don't love anyone. Truly." He said it as a statement rather than a question.

"You know I do, Charles," she replied, keeping her voice calm and steady despite the almost overwhelming desire to cry out in despair that of course she loved him, she adored him, more than anything . . . more than . . . But she couldn't bring herself to say the words in her mind. It would feel too much like a betrayal of her self, her life to this point.

"Not enough, though." Charles knew what lay unspoken in her mind. He tossed her a small, mocking grimace of a smile.

"Enough for what?" she said knowing her voice wavered, knowing he wanted her to say it aloud. She was under pressure now. He'd swung the scrutiny to her own failings.

"To change, compromise your plans." He threw it at her as a challenge.

Libby bit her lip. Did she love him more than her music? It had been her whole life, she'd built her dreams around her ability to play the cello, it was part of her. Could she give it all up for Charles?

He thought not. She'd told him not. But the job she'd applied for allowed flexibility as well as stability. Plenty of room for both her passions.

"Neither do you," she said.

"I don't have any plans. I'm already doing what I want to do."

He turned his back again and stared out the window.

Libby swallowed her rising anger. They shouldn't be talking about her. This was old ground. No solution would be forthcoming on that front this afternoon. He'd neatly deflected the focus away from the other topic, the more crucial one.

"Talk to your mother," she said.

"All right," he cried, spinning to face her. Defiantly. "You go and get her and I'll talk to her. And you can stay right here and see for yourself what she says. You obviously don't believe me."

"Don't move," ordered Libby.

She ran as fast down the stairs as was humanly possible in high-heeled sandals, scanning the living room on the way. No Irene. Out onto the patio. Sun beating onto her head. Heat rising from the paving. Gloria smiling, with Oscar holding her hand as they spoke to Gerald and Cecilia. Bursts of laughter punctuating the chatter. People enjoying themselves at what for almost everyone, was a joyous occasion. Where was Irene?

There! In the shade surrounded by a gaggle of fans. Libby slowed, her feet faltered on the grass, heels sinking into the soft turf. How to approach this woman who was almost a legend in her own lifetime?

But she was just a woman, and she was a mother with a duty to her son. A son whom Libby adored. She edged through the perfumed, chattering circle.

"Excuse me, Miss Temple."

The heavily made up face swung her way, the lips parted in a gracious smile.

"Hello." The speaking voice was quite normal. Unremarkable, really.

"Could you . . . I mean would you be able to spare a minute and have a word with Charles?"

"Oh, my dear, of course! Charles is my son," she announced to the chorus of admirers. "What a question! Where is he? I've hardly laid eyes on him and I've been longing to see him again."

"Charles is upstairs," Libby said.

She grasped Libby's arm expectantly and allowed Libby to lead her into the house. At the foot of the stairs Irene released her grip. "What's your name, my dear?'

"Libby."

"And are you his girl?" Irene's eyes were a shade lighter than Charles'. More green, less brown but the shape and spacing were the same.

"Not really." Irene studied her for a moment. Libby's tone must have given her away or maybe it was the flush crawling up her neck under the silk scarf. "But I'd like to be," she blurted. "Charles is . . . finds it . . . difficult to love."

Too hot. Should have worn a necklace instead of a scarf. Libby undid the knot and slipped the brightly colored square from around her neck, stuffed it in her bag.

"I know nothing about him," Irene murmured. "Nothing at all."

The make-up couldn't hide the sorrow, the regret evident suddenly in the previously imperious, confident features. Irene's age sat heavily on shoulders drooping with the effort of maintaining the public façade.

She indicated with a diamond-cluttered hand they should continue up the stairs. On the landing, heart thumping, Libby opened the door. What if he'd run, unable to confront his past? How would she explain to Irene?

But Charles was standing right where she'd left him. He might have observed them from the window, she hadn't thought to look up. He didn't smile or give any indication of greeting as she entered with Irene close behind. He wore that stony expression she knew so well and stuck his hands in his pockets with blatantly false nonchalance.

"Hello, Irene."

"Charles, my dear, dear boy." Irene rushed to throw her arms around him. "I hardly had a chance to say hello earlier what with helping Gloria. How are you, darling?" She stood back beaming, undeterred by, or oblivious to, his lack of reaction.

He extracted himself from her clutching arms and shrugged.

"Charles?" she said. "Aren't you pleased to see me?" She glanced uncertainly at Libby then back at Charles.

"Not particularly. I've managed to get by most of my life without seeing you."

The silence following that remark sucked the air from the room. Irene stiffened then sagged as though her bones had melted. Charles stood staring impassively. His mother lurched across and sat on the bed. Libby's heart flew to her—an elderly lady, a lonely elderly lady shunned by her only child and coming to the end of her career.

"I know I haven't been a very good mother." Her voice wavered. "I wasn't prepared for it. I didn't know how."

Charles snorted softly, his lip curled in disdain.

"I think I must have missed out on the mother gene." She looked to Libby with a quick, imploring, helpless smile.

"What bollocks! You were more interested in your career," cried Charles. "You didn't want me and you didn't love me. Have you any idea at all what that was like?'

Tears rushed to Libby's eyes. The pain in the tight, controlled words was excruciating. She reached for his hand. He didn't respond. But Irene did. Irene reacted violently. She leapt from the bed and faced him, eyes wide, arms outstretched.

"That's wrong, Charles. I did love you, I do love you. I always did. I just wasn't able to show it. I was so busy when you were little. But I did my best for you. I always hired the best nannies and you were happy with Glory, weren't you?"

"You look like you're in an opera," The same tense voice. "Acting the distraught mother."

But he was touched by her words, some of the violence and disgust had gone. Libby squeezed his unresponsive fingers. He wanted so desperately to believe he was loved. Maybe if he could accept Irene's he would accept hers.

Irene lowered her arms, her spine straightened. "You

made it very difficult for me to get close to you, Charles. When you grew up, you were very hard to talk to. Your father tried but he used to say it was like bashing his head on the wall. Surely you remember?" she demanded. "You threw a plate of soup at him once when you were twelve. And you were very good at long, cold silences. You weren't an easy boy."

Irene's tone had an edge to it now. Charles hadn't changed much in that respect, he was still difficult to get close to, but he had good reason.

"Is it any wonder?" he shouted. Libby grabbed his arm but he shook himself free. "Is it any wonder when I barely knew you? Why would I want to talk to a couple of people who ignored me? You packed me away out of your sight as much as you could."

The silence throbbed in the very air. Charles twisted around and stared out the window again. Turning his back on his mother, turning his back on Libby.

"I can't undo the past, Charles." The dignified star emerged. "All I can do is tell you I was wrong to treat you the way I did. I'm sorry. And I'm sorry you hate me so. But I do love you. I always did. In my own way. The older I get the more I realize how important family is. I have no one, Charles. No one except you and Glory. I want to salvage something from the wreckage if I possibly can."

Charles's voice was dry with cynicism when he replied, "So now, now when you're getting old you want someone to care for you. When your voice goes and no one wants to hear you any more or see you any more and you realize you're all alone." He spun around to glare at her with undisguised fury. "Well, I went through that, mother. And let me tell you in advance—it's hell!'

"I'm asking you to forgive me, Charles." Irene's voice faltered.

Libby squeezed Charles's arm. "Charles?" she whispered.

He looked down at her with venomous eyes. "You see? She's incapable of feeling anything for me. It's always her, what *she* wants, how *she* feels. You're better off having nothing to do with me, Libby. I'm incapable of giving you what you want. I'm better off alone. That's how I was brought up." He looked at Irene and said clearly, "Forgive you? I can't. I'm sorry, but right now, I can't."

He pushed past them both and strode from the room.

Irene slumped on to the bed. All life had drained from the face she raised to Libby.

"He detests me," she said in a bewildered, weak whisper of sound. "I had no idea."

"He's . . . he's. I'm sorry. It's my fault," cried Libby. "I thought he should talk to you and maybe he'd see . . ."

Irene stared at her with vacant eyes. "Your fault? How could it be your fault? It's mine. Mine! I loved him but not enough." She paused. "Who are you?" she asked, frowning slightly.

"I'm Libby McNeill. I'm a cellist. I love Charles but he doesn't think I love him enough. He's afraid I'll . . ."

"Be like me," finished Irene in a hoarse whisper. "Don't let yourself be like me. Don't sacrifice everything for your art. Look at me—my voice is going, I have heart trouble. I can't tour much because my doctor won't allow it. I have no one. No one who cares about me, not the voice, but *me*. It's the price I paid. My pact with the devil, if you like."

Libby grasped Irene's hands in hers. "You will have Charles," she said urgently. "I'll make sure of it. He finds it difficult to express his emotions."

Irene smiled. "Does he? I thought he managed rather well just now."

Charles charged down the stairs. He couldn't stand to breathe the same air as that odious woman. And Libby hadn't helped. It was almost as if she'd planned his humiliation, not forgetting to include a ringside seat for herself.

He had to get away, get right away. Out of the house and into the car. Glory would understand and if she didn't, too bad. It was partly her fault for inviting those people.

Charles' headlong pace slowed as he reached the bottom step. The living room was packed. The noise level verged on deafening. His house was full of strangers. "Wonderful service, wasn't it?" gushed one of Oscar's relatives clutching at his arm.

"Yes," he muttered.

"And Gloria made such a beautiful bride. I don't know how Oscar managed to nab her. But that's just a big sister talking—you know how it is between siblings . . ." She emitted a shrill little gurgle of laughter and gazed at Charles expectantly.

"As a matter of fact, I don't," he replied tersely. "I'm an only child. Excuse me."

"You must be very proud of your mother," she said, clearly undaunted by his half-turned back.

"Charles."

Now Glory and Oscar appeared, hand in hand and positively glowing. No escape.

"We think it's time we did the speeches and the cake." Glory's beaming smile faded, replaced by a frown as she studied him more closely. "What's the matter?"

Her gaze shifted over his shoulder to the stairs behind him.

"Nothing," he replied tersely. "Let's get started, shall we?" He grabbed her arm drawing her with Oscar attached to the patio where the caterers had set up a table with the wedding cake.

Charles clapped his hands together. "Attention please, everyone. Your attention," he called loudly. Several faces turned their way. The sound of shushing carried like a wave through the guests.

His father glowered at him with Cecilia hanging off his arm and that pouty little girl standing smirking next to one of Oscar's grandsons. But then Gerald stepped forward. He stared briefly at Charles, kissed Glory, shook hands with Oscar. Glory smiled happily. To Charles' amazement Gerald faced the expectant assembly, raised his considerable voice and said, "It has been my great good fortune to be related to Gloria indirectly through my dear first wife, the lovely Irene Temple." He was making a speech! The speech Charles had been resigned to making.

"The happy couple, and indeed have you ever seen a happier couple?" A smattering of applause greeted this remark. Gerald smiled indulgently. He had the crowd hypnotized. Exactly the way his mother had, earlier. Blind rage welled inside Charles. This was the way it had always been—always! Libby thought they'd mellowed in their old age but why would they? They couldn't change after forty years of hogging the limelight. Let them take over. Glory was happy, that was the main thing, the only thing, that counted. But he certainly didn't have to stand here and listen.

"I was honored and I must admit, surprised, when Gloria contacted me recently to invite me to her wedding but I was delighted to be able to squeeze today into my hectic schedule." Charles edged surreptitiously away from the table. Glory caught his eye. He blew her a kiss. She smiled and returned her attention to his father. He couldn't see Libby or his mother. Just as well.

"Family is very important. As I grow older I realize just how important . . ." Gerald paused. Charles glanced at him. Was he himself included in this revelation? No. Gerald's eyes were fixed on Cecilia and the girl. "Gloria understands the value of close family ties, she always has. She helped us immeasurably in the old days, generously allowing our son to stay with her on those occasions when Irene and I were unavoidably absent from home.

"Now she has a whole new family to embrace and I'm sure they will soon realize, as has Oscar, what a treasure they have gained." He lifted his glass. "I give you a toast. To the bride. To Gloria."

"To Gloria," rippled around the garden.

"My son Charles has a few words to say, now," said

Gerald. He kissed Gloria and moved across to where Cecilia stood smiling. She tucked her hand in his arm.

Glory and Oscar faced him, hand in hand. Charles cleared his throat. Keep it light, keep it short. Get through it. For Glory. "As the father of the bride . . ." A burst of laughter made him pause. "At least, in my *role* as father of the bride, I have never been so proud in my life. I admit I had misgivings when Gloria and Oscar announced their intentions—not about Oscar because he is clearly a good catch . . ." More titters of laughter ". . . and Gloria is very smart . . ." Light applause as well ". . . but because Gloria is very dear to me and I want only that she be happy. She has been so very good to me all my life." He swallowed, steeled himself to continue. "Embarking on this adventure of marriage is something I've not done . . ." He licked his lips, dry in the warm air. "Yet." A stir of movement at the door caught his eye. Libby and his mother were standing close together, listening intently. Thinking what? He sucked in a deep breath. "But Gloria and Oscar, so clearly happy and in love, make it seem the right and obvious thing to do. I wish them the very best for their life together. May they have many, many years. To Gloria and Oscar."

"Gloria and Oscar," cried the guests.

"Before the cutting of the cake there is one more toast I should like to make." Charles lifted his glass towards his mother. He couldn't raise a smile. He could barely enunciate the words. "To the maid of honor, Irene Temple. Thank you for making this a truly memorable day for all of us."

"To Irene," roared her fans amidst applause.

"Let's cut the cake," said Oscar.

Guests surged forward with cameras clicking. Charles headed for the door to the house. He had to get away, get out of here. Libby and his mother were directly in his path. Unavoidable.

"Well done," said Libby. No smile there.

He stopped. "Thanks."

His mother placed her hand on his arm. She spoke softly, with a certain reserved dignity replacing the distraught desperation of upstairs. "I'm so sorry for everything. Would it be possible for us to talk again? When things are quieter? Tomorrow?" He looked into eyes reddened from tears, a face sagging in distress despite the repair job she'd done with make-up.

"Maybe." He half turned. This was his mother. Pleading with him. Needing his approval, his love, his forgiveness. Too much. "Yes. Some . . . other time. I can't . . . I have to go. I need to think . . ."

Libby didn't say a word. His mother glanced at her. Libby gave her a tiny sympathetic smile.

In his bedroom, Charles collected his keys. He let himself out the front door closing it carefully behind him, went to the garage and backed the car carefully out on to the crowded street. Then he drove, and when he joined the stream of traffic on the expressway, sat in the center lane headed north.

For twenty kilometers nothing entered his head, nothing at all beyond staying within the speed limit, negotiating the car around semitrailers and allowing speedsters to go by. His mind numb, his body blank.

Gradually his hands relaxed on the steering wheel, his stomach unclenched. Thoughts began to filter through the dense, coagulated lump of emotion.

Libby's face flashed before his eyes. Her beautiful soft expression with those two violet-colored eyes vivid with unshed tears. Now she knew what he'd been talking about, what he'd dealt with all his life. His insensitive, loudmouth of a father and that meek little wife. Perfect for him. Biddable and devoted, willing to sacrifice herself to the great man's genius. His mother hadn't. She'd preserved her own identity and isn't that what Libby wanted too? Without the selfishness?

But strangely, his mother wasn't the ogress of his childhood, the monster his imagination had busily constructed over the years. In the reality of adult vision she was a lady past her prime, a well-preserved one but still an aging woman coming to terms with the mistakes of her youth. Wishing to make amends.

Would it hurt to see her again while she was in Sydney? Maybe have a meal together, talk? She probably did love him in her own peculiar way.

And Libby loved him in her special, wonderful way. And he loved her, he'd always known that.

Charles' determination faltered. Where was he going? Was he fleeing from the very thing he'd craved all his life? To be loved. Was he so insular, so stubbornly independent he could live his whole life without love? Without Libby? For she was the only one with whom he could imagine spending his life.

The car slowed and earned a chorus of honking from other drivers. Charles accelerated, keeping his attention on the road ahead, looking for the next exit so that he could retrace his route. To see if Libby still wanted an idiot like him. For the rest of her life.

The house was in darkness when he pulled into the driveway late that night. An accident on the freeway had caused insufferable delays. He hadn't stuck his mobile in his pocket as he left, but rational thought wasn't featuring at the time. Had Glory been worried? At least she had Oscar to calm her down. Libby would think up some valid excuse for him. Glory would take Libby's word and his mother would back her up. Probably.

Charles unlocked the front door and walked through to the rear, switching the hall light on as he went. He paused at the entrance to the living room, checked to see the doors to the garden were closed. The place was neat and tidy, no sign of a party at all. They'd all gone and left no indication of their presence. He was alone just as he'd so vehemently stated he wanted to be. Why did he feel so empty? Leaden inside.

In his bedroom he stripped off his wedding clothes and stood under a hot shower letting the water pour down over his head hoping it would wash away the guilt, dilute the harshness of his own words ringing in his head. Dressed in track pants and sweater he wandered to the kitchen. Maybe they'd have left some food behind. But there wasn't anything, only what he'd had in the fridge before today.

Cheese on toast.

Charles picked up his plate and went to sit on the couch in miserable solitude. He'd ring Libby tomorrow.

No, he'd go to see her. He'd go with his heart in his hands and present his love to her. At least, then, he'd always know he'd tried. If she didn't want him. If she'd had enough of his abuse and stupidity.

Soft sounds from behind made the hair on his neck prickle.

Libby! Coming down the stairs wrapped in his bathrobe, face sleepy, hair awry. So beautiful his heart stopped for a couple of beats. She hesitated when she saw him staring, but continued on with a determined expression until she stood in front of him.

"Are you all right?" Her fingers twisted and rolled the trailing ends of the soft belt of his robe.

He nodded. His restarted heart clogged his throat now.

"We told Glory you had to go out for a few minutes."

"Thanks." The word squeezed its way out. We? His mother and Libby?

"She got distracted then—with everything."

"You stayed," he murmured, his eyes locked on hers.

It was Libby's turn to nod. She was unsure of her welcome, her mouth trembled, she swallowed. She didn't know, whereas he, he had never been so sure of anything in his life and Libby had just confirmed it for him. Gloriously.

She said, "I'll leave now if you like." Hesitant. Reluctant.

Charles leapt up. "No."

"Stay?" Her face softened. Now she knew. The way he did. She smiled. A tear hovered on one lid. Her eyes seemed to grow more and more luminous. Shining with love.

"Yes."

He reached out for her and she walked into his arms with a small sigh that disappeared into his shoulder as he hugged her. "Forever," he said. "Please stay forever."

Libby lifted her face and studied his expression but she didn't slacken the hold she had on him. "With my cello?" she whispered.

"You're not you without your cello," he said. "And I want you, totally and completely."

"You have me, Charles, you have me."